BY THE SHORES
OF THE
MIDDLE SEA

Also by Dana Stabenow

BY THE SHORES
OF THE
MIDDLE SEA

Book II *of* Silk and Song
by
Dana Stabenow

Gere Donovan Press
Portland, Ore.

Gere Donovan Press
8825 SE 11th Avenue, Suite 210
Portland OR 97202
www.geredonovan.com

First Printing, 2014
ISBN 978-1-62858-070-9

*This one is for
Barbara Peters,
who always believed.*

Author's Note

There was no attempt to force my medieval characters to, in Josephine Tey's inimitable phrase, 'speak forsoothly.' When people spoke in 1320, they sounded as contemporary to each other as you and I do when we speak to each other today. I chose to offend neither the reader's eye nor my own oh-so-delicate writer's sensibilities with any *zounds!*-ing.

Cast

Abraham of Acre. Wu Li's agent in Gaza.

Agalia, Jaufre's mother, Robert de Beauville's wife. Sold to Sheik Saghir bin Nazari as the Lycian Lotus.

Al-Idrisi. A Persian mapmaker of great renown.

Alaric. An ex-Templar knight, now caravan guard. Knew Jaufre's father.

Alma. A member of Sheik Mohammed's harem. As close to a medieval philosopher as a Muslim woman can get. Teaches Johanna to write Arabic.

Anwar the Egyptian. Slave dealer in Kashgar.

Basil the Frank. Wu Li's agent in Baghdad.

Bo He. Dai Fang's doorman.

Chi Yuan. A powerful Mandarin at the court of the Great Khan, and Dai Yu's uncle.

Chiang. Edyk the Portuguese's manservant.

Dai Fang. Wu Li's second wife. Johanna's step-mother. Gokudo's lover.

Dayir, aide to Bayan, Ogodei's father.

Deshi the Scout. Caravan master to Wu Li.

Edyk the Portuguese. Merchant trader residing in Cambaluc.

Eneas. Wu Li's agent in Alexandria.

Fatima. Daughter of Malala and Ahmed, betrothed of Azar.

Farhad. Sheik Mohammed of Talikan's son and heir.

Félicien. A Frank, and a goliard or student traveling the world in search of knowledge.

Firas. A Nazari Ismaili from Alamut, the hereditary home of the Hashasins, or Assassins.

Gokudo. Samurai, now ronin. A captain in Ogodei's army. Dai Fang's personal guard and lover.

Grigori the Tatar. Wu Li's agent in Kabul.

Hari. A monk from India.

Hayat. An inmate of Sheik Mohammed's harem. A dyer and weaver.

Ibn Tabib. A doctor of Kabul.

Ishan. Stable master to Sheik Mohammed of Talikan.

Jaufre. Orphaned on the Silk Road, rescued by Johanna's family, brought up as her foster brother and personal guard. Son of Agalia and Robert de Beauville.

Jibran. Headman of the village of Aab.

Joan Burgh. English pilgrim on the Jerusalem Journey.

Johanna. Trader, singer, adventurer, thief. Daughter of Wu Li and Shu Ming, granddaughter of Marco Polo and Mei Lin. Known in Sheik Mohammed's harem as Nazirah.

Kadar, the chief eunuch in Sheik Mohammed's harem.

Mohammed bin Assad. Sheik of Talikan. Father of Sabir.

Ogodei. A Mongol lord of Cambaluc. Son of Dayir who was friend to Wu Li. Began as a captain of a ten thousand and rose to one of the twelve barons of the Shiang and general of a hundred thousand. Named for Genghis Khan's successor.

Marco Polo. Venetian merchant, c.1254-1324. Traveled to China with his father and uncle where they spent twenty years working for Kublai Khan.

Rambahadur Raj. Havildar of the first caravan into Kabul in 1323.

Robert de Beauville. English knight, ex-Templar, caravan guard on the Silk Road. Jaufre's father, Agalia's husband.

Shu Lin. Shu Ming's mother, Marco Polo's concubine, the Khan's gift to Marco Polo, Johanna's grandmother.

Shu Ming. Johanna's mother, Wu Li's wife, Shu Lin's daughter, Marco Polo's daughter.

Shu Shao. Called "Shasha." Nurse, friend, healer, wise woman. Foster sister to Johanna.

Tabari. A clerk of Kashgar.

Tarik. With Mahmoud, one of Johanna's guards in Talikan.

Wu Cheng. Wu Li's brother. A eunuch who was gelded by his parents for advancement at court. Fell out of favor when the old Khan died and with the help of his brother went into business as a trader on the Road.

Wu Hai. Marco's friend and Wu Li's father.

Wu Li. Merchant and trader of Cambaluc. Johanna's father. Wu Hai's son, Shu Ming's husband, and later Dai Fang's husband.

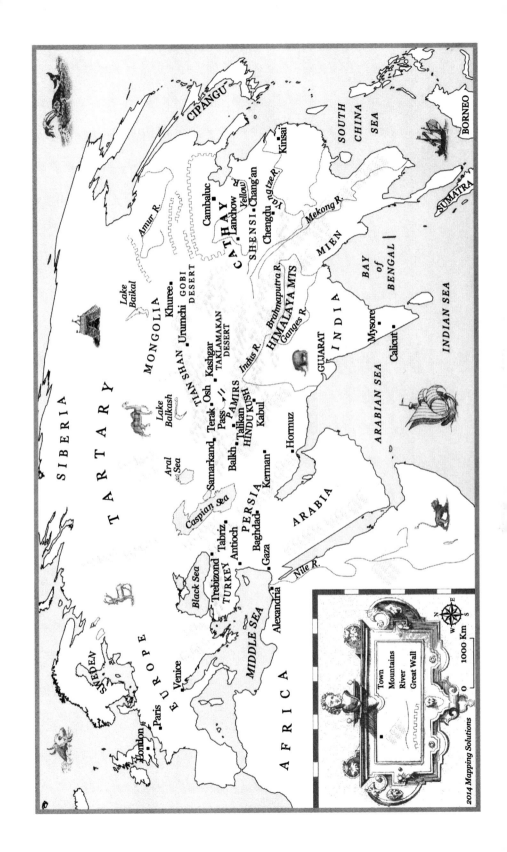

SIBERIA

TARTARY

SWEDEN

EUROPE

London
Paris
Venice

Black Sea

Trebizond
TURKEY
Antioch

Tabriz
Baghdad
Gaza

Alexandria

MIDDLE SEA

AFRICA

Nile R.

ARABIA

PERSIA

Kerman

Hormuz

Caspian Sea

Aral
Sea

Lake
Balkash

Samarkand
Balkh
Talikan
HINDU KUSH
Kabul

PAMIRS

Terak
Pass
Osh
TIAN SHAN

Kashgar

TAKLAMAKAN
DESERT

Urumchi

MONGOLIA

Khuree

Lake
Baikal

Amur R.

GOBI
DESERT

CATHAY

SHENSI

Cambaluc

Lanchow

Yellow
Chang'an

Yangtze R.

Chengdu

Kinsai

CIPANGU

SOUTH
CHINA
SEA

MIEN

Mekong R.

Indus R.

HIMALAYA MTS

Brahmaputra R.

Ganges R.

GUJARAT

INDIA

Mysore

Calicut

BAY
of
BENGAL

ARABIAN SEA

INDIAN SEA

SUMATRA

BORNEO

Town
Mountains
River
Great Wall

N
W   E
S

0   1000 Km

2014 Mapping Solutions

BY THE SHORES
OF THE
MIDDLE SEA

⋆ Part III ⋆

· One ·

┝━━━┥

Johanna had never been so bored.

There was no lack of comfort in the harem, that was true enough. The blue-tiled floors had been built over a hypocaust, and were warm both winter and summer. So was the water in the rectangular bath that stretched the length of the main room. The silk cushions were large and comfortable, if a little gaudy in their brilliant red and orange and purple and green stripes, and so were the beds. The food was plentiful and most of it delicious, if the cook did have a heavy hand with sugar and spices. Each inmate had her own room and her own personal servant. The larger suites, assigned to the sultan's favorites, had their own kitchens, their own fountains and some their own heated pools.

There were no doors to these rooms, of course. Who knew what those women would get up to behind closed doors, if they had them?

They got up to plenty without them.

Concubines had been a feature of life in Cambaluc, too. Johanna's own grandmother had been concubine to the great Kublai Khan before being given in marriage to her grandfather, the honored Marco Polo. It was natural for men of power and wealth to accumulate women much as they did other possessions, as a way of measuring themselves against their peers and as a means of demonstrating their elevated status in society. More women also meant more heirs of the body, although Johanna, familiar with the stories of internecine warfare among the descendants of the Great Khan, wondered what any man needed with that many sons. Too many heirs only guaranteed long and extremely bloody fights over who would one day occupy the throne. Those fights inevitably spiraled out from court to city to countryside, and never ended well for the innocent bystander. Johanna's own grandmother had died in prison after one such dynastic disturbance.

But in Cambaluc, concubines could walk the streets unveiled, could shop in the markets, could visit their friends and relatives, could attend the horse races and bet on the outcome. They traveled, with personal guards of course, the number according to their consequence, but one saw them everywhere, Chinese and Mongol alike. The Mongol concubines could even own and ride their own horses. Here in Talikan, under the absolute rule of Sheik Mohammed, the only time the concubines left the harem was when the sheik called for their presence in his rooms for the evening.

With one exception.

The knock landed heavily on the other side of the great mahogany door, the sound echoing off the tiled walls. Before the second knock fell Johanna was on her feet and running. The third knock sounded and she was standing before the great door, fidgeting, waiting for Kadar, the chief eunuch, to deign to open it. He disapproved of Johanna's daily excursions to the stables and expressed his disapproval, in so far as he dared flout his master's will, by delaying as long as possible her departure.

She heard the sound of robes swishing over tile, and turned to see Kadar approaching with a deliberately unhurried stride. Concubines peered from behind him and whispered furiously among themselves, watching the Easterner with her odd-colored eyes, who had never been invited into the sheik's bed, not even once, be granted yet again this unheard of, this extraordinary, and some even alleged this blasphemous freedom. She didn't even wear a veil outside the harem!

After six months one would think her mornings out would occasion little comment, but no. Their lives were so monotonous and so entirely absent of event, they had so little else to talk about.

And she was here as a result of betrayal, kidnapping and blackmail. They might not speak of it directly, but they knew – and she would never forget. The sheik and his son and their men had ambushed her party on the trail down from the high pass through the mountains because the sheik had wanted North Wind, and because the big white stallion wouldn't go anywhere without Johanna.

She remembered again the blade of Farhad's sword sliding so easily into Jaufre's back, and closed her eyes against a wave of nausea. She took a deep breath and let it out, slowly. When she opened her eyes Kadar was sweeping past, and she stiffened her spine because it was a point of honor never to show weakness before the chief eunuch. A tall man of massive girth with a broad, impassive face clad in skin the color of tar in which no single hair could be found, he ignored her to shake back the elaborately embroidered brocade of his long, wide sleeves and draw the filigreed bronze bolt on the door. The bolt was more an ornamental badge of Kadar's office than it was any serious kind of deterrence to forced entry. The locks on the other side were far more substantial.

Johanna had refused all attempts to indoctrinate her into the Islamic faith, to the further scandalous twittering of the harem inmates, but she had embraced the opportunity to learn Persian, because another language was always a useful skill. When she discovered that Kadar meant "beloved" in that tongue she had been hard put to it to conceal her amusement. As with everything else in the harem, excessive mirth could draw unwanted attention.

The door began slowly, oh so slowly, to swing wide. Johanna was leaning forward, almost on her toes, every fiber of her being yearning toward the other side.

"Nazirah! Wait!"

A small, slim figure slipped through the crowd of women and rushed forward. She had dark flashing eyes, an infectious smile and a merry disposition. She reminded Johanna of Fatima, a childhood friend. "Hayat," she said, striving to sound patient. "What is it?"

"Only this," Hayat said, seizing Johanna's hands in her own. "I need more indigo. Could you ask the guards to stop at the dyers' shed on your way back?" Hayat dimpled at Kadar. "You don't mind, do you, Kadar?"

Even the chief eunuch was not proof against Hayat's wiles, as indeed few of them were. Nevertheless he said sternly, "The master's orders are specific, Hayat, as you well know. Nazirah is to go directly to the stables and to return directly to the harem."

Johanna felt a scrap of paper transfer into her left palm. Her own closed over it. She gave Kadar a sunny smile that was not meant to be friendly and the chief eunuch was not so foolish as to take it so. "The dyeing shed is along the way," she said to Hayat. "If they have it, you will have indigo when I return."

She turned back to the door, smoothing back her braid and brushing the front of her tunic. In the process she slipped the scrap of paper into her sash.

With conscious ceremony Kadar bowed her through the doorway. Was the bow a little too exaggerated, a little over-elaborate? No matter. The door shut behind her with a thud that resounded off the blue-tiled walls of the harem's antechamber, vying with the trickling water of the inevitable fountain for precedence.

She felt rather than saw the two armed guards falling in behind her, fierce with scimitars and daggers. She knew the way by now and her pace quickened, until she was almost running again by the time she reached the next door. She didn't wait for the guards, she flung it open and burst into a walled garden. She threaded through roses red and white and pink and yellow—forever after she would associate the scent of roses with a feeling of imprisonment—and reached yet another door in the wall on the other side. She didn't wait for the guards to catch up with her, she hammered on the door with her fist. "Ishan! It's Johanna! Open the door!"

A horse's whinny, imperious and insistent, was heard, and Johanna laughed. "Ishan! Open the door before North Wind opens it for you!"

The door opened and Johanna shot through the opening as if she had been loosed from a bow. Still, North Wind was there before her.

Ishan, the stable master, was the only man in Sheik Mohammed's entire stables who could even marginally handle North Wind without injury. He was certainly the only one courageous enough to saddle and lead the stallion from his stall, and smart enough to flatten himself hastily against the stable wall as the great white stallion moved past him at a gait unsuitable for the relatively cramped quarters of the stable yard. She laughed again, caught a handful of mane and swung herself up on North Wind's back. He didn't stop as she settled into place, continuing on toward the double doors of the stable yard, his intent obvious. Either someone would open the doors or North Wind would go right through them.

Johanna was disinclined to slow him down. Indeed, she urged him on. She heard Ishan shouting and two brave or well-bribed souls ran for the gates and dragged them open just in time for North Wind to thunder through. She caught a confused glimpse of a man or men on horseback outside the gates and flattened herself on North Wind's neck. "Run, North Wind, run!" she cried, and felt his stride lengthen. The wind flattened her clothes against her flesh and tore her hair loose from its braid. The looming shadow of the palace walls fell away and they were at last gloriously out on the ribbon of sand groomed soft for the sheik's racing horses.

The trail ran next to a wide canal shadowed by date palms and almond trees, beyond which a horizon of undulating hills beckoned more alluringly than any line of hills on any horizon she had ever seen. Freedom. The hills seemed to whisper the word in her ears. *Freedom.*

In the sheer pleasure of the moment the rigid guard she held on herself at all times slipped, just a little. Jaufre. Shasha. How far beyond those hills were they? Had Shasha kept her promise?

Was Jaufre even still alive?

The great white horse, always sensitive to her moods, broke stride. She tightened her knees, banished thought, and bent over North Wind's neck again. Reassured, his stride lengthened and he ate up the track, a league and more of immaculately groomed sand filled with gentle rises and falls of ground and easy curves, meant to test and build speed and endurance. His gait never faltered, his spirit never flagged, and on his back Johanna felt that no distance was too great to travel so long as North Wind carried her on his back and her friends were at the end of the journey. For one precious moment, the moment she lived for every day, the moment that allowed her to possess her soul in patience for the other interminable hours she had to endure to arrive at it, she could imagine this was the day she would begin that journey.

And it seemed only a moment before the last of the palms flashed past. She sat up. North Wind's stride began to slow. After a few moments another horse drew level with them, flanks white with foam. It wasn't easy, trying to keep up with North Wind.

She knew without looking who rode the second horse.

North Wind slowed to a canter and at last to a walk. He was barely sweating. Johanna swung her leg over and slid to the ground, there to run her hands down his legs and pick up his feet to examine his hooves. He raised each foot obediently at a slight pressure of her hand.

"Still he obeys you as he does no one else," a rueful voice remarked. She stiffened, and tried to hide it.

After a slight pause, which she did nothing to fill, the voice said, "He ran well today."

"He runs well every day," she said, and stood up to see Farhad's eyes gleam with satisfaction. It wasn't often that he was able to goad her into speech.

This was the time she craved most, to be alone with North Wind, or alone if she discounted the omnipresent guards. Farhad did not ride with them often, but he was always an intrusion when he did, and she made sure he knew it. Very well, if he wouldn't let her ignore him, she would attack. "Has your father reconsidered giving me rooms in the stables?"

"This again?" He sighed. "As I have told you, repeatedly, an unmarried woman is safest in the harem." He smiled at her.

She didn't smile back. He didn't dismount, not even to wipe down his mount. That was a task for lesser beings. "As you saw this morning, North Wind dislikes it when I am kept from him."

He smiled again. "He can still run. As you both just proved. It is all my father requires of him."

She had already thought of ways of making North Wind physically ill and claiming it as proof of the great horse's sickness of spirit, but she hadn't been able to bring herself to do it. Not yet. Although it might come to that in the end. She leaned against the stallion and he responded with a reassuring whicker, a comforting bulwark against Farhad and his most unwelcome attention.

The sheik's son gave a nod and his guards nudged their mounts into a trot and fanned out in a dozen different directions. A dozen, Johanna thought, interested against her will. When the sheik's son rode with her his guard was usually two men, no more, the same as her own escort. She looked more closely at the retreating figures and saw that they were not guards but scouts, equipped with water skins and full saddle bags. They were dressed in layers of sturdy clothing, cheches wrapped securely around their faces and heads so that only their eyes were showing, and they wore braces of daggers and swords. "Where are they going?" she said.

The sheik's son gave a negligent shrug. "To see what there is to see, merely."

She didn't believe him. There was a tension about his shoulders that she had not seen before. "Are we expecting trouble?"

He smiled, although the expression seemed forced. "How nice to hear you say 'we.'"

"Your father," she said thoughtfully, ignoring the provocation. "He is well again?"

Sheik Mohammed's son sobered. "He is not," he said. "The doctors fear the worst."

He looked at her, slowly, deliberately, all of her, from the crown of now-tumbled bronze hair to the hostile gray of her eyes and down, over slim shoulders, full breasts, narrow waist, and long legs. She was attired in the raw silk tunic and trousers she had worn from Cambaluc, which they had let her keep for riding. Kadar had forbidden her to wear them in the harem except when she was going to and from the stables.

The clothes, sturdy, unglamorous, workmanlike, did nothing to deter Farhad's attention. He wanted her. Johanna, no blushing virgin, saw his desire and recognized it for what it was. She did what she always did: she ignored it, vaulting again to North Wind's back. Again, the stallion was quick to sense her mood, and she felt the great muscles contract beneath her.

He would kill Farhad for her, if she willed it so.

Oblivious, Farhad nudged his mount to come up beside them, and dropped his voice to what he apparently had decided was an irresistible growl. "When you are my wife, Nazirah, when you are in my bed, I will keep you too busy to brood."

She faced forward and nudged North Wind into a walk. "Your father promised that I would be freed in his will."

"In his will," Farhad said, his smile fading. "Not in mine. And when I am sheik of Talikan, my will rules."

She gave him a considering look, carefully maintaining her own mask of polite civility. He was a young man, strong, not ill-favored and, inescapably, would one day in the lamentably near future be the most powerful man in Talikan. It would be unwise to offend him too soon, and if it came to that—here she swallowed and set her teeth—she could tolerate his attentions long enough to find a way, both to exact revenge for his treacherous attack on Jaufre and to find a way out of this silken trap.

Because if she didn't, Johanna would never see the outside of the harem again. The mere thought of that great wooden door closing between her and the rest of the world for the last time made her throat close up. For a moment she couldn't breathe.

Farhad saw her distress and mistook the reason. "Come, Nazirah," he said in a soothing voice, "surely the prospect isn't so bad as that. You—"

She turned North Wind and kicked him into a canter. Her guards scrambled to get out of the way and for the first time that morning she saw their faces. One of them was new.

But not, she realized, first with a shock and then with a thrill of mounting excitement, new to her.

The new guard was Firas.

· Two ·

Spring, 1323 A.D.
Talikan

┝━━━┥

Johanna spent as long as she could in caring for North Wind after her ride, feeding him, watering him, grooming his coat, polishing his hooves, partly because his company was so much more acceptable than that of anyone behind the harem doors, and partly in hopes that the sheik's son would be called away before she finished. In this she was successful, emerging at last to find Farhad gone and the two guards waiting with varying degrees of patience to escort her back to the harem.

"Oh," she said, looking at Firas as if she was seeing him for the first time. "Where is Mahmoud?" she said to Tarik.

He addressed the area above and behind her left shoulder. In the entire city of Talikan it was by now well known that she did not share the sheik's bed, but one never knew what might happen in the future. She resided in the sheik's harem and she was subject to his will. At any moment the fancy could take him to sample this exotic, self-willed creature. She could end as his favorite, a wife, even. Thus no sensible man of the city of Talikan would dare trespass by addressing her with less than the utmost respect, but that didn't mean that Tarik, a deeply religious man, had to look at her face as she flaunted it with no veil before men not of her family.

Besides, she was the only person who could handle that very *afreet* of a horse, and Tarik had won a month's salary on North Wind's last race. He answered her with civility, familiar to a demon though she might be. "Alas, Mahmoud is dead, lady. Inshallah."

"Dead?" Johanna was all polite incredulity. "What happened to him?"

A shoulder raised and fell. "He fell from his horse and broke his neck, lady."

"Now, how did he come to do that?" Johanna said, marveling. "I would have thought Mahmoud much too good a rider to be so careless as to fall from his own horse."

"Yes, lady, and so would we all." A note of condemnation crept into Tarik's voice. "Nevertheless, what is one to think when his horse returns riderless and a search discovers Mahmoud's lifeless body at the bottom of a cliff?"

"What else, indeed," Johanna said gravely, and turned to Firas. "And this is?"

"Firas, lady."

She nodded at him, schooling her features to courteous indifference while her heart beat so loudly it roared in her ears. "Well met, Firas," she said, in a voice, no matter how hard she tried to control it, not quite her own. "Let us hope you manage to stay on your horse."

"Let us hope so indeed, lady," Firas said, his face bland.

Bland, but for the merest hint of a wink.

A wave of relief and joy swept over her, so intense that her vision grayed a little. When it cleared she found his dark eyes still steady on hers, compelling her to composure. She could betray by neither word not deed that they were known to each other. It would be worth his life, and possibly even her own.

Jaufre lived.

He lived.

It wasn't safe to say any more in Tarik's hearing, who already appeared quizzical at a courtesy she had never displayed to her other guards, but she could wait. She had absolutely no doubt Firas would find a way to speak to her again. She was even, now that her heartbeat had steadied, a little curious to see how he'd manage it. "Tarik, I am done here for the day," she said, regaining her composure, with an effort she hoped she had masked. "I return to the harem by way of the dyers' cottage." She had not and she would never call the harem home.

"Lady—"

Johanna turned her back on the protest Tarik felt obliged to make every time she deviated from a direct path back to the harem and strode off, letting them catch up to her or no, as they wished. Follow they did, Tarik's whine degenerating into a grumble. Firas said nothing at all.

The dyers' shed was one of a row of artisans' cottages built against the thick, continuous wall two stories high that formed first a barrier around the palace, which was then enclosed by the city itself and by the city wall, twice as thick and twice as high. These craftsmen, each deemed the best in the city at their individual trade, had been granted their places inside the royal enclosure by royal warrant. In return they received a rent-free workshop and handsome prices for their work wherever they sold it, although the sheik had first right of refusal on anything they made. There was a saddler, a weaver, a cabinetmaker, a glassblower, a goldsmith, a jeweler, and more. A tanner was off by himself in a location predetermined not to waft any noxious fumes in the direction of the royal nostrils.

The dyer's shop was between the weaver and the herbalist. Johanna knocked once, and went in. "Halim, well met the day."

"Salaam, Lady Nazirah!" Halim, sleeves rolled back and red to the wrists with the blood of cochineal bugs, bowed as best he could. "It is a joy to see you well and flourishing. And that great white monster you persist in riding at peril of your very life and limb?"

Johanna, once more fully in command of herself, patted herself down ostentatiously, extracting Hayat's scrap of paper from her sash as she did so. The guards remained outside, but she was never careless on the errands she ran for Hayat. "I survive, as you see, Halim, and North Wind, too, is in fine health. You may bet freely and with confidence on his next race."

"Hah!" Halim said, grinning. "And that I will do, my lady." If Halim, like Tarik, thought it a scandal and an abomination for a woman to ride a horse at the public races—and a stallion, no less!—he did not say so. Of course Tarik never said so, either, or not outright, nor did anyone else. The word of the sheik was law. Questioning that law had consequences, usually involving a whip, or even the edge of a sword.

The dyer's shop was sturdily built, and Halim was prosperous enough that his floor was tiled, but not so prosperous as to have his own fountain. Instead, a large urn glazed a deep blue was sunk into the floor up to the lip and filled daily by a small boy who came round with a donkey laden with sacks of water. The walls of the shop were white, with small, rectangular windows cut near the ceiling so as to let in the light and let out the heat. In spite of the messiness inherent in the craft of dyeing, it was scrupulously neat, with hanks of wool in various stages of drying looped over wooden trees as tall as Halim that surrounded vats of various sizes. The grate of a large brazier glowed with live coals beneath a large pot bubbling not quite over with a rich purple liquid.

It was a scene that looked both industrious and efficient, and indeed Halim was both. He was also a skilled smuggler.

"A lovely color, Halim," she said of the cochineal.

"Is it not, lady, is it not, indeed." Halim slid the bowl across the table for her to examine more closely.

Johanna tipped the bowl to admire the swirl of scarlet liquid, at the same time slipping the scrap of paper beneath it.

Halim slid the bowl back to his side of the table, hand beneath the table to catch the paper when it fell from the edge. "Is it the cochineal the lady Hayat is in need of this day?"

"It is not, Halim," Johanna said. "She hopes you have indigo in stock, a small amount only."

Halim made a wry face. "The lady Hayat will soon be setting up her own dyers' shed in competition with me."

"I think Lateef the weaver has more to fear," Johanna said with a smile.

They continued to pitch their voices to be heard beyond the cottage's walls, demonstrating to anyone within listening distance that there was nothing untoward or conspiratorial going on therein. "Let me see," Halim said, shifting boxes and jars and bags from the vast array on display. "Indigo, indigo, yes, I have some here." The lid of a cedarwood box was raised to display its contents, small square cakes wrapped in bright scraps of fabric and tied with dyed jute in elaborately decorative knots. Halim knew a thing or two about presentation and marketing.

"Excellent," Johanna said. "Could you spare two, most worthy Halim?"

"I believe I can," Halim said, and conjured a small silk bag with a thick bottom, into which he ceremoniously placed two cakes of the indigo. "Did you know, lady, that the flowers of the indigo plant are pink in color?"

Johanna, who had seen entire fields of indigo in bloom in Cipangu, widened her eyes. "No? Pink? Really? How curious, Halim, that a plant should camouflage its true nature in such a way."

"As you say, lady." Halim produced a length of jute and tied the mouth of the little sack with an even more elaborate bow. "I have often wondered how the first dyer discovered indigo's secret."

"Probably by accident," Johanna said. "A cut branch leaking sap on the leg of someone's trouser. Which then turns blue."

"But that would require the owner of the trousers to notice." Halim presented the bag to her with a flourish.

She accepted it, and felt the shape of the third item through the bottom of the bag. She beamed at him. "Thank you, Halim. Salaam."

"Salaam, Lady Nazirah."

There was no opportunity to speak further with Firas on the journey from the dyer's shop to the harem, and Kadar was of course waiting for her at the door. "Until tomorrow morning, Tarik, Firas," Johanna said to Tarik, meeting Firas' eye with a very fleeting glance.

"Lady."

"Lady."

The door closed on their bows.

"Kadar," Johanna said with a pleasant smile.

No smile of any kind was returned to her, not that she had expected one. "You are late, lady."

"Am I?" She held out the little silk bag with a hand she was pleased to note was rock steady. "Would you care to examine the indigo Halim the dyer sends to the lady Hayat?"

He gave the bag a perfunctory shake and dropped it back into her palm. "We would be pleased to see you in proper clothing as soon as possible, lady."

She smiled again without answering and strode down the tiled hallway, eschewing the seductive, hip-rolling stroll of the harem inmate for the vigorous, ground-eating stride of someone accustomed to wide open spaces, one with no limits placed on her activities. It was a rebuke of him and of the constraints of his realm, and they both knew it. Johanna reveled in it. Kadar, she was sure, marked it down in the column of her sins. By now, it had to be a very long column.

She went to her room and changed into the hated harem clothing, the briefest of sleeveless vests and diaphanous trousers gathered at waist and ankle with, of all things, tiny bells. They tinkled as she walked. The sound was meant to be seductive, but all it meant to her was an easy alert to her location. Her feet might as well be bound.

At least she got to remove the bells once a day.

The veil she refused to put on. Instead she brushed her hair and reworked it into its single braid. She folded her riding clothes away, her hand involuntarily smoothing over the lumps in the hems of her trousers. She washed her own clothes herself, by her own hand, ignoring the scandalized looks of the other harem ladies and the reproving admonishments of the chief eunuch, saying only that they were made of a special kind of silk from her home and required a certain kind of care. She had no idea how long she would be able to continue to get away with such specious excuses.

She thought of Firas. Perhaps she wouldn't have to for very much longer.

It was quiet and still in her room, the only movement the slight breeze stirring at her window, the only smell a slight scent of roses, the only sounds the calls of doves. She stood very still in the luxury of this brief moment of private peace to remember that tiniest of winks that Firas had given her.

She had not grieved for Jaufre. She had refused to do so. If she had grieved him, then he would have been dead, and lost to her forever. She would not admit such a thing to be possible, and so it wasn't. Jaufre was alive, had been alive all these months, even though the sheik's son had stabbed him most treacherously in the back and left him laying in the middle of the trail, there to bleed to death.

Stay with him! she had shouted at Shasha, who was preparing to follow Johanna as the sheik's men crowded around North Wind, forcing him down the trail. In the ensuing mayhem created by one determined stallion, Johanna had managed to drop her belt and her pack. *Stay with him! Heal him! Make him live! Promise me!*

And Shasha, eyes stormy with rebellion, had cried out, *He will live. I give you my word.*

He was alive.

Jaufre was alive. The wink could mean only that.

For a moment, for one precious moment stolen from the unrelentingly public life of the harem, she let her proud head fall, let the hot tears fill her eyes, let her shoulder shake with silent sobs. All these horrible months, frozen in a state of unknowing despair, suffering the loss of her freedom and the absence and possibly the death of her family of friends, while at the same time aware of the absolute necessity of maintaining a facade of calm control in a place as competitive and potentially homicidal as a harem, she had allowed herself neither hope nor despair, only certainty, that Jaufre and Shasha were alive and on their way to Gaza. It had always been the plan, that if they became separated, to travel to Gaza and wait there for the others. It was all she had had to cling to.

Just this once, she let the tears fall. Just this once, she let herself realize how frightened she had been.

The tears stopped. She wiped her eyes carefully, raised her chin, and squared her shoulders.

There was no perhaps about it. Firas was here, which meant that Johanna was not long for the harem. She would admit no other possibility for that, either.

"Nazirah! Nazirah, you stand there daydreaming while the greatest weaving of my whole entire life sits waiting!"

She looked around and saw Hayat standing in her doorway, a hand holding the gauzy curtains to one side. The other woman's face changed when she saw Johanna's expression. "What is it? What's wrong?" She took a quick step forward and dropped her voice to a breath of sound. "Did Kadar—"

Johanna summoned a smile and shook her head. "No," she said, "no, nothing like that. I was missing—I was missing my family, that is all."

Hayat pounced on her hands and towed Johanna out of her room and down the hallway to her own room, larger than Johanna's and much more crowded with belongings. "You spend too much time on your own, Nazirah," she said. "It leads to brooding, which is unpleasant, unhealthy, and unattractive. Not this afternoon, however. This afternoon you will come and admire me as I weave."

"I'm not to admire the weaving?"

Hayat laughed, and the other woman in the room looked up with an annoyed expression, which cleared when she saw who it was. She dipped a pen into ink and bent back over the sheet of vellum. The lady Alma was always in the throes of another poem. Some of them were quite good, in Johanna's opinion, but she regretted the lady Alma's need to read them out loud to whatever audience was present at the time. Although she could only approve of anyone in the harem who took up an activity other than gossip and quarreling while waiting to be called upon to service their lord and master.

A corner of the room was dominated by a standing loom holding a half-finished tapestry three ells in width and at least that much in length. To one side of it, wooden stands were loaded with hanks of fine spun wools dyed in yellows and browns. A basin stood ready, filled with water, and Johanna handed over the little bag. Hayat opened it and took out one of the squares of dye and dropped it into the basin. She lit the brazier beneath and gave the dye an admonitory stir with a large wooden paddle. "There," she said, "we will leave that to be getting on with itself." She knotted the mouth of the bag again and tucked it into her belt, giving it to what all outward attention was an absent-minded pat. She smiled at Johanna and said teasingly, "Will you sit at my loom, Nazirah?"

It was the custom of the harem to rename all of its inmates at the time of their incarceration (Johanna never thought of it any other way). The sheik himself had bestowed the name on her, which she later learned mean "like," or "equal" and which she at first took as a joke at her expense. Later she realized he was sending a subtle signal to the other inmates and most especially to Kadar, that because she was not called to the sheik's bed didn't mean she was not entitled to the same rights and privileges as the rest of the harem. Such rights and privileges as they were. When the anger had subsided, and whenever Farhad had been especially caressing on their morning rides, she wondered if his father knew of his son's interest in his "guest." If he did, it was possible that he had done his best, within the strictures of Persian society, to protect Johanna from that interest.

Although she resisted ascribing anything like benevolence to her kidnapper.

"I will not, Hayat," she said, as she had said every day since Hayat had first invited her to. Weaving was barely a step above embroidery, and Johanna had stringent opinions on learning anything to do with a needle and thread over and above the call of mending ripped out seams or darning tears.

Hayat laughed, a joyous sound very like bells ringing. Hayat meant "life," which was certainly appropriate, because Hayat was bursting with it, sometimes so much so that Johanna thought privately she would one day break right through the imprisoning walls from sheer exuberance.

Alma snorted, scraping busily at her vellum with a penknife. Alma meant "learned," given probably because of her ability to read and write.

So far as Johanna had been able to discover, Alma was the only other member of the harem besides herself and Hayat who could.

"If the lady Alma is willing," Johanna said, "I would like to continue my writing lessons."

Alma looked up and smiled, brushing a strand of hair back from her face and leaving a smear of ink behind. "Of course, Nazirah," she said. "Especially as this pestilential poem has gotten hopelessly stuck."

Johanna did not ask how because Alma would have told her, at length. She curled up on a nearby cushion instead and Alma provided her with a sheet of parchment, almost transparent from being scraped and reused so many times. Spoken languages came easily to her, written ones less so, but Persian was infinitely less complicated than Mandarin and every bit as beautiful in written form. Every sentence looked like it should be framed and hung on a wall.

Today, Alma had chosen a poem by her favorite poet for Johanna to translate, working from a Uighur translation, which language Johanna had learned young and well from Deshi the Scout. "That way," Alma explained, "you can compare your translation to the poem as it was originally written in Persian."

Johanna surfaced hours later, hand cramped, shoulders stiff with the effort of concentration, to the sound of a distant bell, accompanied by the patter of bare feet on tile. She looked up to see that the sun had set and that while she was absorbed in her work, a servant must have come in to light the oil lamps hanging from brackets on the walls.

"Let me see," Alma said, extending an imperious hand. It was said in the harem that Alma was the daughter of a king, an incentive to a trade agreement between the two kingdoms, and at moments like these Johanna was inclined to believe the rumor. She handed over the parchment.

"'Come, fill the Cup, and in the Fire of Spring,'" Alma said, "'The Winter Garment of Repentance fling/The Bird of Time has but a little way/To fly—and Lo! the Bird is on the Wing.'" She lowered the paper and smiled at Johanna. "Well done, Nazirah. Wait, let me read out the same verse in the original." She searched for and found a small book, parchment pages bound between covers, handprinted, a little faded but still legible. "Here, you read it."

Johanna read it slowly all the way through, the words in the original Persian lovely, graceful, as natural in flow as water moving downstream.

The image of a bird on the wing worked powerfully on her in her present state of mind, and to distract herself she said, "This poet of yours? What did you say his name was?"

"Umar al-Khayyam," Alma said. "He was born not far from this very spot. He studied in Samarkand and then he went to Bukhara, where he lived out his life."

Johanna remembered seeing Bukhara in her father's book. It was north of here, a little north and west of Samarkand. It was a major city on the Road, known for its fine carpets.

"He was not only a poet, Nazirah, he was a philosopher who studied everything from the rocks on the ground to the stars in the sky." Alma's voice was reverential, and perhaps even a little envious.

"You would like to study the stars in the sky yourself," Johanna said.

Alma raised her eyes, an eager expression on her face, only to have it fall again when the arcaded ceiling got in the way. "They move, you know," she said in a low voice.

"What moves?"

"The stars."

Johanna looked at her, puzzled. "Of course they move, Alma," she said. Any dark night on the Road proved it beyond doubt.

"But some of them wander," Alma said. "I have read that it is so." Her face was the picture of yearning. She was a true scholar, a seeker after information for the sake of the information itself. "One must observe, over a period of time, to see them move. I had hoped to observe them for myself one day."

Johanna's brow creased. "From the garden, at night—"

Alma shook her head. "I asked. Kadar said no."

You shouldn't have asked, Johanna thought, but was just—barely— smart enough not to say so out loud. Accustomed to a life of freedom, in the harem it was an ongoing difficulty to master her tongue. If Kadar couldn't punish her, he could yet punish others in her place. "Perhaps the rooftop?" she said instead.

"There is no access to the roof from the harem," Alma said.

Alma was still called to the sheik's bed from time to time. It was the proximate cause of Johanna's smuggling activities.

Well. That was her excuse. Hayat had approached Johanna for help during Johanna's first month in the harem. "You walk from the harem to the stables every day," Hayat had said. "Halim's cottage is hardly out of your way."

Hayat's words, did she but know it, fell on fertile ground, as Johanna had lived that first month after her arrival in a state of bubbling rage. She was ripe for any act that directly or indirectly exacted revenge on her captor, even if it was only depriving him of children by at least one member of his harem, and she was utterly reckless of any consequences. It was another month before she gave any thought to what it was she was smuggling in, and another month after that before she asked. By then, Hayat and Alma were her firm friends, and she had seen with her own eyes how joylessly Alma responded to a summons from the sheik. Hayat had not been called to the sheik's bed since Johanna's arrival in the harem.

Thinking of all of this now as she gathered her parchments together, Johanna said, her eyes on her task, "Your master the sheik is known to entertain and sponsor philosophers here at Talikan. Perhaps he could be, ah, persuaded to access the roof for you." She quirked an eyebrow.

Alma tucked her ink and pens into an exquisitely carved sandalwood box. "Perhaps," she said slowly, her brow puckering. "It would have to be phrased in the right way..."

Johanna left it at that, contenting herself with imagining the expression on Kadar's face should such a thing be commanded of him by his lord and master. "Alma," she said. "How long have you been in the harem?"

"Eleven years," Alma said. "And ten months." She paused. "And sixteen days."

She stopped short of enumerating the hours and minutes. Almost twelve years, Johanna thought.

It had been seven years ago that Jaufre's caravan had been attacked on the Road, his father killed, his mother kidnapped and sold in the Kashgar slave market. She had not dared ask before, but the appearance of Firas that morning had woken her to the realization that her escape might be nearer than she had thought. And besides, she could trust these women. She dropped her voice. "At any time here in the harem, Alma, did you perhaps meet a Greek woman? She would have been older but lovely, dark hair and eyes. Her name was Agalia. She might have been called the Lycian Lotus."

Hayat's loom slowed. Alma met Johanna's eyes and said gently, "No, Nazirah. To my knowledge, there has been no one of that name in the harem during my time here."

Alma would not ask, Johanna knew, but she could feel Hayat's curiosity burning from across the room.

The distant bell sounded a second time, followed by another, larger patter of footsteps and many voices chattering. Hayat tidied away her bobbins and shuttles and racked her loom, and rose to stretch out her back. She checked the pot of dye. "Perfect," she said in a satisfied tone, and dropped in two hanks of undyed spun silk and addressed it in stern accents. "A beautiful blue you will give me, the color of the sky at dawn."

Johanna laughed.

Hayat looked around. "Hungry? I am famished!" She smiled at Alma, and Alma smiled back. Their gazes held, and Johanna, unnoticed, excused herself.

She had to admit that the privies in the palace were lovely, raised above their humble function with more tile and smooth seats, each separated from the others by a half wall, and so well constructed and maintained that the smell never became noxious.

She laughed silently to herself, sitting there alone in the dark. It was a measure of her dissatisfaction with her current position that the best thing she could find to say about it was that the necessaries were comfortable.

She thought of Firas, and decided that she would enjoy such comfort while she could, because very soon it would be back behind a bush on the side of the Road. She couldn't wait.

Back in Hayat's room someone had extinguished the lamps and the darkness of evening gathered in the corners. "Hello?" she said.

There was a scrabbling sound and a rustle of clothing, and first Alma and then Hayat came forward. Alma looked panicked, Hayat rebellious, and both women were flushed and rumpled.

She couldn't pretend that she hadn't seen, so Johanna bowed slightly. "Forgive me for disturbing you," she said, and passed on down the hall to the common room.

She had traveled the Road since birth and had learned at an early age that love came in many forms, and Shu Ming had been wise enough to instruct her daughter in the ways of the flesh. "Desire is a powerful thing, especially in the young," she had told Johanna. "There is no stronger urge to satisfy, except, possibly, hunger."

"And this is how children come into the world?" Johanna said.

Shu Ming had cupped Johanna's cheek and smiled into her daughter's curious eyes. "It is," she said, "and it can be so much more."

What Johanna found so offensive in harem life was that it contradicted everything her mother had taught her. There were at a rough head count a hundred women in the sheik's harem. For lack of anything better to do, Johanna had worked it out mathematically. Even if he distributed his favors equally, which he did not, even if to be fair he rotated each woman through his bed one at a time, the harem inmate would see his bed an average of three nights out of 365. If a harem woman was in need of a presence in her bed for purposes other than sleep, she would do best to cultivate a relationship with another member of the harem.

Which it appeared that Hayat and Alma had done.

Johanna remembered those three days at the summerhouse with Edyk the Portuguese, her last days in Cambaluc but one, and that one the day of her father's funeral. So much joy, attended by so much sorrow, the both to send her down the Road and out of Cambaluc and by the carelessness of fate to her confinement here in the harem.

She knew a sudden, fierce ache to feel again Edyk's hands touching her, his lips on her own, the intoxicating escalation of pleasure that led to such a bright, exquisite culmination of feeling in body and mind. What she had had with Edyk bore no resemblance to what the members of any harem experienced with their owners.

Shaken at how vivid those memories were, at the yearning they awoke in her own body, she went soberly into dinner, the sound of two pairs of slippers on tile close behind her.

If Hayat and Alma were discovered, they would be killed. Three months into Johanna's stay, one of the women had been caught with one of the eunuchs, who was found to be not so much a eunuch after all. The eunuch had been splayed like a fan in the courtyard, castrated, and disemboweled. The woman had been tied in a sack and thrown into the river. The screams of both lingered still in the thoughts of everyone in the harem for days afterward.

Which was, Johanna thought now, part of their purpose. If Johanna had found them out, someone else would. Spies were rewarded in the harem.

Perhaps they wouldn't be discovered, she thought, her step slowing as an idea struck her.

Perhaps Johanna would take them with her when she left.

She woke early the next morning and was dressed to leave her silken prison at the appointed time. Kadar, silently disapproving as always, met her at the door. Tarik and Firas were waiting on the other side, North Wind in the yard, and moments later she was riding the wind, her guards faint but pursuing. The sheik's son was not with them today and her spirit rose accordingly. She lay flat on North Wind's neck and cried out, "Run, North Wind! Run!"

North Wind needed no encouragement. He lengthened his stride and the almond trees and the date palms and the canal beside the track melted into a green and silver blur. The thunder of his hooves and the wind of their passage roared in her ears. She heard a voice crying behind her and ignored it for as long as she could. "Young miss! Young miss!" The voice changed. "Wu Li's daughter, stop that monster this instant!"

She sat up and North Wind's stride slowed. Firas came galloping up and reined in beside her, out of breath and evidently out of temper as well. "Did you not hear me calling you, young miss? We don't have much time, and we must speak!"

"Where is Tarik?" she said, looking around.

"His mount threw a shoe just outside the door to the stable yard," Firas said, adding no explanation as to how such a thing might have happened.

Johanna laughed. It was impossible not to.

"Yes," Firas said, "it is all very well for you to laugh, young miss, but we will be out of his sight for a very few moments only and if we are out of his sight for longer than that I will answer for it with my head! Please slow down!"

North Wind slowed to a walk. "Jaufre," she said. "He is alive?"

His expression softened. "He is alive, young miss," he said. "Jaufre is alive."

She turned her face away from him, battling once again for control. North Wind, always sensitive to her moods, moved uneasily beneath her, and she drew in a deep breath and sat up straight. "I saw you wink at me. I was sure that was what you meant, but—"

"He is alive, young miss, my hand on my heart," Firas said. "He lives. I wouldn't call him well, but I believe in time he will be."

"Where?"

"I left them in Kabul, but it was Shasha's intent to join the first caravan going to Gaza. She said that was the plan, if you became separated."

"It was," she said. "But Kabul is so near, and Gaza so far. We should go there." She looked hungrily at the rolling hills on the western horizon. They beckoned her even more strongly now than they had every morning she had ridden out. "We could go now."

"They would be after us in minutes," Firas said.

"We should go, Firas!" she said. It was agony, to feel the taste of freedom on her tongue and not be allowed to swallow. "We may never have a better chance! This isn't a tale of the Genjii, I'm not a princess and a magic carpet isn't going to appear to whisk us out of here! We should go! Now!"

"The sheik's men would be after us, and would catch us, in minutes," Firas said, his own voice rising in turn. He looked over his shoulder and lowered his voice. "We need some kind of distraction, something to draw their attention while we escape."

North Wind whinnied and tossed his head. Almost Johanna could believe that he agreed with what Firas was saying.

"Besides," Firas said, "they may have already left Kabul. Indeed, it would be best if they had."

"Why?"

"Ogodei is coming, young miss," Firas said. "And Gokudo is alive, and he is with him."

Ogodei was the Mongol baron, the head of a force of a hundred thousand men assigned by the Khan in Cambaluc to patrol the western reaches of Everything Under the Heavens. Gokudo had been the mercenary soldier from Cipangu who had been her step-mother's lover and her father's murderer.

Johanna stared at Firas, shocked. "Gokudo! But he's is dead, Firas, we all saw him put to death at Ogodei's word!"

"He lives, and he is now Ogodei's favorite captain."

"That cannot be true," she said hotly. "Ogodei was my father's good friend! He would not dishonor his memory so!"

"Gently, young miss, gently," Firas said. "I merely report what I hear on the Road."

Her brow cleared. "Then it is only rumor."

He looked at her, and her heart sank at the pity in his eyes. "I have also met refugees on the Road, young miss, from the cities and oasis towns that Ogodei and his army have attacked and destroyed." He pressed his lips together for a moment. "They are few in number, admittedly, but they almost all speak of one of the Mongol captains who wears black armor, who wields a tall staff with a curved blade. He is the fiercest of the captains, they say, with no mercy for anyone, men, women, children, the aged. He slaughters them all, at his master's bidding."

She stared at him, white to the lips.

"I believe Ogodei has determined to carve his own empire out of this part of Persia," Firas said. "And a ronin samurai from Cipangu would be a valuable asset to him in this endeavor."

But she was no long looking at him. "Young miss?" Something in her expression must have alerted him, and he pulled his horse around.

Tarik found them there when he came galloping up, staring numbly at the bodies of all twelve of the scouts sent out by Farhad the previous morning.

They lay side by side in a neat row. Each one of them had been expertly flayed, castrated, and had had their genitals stuffed into their mouths.

· Three ·

Spring, 1323 A.D.
Kabul

⊢———⊣

t had been a cold winter, one snowstorm after another, followed
by thaws and rain, followed by freezing temperatures that turned
everything to ice, followed by more snowstorms. The people of Kabul
emerged from their homes like pale, thin ghosts of themselves, blinking
dazedly in the sunlight of longer days, not quite trusting in the warmer
temperatures. Shutters and doors opened and remained so. Neighbors
greeted each other with no memory of past quarrels and vied with one
another in the clearing of communal toilets and fountains and streets,
and in the cultivation of garden plots barely thawed.

The weeds around the dilapidated fountain in their tiny courtyard
sprouted in a welcome show of green, and one day Félicien came home
from the market with a basket of fresh strawberries. They devoured them
on the instant.

With the sweet juice of the berries lingering on his tongue, Jaufre
had the curious sensation of waking up. The room he was in seemed
familiar and at the same time unfamiliar to him, small and square, and
while obvious effort had been made to keep it clean the dirt bricks that
formed the walls were crumbling beneath several layers of whitewash
to form tiny piles of debris in odd corners. What had once been a small
window had been inexpertly hacked into a larger one, and a roughly
planed wooden sill recently plastered into place to form a seat. Light
poured through it, illuminating the neatly rolled bedrolls in one corner
and the packs heaped in another. There was a pot and a pan and four

bowls stacked on a small table. A large brown urn stood next to one a size smaller, the mouths of both covered with plates. An unlit brazier sat nearby, next to a bucket of charcoal.

His own bedroll was arranged against the east wall of the room, out of the direct sunlight streaming. Félicien, Hari, and Shasha were seated around it in a solemn half-circle, watching him. He stared at them in silence, and in silence, they stared back, all with the same expectant expression on their faces.

Félicien. A slim presence in a worn dark robe, a thin, beardless face with high cheekbones and a wide, thin-lipped mouth. A student, no, a goliard he called himself, from a country far to the west, who had been traveling the Road for years. There was a lute, well played, and a light, pleasant voice given to ballads about love and war. He collected coin in his bowl around the fire each night. He was a self-styled seeker after truth, who had joined their caravan...where was it? Chang'an? Yarkent?

He couldn't remember, and the inability to do so bothered him, so he let his gaze move to the next person. This name was slower in coming. Hari. Skin and bones barely clad in a length of saffron fabric that wrapped around his waist and over one shoulder. Dark, steady eyes that implied knowledge and experience, and an unquenchable need to gain more. The priest from the lands south of the Hindu Kush, whom they had first seen being beaten before the gates of Kashgar. He couldn't remember why.

And Shasha. Proper name Shu Shao. His foster sister, adopted by Wu Li. Trim and neat in her Cambaluc robes, and supremely capable at whatever she decided to set her hand. A cook. A healer. A...trader.

A trader. Like himself.

It was Shasha who at last broke the silence. "Jaufre?"

"Shasha?" he said. He tried to sit up, and was incredulous to realize that he was too weak to do so unaided. Hari and Félicien each took an arm and Shasha tucked a bedroll between him and the wall.

Birdsong sounded from beyond the window. He took a deep breath and put a hand involuntarily to his back, where there was a dull ache in one spot. He prodded it with a cautious finger, but the ache was all there was. Why that was important he could not immediately remember.

"Drink this," Shasha said, putting a cup beneath his nose.

Perforce, he drank. The herbal decoction wasn't noxious but it wasn't delicious, either. Hari dipped a new cup from the large urn, which he was relieved to find was water, cool and fresh. Exhausted from the effort of draining it, he leaned back against the wall, his eyes closed. "Where are we?"

"Kabul," Shasha said.

"Kabul? But—" He frowned. Surely they had only just been in that great pass, high and flat, between the mountains of the Hindu Kush and the Tian Shan? No, coming down from it. He remembered the steep, crooked trail choked with pine and juniper, slippery with rockfalls, riddled with blind curves. A route perfect for ambush and attack.

He opened his eyes and looked out the window. A drape of gauze had been tacked over it, now drawn back to allow the sun to brighten the corners of this otherwise very dark room. A small, dusty courtyard lay beyond it, where he could hear a trickle of water. "Kabul," he said again, and despised how weak his voice sounded.

"Not Kabul, precisely," Shasha said. "More on the outskirts of it."

"Don't you remember, Jaufre?" Félicien said.

"Gokudo?" Hari said. "Ogodei? The sheik?"

"Johanna," Jaufre said, and shook his head, frustrated. "Where is she?"

A heavy silence fell. Shasha got up to refill his cup from the urn. "Have some more water," she said, offering it to him.

He shoved it away, spilling the contents of cup on the floor. "Johanna," he said again.

"I'll get more water," Félicien said. He took the urn and left the room.

"Do you remember?" Shasha said.

He did remember it all now. It all came back in a rush of brief, too vivid scenes. Shu Ming's death. Wu Li's remarriage. The secret departure from Cambaluc. Joining Wu Cheng's caravan at Chang'an. The months on the Road. Leaving the caravan in Kashgar to traverse the mountains through Terak Pass. The nearly successful attack by Wu Li's widow's paid thug, Gokudo. Their rescue by Ogodei, Mongol general and family friend. Gokudo's execution, Ogodei's parting gift. The trail down from the pass.

And then the sheik and his men. The sheik's son, Farhad. The sharp metal piercing his back. The shock and the subsequent searing pain. Falling. North Wind's angry neigh. Johanna shouting. And then the images faded to darkness.

"He stabbed me," Jaufre said.

"The sheik's son," Shasha said. "Farhad. Yes. In the back." She indicated. "Where it hurts. Does it still hurt?"

"It aches, but…" He felt his back again. The area was tender and his muscles protested. In sudden fear he raised his arms and lowered them, flexed them at the elbows, made fists and opened them. He threw back the covers. His feet and toes and knees, everything functioned, but his skin hung on his bones.

Félicien returned and he lay back, pulling his covers up. Félicien poured out another cup of water and this time he accepted it and drank it down, suddenly aware of how thirsty he was. He handed the empty cup to Shasha and said in a voice he hardly recognized as his own, "Tell me."

"Johanna, so far as we know, is with North Wind," Shasha said, answering the question she knew he wanted an answer to first.

"And North Wind is with Sheik Mohammed."

"Yes."

"And Sheik Mohammed is where?"

Shasha exchanged glances with Félicien and Hari. "All we know is that it is a place called Talikan."

"Do we know where Talikan is?"

Shasha hesitated. "As yet, no. Not precisely. But—"

Jaufre summoned up enough energy for a glare. "Why aren't you with her?"

Shasha glared right back. "Because I had my hands full keeping you alive."

"You should have gone with her," he said.

"And you should have known better than to turn your back on that poisonous little spawn of the sheik," she said smartly.

Hari raised his hands, palms out, smoothing the air between them, and spoke for the first time. "Gently, my friends, gently. Harsh words will not change our dilemma."

"How long?" Jaufre said.

Shasha met his eyes squarely and said, "Six months."

"What!" He sat up again and swung his legs to the side of the cot. Shasha didn't try to stop him, merely watched as struggled to his feet. His legs would not hold him up, and worse, a wave of dizziness forced him back down, sweating and swearing in a breathless voice. He subsided as they rearranged his limbs and pulled the covers up over them again. "Six months, Shasha," he said. "In the name of all the Mongol gods, what is wrong with me?"

"You mean other than being stabbed in the back with one of those curved pig-stickers the Persians call swords?" She huffed out a breath. "It was everything we could do to keep you from bleeding to death on the spot. When I was marginally sure you wouldn't, we fixed up a litter and carried you down the trail. Firas scouted out a village and we took you there. It was filthy and in spite of everything I could do your wound became infected. You got through that, believe it or not, and then the village came down with typhus, which you also got."

"I don't remember any of this," Jaufre said faintly.

"You were delirious," Shasha said. Also coughing hard enough to bring up an organ, covered in red rash and complaining constantly of severe headaches, but she didn't say so. For a few horrible days she had been certain he was going to die, but she didn't say that, either. "You were delirious for a long time. Even after we left the village you were delirious off and on again." For months. "We brought you to Kabul because I thought we might find a doctor here who could help you."

"You left her behind," he said, his eyelids drooping, his voice even fainter now.

"She ordered me to stay with you," Shasha said. His eyes closed and his breathing deepened. "The last words she said were of you," she said in a softer voice. She smoothed his hair back from his forehead, and whispered, "She commanded me to save your life, Jaufre. And I promised her I would."

That afternoon Jaufre woke to the presence of a man in a crooked turban and a once handsome robe covered with unidentifiable stains, some of which had eaten right through the fine wool. "This is Ibn Tabib," Shasha said. "He is the doctor who has been treating you."

"Hah," the doctor said, beaming. He was Persian, short, dark of skin and hair, and of a cheerful rotundity. "It is good to see you back in your own body, young sir. It was start and stop there for a while, I can tell you." He had a brisk manner and deft but gentle hands. He peered into Jaufre's eyes and mouth, sat him up and prodded his wound, manipulated his abdomen, and placed his ear first against Jaufre's chest and then his belly.

He pinched the flesh of Jaufre's upper arms and thighs between thumb and forefinger and shook his head over the result.

At last he sat back. "Well," he said. "How much do you know about your illness?"

"Nothing," Jaufre said. "How much do I want to know?" He was feeling better, and in spite of nagging fears concerning Johanna he was able to concentrate on the here and now.

"Hah! You make the joke! A good sign." The doctor settled onto a pillow, his legs crossed, sipping from a mug of sweetened mint tea provided by Shasha. Hari and Félicien had absented themselves from Jaufre's examination. "Well, you know how you were injured initially." Ibn Tabib cocked his head, his bright eyes inquiring.

"Someone stabbed me in the back with their sword," Jaufre said. "It's about the last thing I really remember." Although nightmarish visions of dark, dirty rooms and endlessly painful rides swam at the edge of his memory, interspersed by occasional glimpses of Shasha's face, pale and tired, her strained voice telling him to roll over, stay still, drink this.

"Hah," Ibn Tabib said. It was an utterance he made frequently, used to punctuate many different meanings. "Yes, indeed, young sir, you were stabbed, but either your assailant was particularly inept or he meant to do you as little harm as possible."

"What?" Jaufre looked at Shasha, who was regarding her tea with interest. "He meant to kill me."

"Then we must assume ineptitude, and praise Allah for it," the doctor said. "The blade entered your back, glanced off your ribs and slid someway between flesh and bone to come out more than a handspan later." He paused to consider. "There was a great deal of blood, of course, which led Shasha here to fear the worst. She bound up the wound to stop the bleeding and moved you to shelter as soon as possible, where she could look at it more closely. All very proper." He beamed at Shasha and raised his cup in salute.

Shasha thought of those nightmarish days before they found a village far enough off the beaten track to be reasonably confident that they might escape the notice of passing travelers, who might in their turn find what belongings Shasha and Jaufre and Hari and Félicien had left too enticing to ignore. She repressed a shudder.

"Unfortunately, by the time she was able to determine that your insides were, in fact, not at risk, infection had set in. She cleaned the wound as best she could and stitched you up—a very neat job, I must say. It's a large scar—two, in fact—but they will fade in time." He sipped tea. "There was nothing she could do for the infection but keep the wound clean and dose you with willow bark. You were in a very bad way for some time—"

Eleven of the longest days of Shasha's life.

"—and then your fever broke. You were on the mend when, would you believe it, the village you were in came down with an outbreak of typhus, which you contracted. So did the young scholar traveling with you."

"Félicien? He's all right?"

"Yes," the doctor said, looking at Shasha with an expression impossible for Jaufre to interpret. She stared back, impassive, until the doctor coughed and returned to his tale. "I understand that your priest got it, too, but his case was less severe. He tells me he has suffered this malady before, which may explain it."

"Is that all?" Jaufre said.

"If you don't count the food poisoning, the near starvation and dehydration because of your inability to keep down anything down," the doctor said drily, "that was quite enough to be going on with, wouldn't you agree?" He nodded at Shasha. "You would have died three or four times at least, were it not for her, and for the devotion displayed by your other friends. Hah. Indeed, you are very lucky, young sir."

Jaufre looked at Shasha. A little color had risen into her cheeks. "Thank you," he said.

"I had to," she said. "I promised her."

He took a deep breath, and nodded once. What else was to be said could not be spoken of before strangers.

The doctor looked from one to the other. "Hah," he said, smacking his hands on his thighs. "It is not often that such a chapter of incidents leads to so happy an ending. I am very pleased with you, young sir, very pleased indeed. Now, as to your recovery." He bent a stern eye upon his patient. "You have lost perhaps a quarter of your body mass, much of it muscle. You may not rise immediately from your sick bed and pick up your sword." Jaufre followed the accusatory finger to the leather scabbard that hung from a makeshift peg on the wall. "You have been ill for months.

It will take weeks for you to recover your strength, and months to recover it completely."

Jaufre remembered the humiliation of failing to stand on his own feet that morning and felt his face grow hot.

"Hah," the doctor said, not without satisfaction. "So you have already tried. Good. I find empirical evidence always works best with stubborn patients, and soldiers are above all determined to prove their invincibility, young ones in particular."

"I'm not a soldier," Jaufre said. "I'm a trader."

Ibn Tabib ignored this. "Learn to stand again first. Then walking short distances." He raised an admonitory finger. "With aid, young sir. With aid. As you grow stronger, longer distances on your own." He looked at Shasha. "You may start him on solid foods, but bland, and in small amounts. Soups and teas for fluids, as much as he can swallow. A little wine once a day. Is the water from the fountain good?"

"Yes, effendi. We have all been drinking it. It is clear and cold and seems pure."

"Then water, too, as much as you can pour into him."

"Yes, effendi."

"Ha." The doctor rose fluidly to his feet. "Will I see you at my clinic tomorrow? Our patient from last week is returning."

Shasha looked up. "The young woman with the head injury?"

"Hah. Yes. It may be that we have saved her for many more years of abuse at the hands of her so detestable husband." They went out together, conversing.

Jaufre pushed back the bedding and heaved his legs over the side of the cot and looked down at his body, His skin, once a smooth healthy pink stretched over bunched muscle, was pale and loose. He pushed himself to his feet, grunting with the effort, and shut his eyes and clenched his teeth against the resulting wave of dizziness. He didn't fall. It was a minor triumph.

He opened his eyes again to see Shasha standing in the doorway, watching him. "With aid," she said.

He swayed, but shook his head at her when she took a quick step forward. She halted in mid-stride, and he lowered himself to the cot, the last few inches more of a controlled fall. "Tell me," he said. "All of it, this time."

"You should rest."

"Now," he said. "I remember everything that happened up until the time that son of a bitch stuck me. I heard screaming, and then—" he gestured "—nothing. Or not much."

"Let me make fresh tea." She served them both and sat down on a cushion opposite him. "You had fallen to the ground and were bleeding so profusely—" She took a deep breath and let it out slowly. "I got down to see to you. In the meantime, the Sheik and his men figured out soon enough that all they had to do was take Johanna and North Wind would follow."

She took another breath and said, with more difficulty, "She shouted to me as they took her. She ordered me, she commanded me, Jaufre, not to let you die. And I was the only one among us who had any experience with caring for the sick. I could go with her and let you die. Or I could let her go and you would live."

"And if I'd died?"

Her face darkened. "Don't you dare question my decision, Jaufre. Or Johanna's." She stood up and shook out her trousers. "Now, we get you well."

He stood up with her, slowly, shakily, but he was on his feet, without aid, no matter what the doctor had said. He knew a tiny spurt of triumph, and then he looked again at his sword, hanging from the wooden peg obviously placed there for it. He had been taking lessons from a master swordsman right up until the attack. He had been in peak physical condition. How long would it be before he was there again? How long before he could even raise his sword single-handedly? "Firas," he said suddenly. "Where is Firas?"

Shasha looked suddenly older and more careworn. "With Johanna."

All he could think of to say was, "Why?"

"Because I asked him to," she said. Before he could say anything else she said, "No, we have had no word. But he is with her. I am certain of it."

He closed his mouth on all he might have said. That Firas was new to their company. That they had no reason to entrust him with the well-being of one of their own, let alone when that one was Johanna. That he was Persian, like the Sheik, and could be counted on to sympathize more with a man of his own world than with a woman of Cambaluc, especially one who had abandoned the safety and security of home and family to hare off over the horizon on an adventure that a man of his culture would see as most ill-advised, not to mention scandalously unchaperoned. But Shasha was his sister in everything but blood and he would not willingly hurt her, no matter how great his fear for Johanna's safety. He cast about for another topic. "What assets do we have left to us?"

She looked relieved. "The sheik's men tried to take everything but Firas got away with my horse and Félicien and Hari on their donkeys, and one of the camels, the one carrying the spices. I've been trading them in the marketplace here for food and supplies." She cast an involuntary glance over her shoulder and lowered her voice. "I gave Firas one of my hems."

Johanna's father had left her a quantity of loose gemstones, mostly rubies, which the three of them had sewn into the hems of their garments before they left Cambaluc. Until now, they had had no need of them. "What did he say?"

"That it might be enough, but that he would return with Johanna regardless."

Possibly his judgement of Firas had been hasty. Possibly. "Have you spoken to Grigori?" Grigori the Tatar was Wu Li's agent in Kabul.

"I have," she said. "He recognizes Wu Li's bao, and he stands our friend. He found us this house." She gave a disparaging wave. "It's not much, I know, but all the better houses are too near the market. I thought it best if we could remain as much as possible unnoticed." She paused. "We are still too close to Cambaluc for my comfort."

"We have the bao?" He thought of the leather purse that never left Johanna's waist. "How?"

"We also have Wu Li's book." She smiled a little. "When they pulled her from North Wind's back, North Wind took exception."

Jaufre thought of the massive white stallion whose affections had fastened so oddly and inflexibly on the girl so much at the forefront of their thoughts. "I can imagine."

Her smile faded. "In the ensuing, shall we say, fuss? Johanna managed to drop her purse. They didn't notice."

"Was she hurt?" He heard the panic in his own voice, and tried to steady his heartbeat.

She shook her head. "I don't think so."

There was a momentary silence, fraught with memory. Twice in two days, he thought.

Shasha raised her head to look at him. "What?"

He realized he had said the words out loud, and his mouth twisted. "Twice in two days," he said. "First I let myself be knocked unconscious by Gokudo. Twenty-four hours later I let myself get stabbed in the back by Farhad. I was so amazingly useful."

Her eyes narrowed. "Self-pity is never useful, Jaufre," she said sharply. He felt himself flush and looked away.

"We were all attacked," she said, with emphasis. "You, me, Johanna, Hari, Félicien. Even Firas. Johanna was kidnapped. Don't you dare be such a child as to think for one moment that you were alone in this, or that you alone could have stopped it!"

She realized that her voice had risen, and she got to her feet to take a hasty turn around the room. When she passed the door she caught a glimpse of a shadow on the other side. Félicien or Hari or both, keeping out of range. Intelligent of them.

She took a deep breath, centering herself with the intonation that began any practice of soft boxing. Root from below, suspend from above. Root from below, suspend from above. Her anger still flickered beneath the surface, but now it was under control. She returned to her seat.

"We have to go after her, Shasha," he said, and the agony in his voice was enough to cause her anger to evaporate.

"No," she said, not without sympathy, because she had suffered through her own guilt over remaining with Jaufre, no matter what promises she had made.

"We have to go after her, Shasha!" He leaned forward, groping for her hand.

"No," she repeated, in a voice much firmer than she felt. "We talked about this, Jaufre. We decided, even before we left Cambaluc, that if we were separated on the Road that we would make for Gaza. She will make her way there, too." And Firas, she thought. Whether he helped her escape or not, he would meet them there as well. He had promised, and Firas the Assassin was not a man to give his word lightly.

"Besides," she said, "we don't even know where Talikan is. We only know that it is the sheik's home. It could be as far as Bagdad, or as near as Balkh, but without direction we could spend the rest of our lives traveling every spur and trail of the Road and never find it."

He was silent for a moment. "It's not on Wu Li's map?"

She bit back a quick retort. Her temper seemed to be deteriorating in direct proportion to Jaufre's recovering health. "No," she said. "I looked, of course. We all examined every page before Firas left. There is no location of that name anywhere in Wu Li's book, and we asked in the marketplace before Firas left. The name is familiar to many, but it is no better known than any of the thousand and one sheikdoms scattered from Terak Pass to the Middle Sea. The more the Mongols retreat to the east and the north, the more local warlords appear. You know this, Jaufre." She made herself take a calming breath, and said more patiently, "Which means that all we know is what we picked up in passing from the Sheik's men during our time together on the Road. The northeast of Persia. South and west of Samarkand. We believe."

"You believe," he said bitterly.

"Yes," she said. "It gives Firas a place to start, at least." Before he could speak, before he could think up something even nastier to say to her, she added, "The instant you are well enough to sit on a camel, we start for Gaza with the first caravan of a decent size heading west. We know where Gaza is. So does Johanna. Wu Li had a factor there."

"Abraham of Acre," Jaufre said.

"If he's still there, we have the bao. Like Grigori, he will help us. When she can, Johanna will meet us there. She might even get there before us." Unlikely, but not impossible, she thought. She took a deep breath and let it out slowly, preparing herself to give him the worst news of all. "There is another reason we need to start moving west, as fast as we can."

The tone of her voice made him look up. "What?"

"Ogodei." To her shame, her voice trembled. With an act of will she steadied it.

He stared at her. "Ogodei?"

Her eyes dropped to her hands, which were curled into fists. She straightened them, and smoothed one over the other, a nervous, wasted motion totally out of character. "Ogodei has brought his one hundred thousand down this side of Terak."

"Why?" he said, when she did not go on.

"He is…laying claim, I think is the only way to describe it. He's marching up to the front doors of every walled city, of every town and city of a size to make it worthwhile, and demanding that they surrender. If they do, he lets them live. If they don't, he destroys them."

"Destroys them?" Later he would think his prolonged illness had slowed his ability to think rationally.

"Destroys them," she said. She put a hand to her mouth and then with what looked like a determined effort dropped it and sat up straight again. "Refugees arrived in Kabul over the past month. Pitifully few of them, and the stories are horrific." She made a poor attempt at a smile. "He seems to imagine himself the reincarnation of Genghis Khan himself."

"Is he acting on orders from Cambaluc?"

"I doubt it."

"Why?"

"Shidibala Gegeen Khan is dead, murdered. The news came earlier this month, when the trails over the mountains opened. I think Ogodei is taking advantage of what always follows a change of power in Cambaluc to set up his own empire."

Jaufre was silent, digesting this. "He was always ambitious, Wu Li said." She nodded.

"Which cities?"

"Jaufre?"

"Which cities, Shasha?"

"While we were on our way here, he went first for Samarkand and then Tashkent, and from what they say didn't miss any of the oasis towns between. So far he's staying out of the mountains."

"So far?"

She met his eyes, and only then did he really see how worried she was, and how tired. "Rumor in the market has it that he is turning his attentions south."

"India?" he said.

She shrugged.

Realizing, he said, "And everything in between. Including Kabul?" Talikan? he thought.

"There's worse," she said.

He gave her an incredulous look.

"They say he has a new captain," she said. "A warrior, from a land far to the east."

He stared at her. "No," he said.

"He wields a tall staff, they say," she said. "One with a curved blade."

"Gokudo," Jaufre said, his voice barely above a whisper, and a chill chased down his spine.

· Four ·

Spring, 1323 A.D.
Kabul

⊢———⊣

I t took a month for Jaufre to force himself back into health, or enough so that he could walk some distance mostly without aid. He never sat where he could stand, never stood where he could walk, and if he could only run ten steps before he had to stop, breathing hard, then he ran those ten steps. He had begun to practice form with Shasha every morning and again every evening, Félicien joining in, Hari off to one side chanting his interminable oms. Yesterday he had taken down his father's sword and practiced some of the parries and thrusts that Firas had taught him, no matter that after five minutes the yard had begun to revolve slowly around him and he'd had to let Shasha replace the sword because he could no longer raise his arms that high.

This morning Félicien had announced his intention of walking into the city to see if the first caravan of spring had arrived. "They say in the market that there should be one any day now," he said.

"I'll go with you," Jaufre said.

Félicien glanced at Shasha. "There isn't much to see," he said.

"Go ahead," Shasha said, waving a hand in airy dismissal. "Kill yourself."

When they had left, Hari said gently, "He is sick at heart."

"He is sulking," Shasha said, and stalked from the room.

The city of Kabul was a claustrophobic wedge crowded into a narrow valley, an unlovely jumble of square buildings constructed of mud bricks, interspersed with the inevitable neighborhood mosque. On all sides rose the sharp-edged peaks of the Hindu Kush, still clad in a receding layer of winter snow, leavened here and there by tiny patches of green. On closer examination those patches proved to be the smallest of terraced gardens jostling for place with granite outcroppings and small avalanches of broken shale, reclaimed from the mostly vertical landscape with waist-high walls made of loose, readily available rocks. The nearest arable land was far to the north, on the other side of the mountains, and those citizens of Kabul too hungry to wait for the first spring caravans to arrive with fresh fruits and vegetables scrabbled in the hard dirt to grow a few of their own. It was at best a vain effort, thought Jaufre, viewing the scraggly results of one such, but still they tried, toiling up and down the steep trails and stairs to their homes with sacks of water on their bent backs. Here and there a poplar bravely raised a spindly, trembling head.

"There isn't even a university," Félicien said, regarding Kabul with manifest disgust.

"There's a madrasa at the grand mosque, surely," Jaufre said mildly.

"Teaching religion. What of mathematics and rhetoric and philosophy?"

Jaufre, out of breath from their short climb, didn't answer.

"Look," Félicien said, pointing. "There is the caravansary. Such as it is." He led Jaufre through a cluster of one-story buildings that formed their little neighborhood. Most of the men who lived there were employed in the construction of a new mosque not far away. Religion was the only industry that paid and paid regularly in Kabul. "They can't dig a well to water their gardens, but they can always find enough money for another mosque," Félicien said.

The women remained sequestered in their homes while their children too small to work played in the dirt outside their doors. A cloud of dust was already beginning to rise over the city and it wasn't even noon.

"An unlovely place," Jaufre said.

"It does not improve on closer inspection," Félicien said, and then clutched Jaufre's arm. "Look! Look, Jaufre, look there, you see!"

A cloud of dust, thicker than the one over Kabul, rose at the top of the pass leading into the city, and as they watched the first in a line of camels minced down the trail and approached the northern gate.

"Come, Jaufre!" Félicien said, his face alight with excitement. Jaufre couldn't blame him. His companions had not slept the winter away as he had and by now were heartily bored with Kabul and environs.

They arrived at the caravansary at the same time as what appeared to be at least half the population of Kabul. When Jaufre saw what was in the caravan's train, he curled a lip in disgust. "Slavers," he said.

Félicien eyed him. "It's not illegal."

"No, just disgusting. Let's get something to eat while they sort themselves out."

Jaufre fended off an offer for ground testicle of sheep—"Guaranteed to rekindle the interest of the most indifferent lover, truly, sahib!"—and found a kebab vendor next to a fountain in an adjacent square. Jaufre, whose appetite had returned with full, pre-injury force, ate three of beef and one of goat's liver. Félicien had one of chicken. No vegetables, of course, but they found an old man with a fruit cart piled with last year's apples. They were wrinkled and a little dry but still sweet.

When they returned to the caravansary, the novelty of the first caravan of the year had worn off and the crowd had dispersed, at least until the merchants had offloaded their goods and set up their tents. Jaufre inquired for the havildar, and was introduced to a Gurkha named Rambahadur Raj who wore a kukri as long as his arm in a worn but well-cared-for leather sheath. He was a foot shorter than Jaufre but he stood with an easy assurance that reminded Jaufre of Firas.

"I am Jaufre of Cambaluc, havildar," Jaufre said, inclining his head in a show of respect. "This is Félicien of the Franks."

"Salaam, Jaufre of Cambaluc, Félicien of the Franks," the havildar said, bowing his head less deeply in return. "Let us retire out of the sun and send for tea."

"That would be welcome," Jaufre said, not lying.

They settled beneath the awning at the front of the havildar's yurt and discussed the weather until the tea came on a round tin tray. The havildar brewed the tea with his own hands, poured it into earthenware cups and handed it around with a plate of hard biscuits. He sat back with a sigh, blowing across the top of his cup. "I confess, it is a pleasure to be at rest."

Jaufre sipped. The tea was hot and heavily sweetened and scalded his throat as it went down. "Has your journey been a long one, then, havildar?"

"As long as necessary, Jaufre of Cambaluc, but certainly more interesting than usual."

Jaufre raised an eyebrow. "Bandits? Raiders?"

Rambahadur Raj grimaced. "Armies, more like."

"Kabul talks of armies as well," Jaufre said. "In particular of a Mongol army, come recently over the mountains from Everything Under the Heavens."

The havildar nodded. "If rumor is true, this army has a general who regards himself as the living reincarnation of the great Genghis Khan himself."

Shasha had said almost exactly the same thing.

"But you yourself are of Cambaluc," Rambahadur Raj said. "If rumor is true and he is a Mongol, surely he is known there."

"He is, if rumor is true," Jaufre said. "It is said his name is Ogodei. A Baron Ogodei was recently named to the head of a hundred thousand and posted to the West."

The havildar's eyebrow went up. "Possibly an attempt to move an overly ambitious lord from the seat of power?"

"Possibly," Jaufre said, and shrugged. "I don't pay much attention to politics, but it was said that the late khan was…cautious in the men he chose to hold office near to his person."

"Not cautious enough," the havildar said drily.

As the last khan's tenure had been less than two years, Jaufre could hardly disagree. "As you say."

"This Ogodei, rumor says that he is bent on conquest," the havildar said. "That if a city surrenders to him that he will spare it, but that if it does not, he destroys it and kills all of its people, down to the last child."

Jaufre thought of his last sight of Ogodei, sitting at his ease on a pile of carpets before a yurt very like this one, drinking koumiss and watching with equanimity the death of one of his men by the riding of horses over his body. Next to him Félicien stirred, and he touched the boy's arm briefly in warning. It would not do to have it known that they knew Ogodei.

Besides, it was glaringly obvious that they didn't. If rumor did not lie, he had not, in fact, executed Gokudo, and there was no question that he had betrayed them to the sheik. "He is in the north of Persia now, if rumor is true," he said.

"If rumor is true," the havildar said, nodding. "But rumor also says that his army moves very fast. Samarkand fell in a matter of days, and is said now to be moving south."

Where Talikan might, or might not, lie. Jaufre did his best to keep his face without expression. "You will be leaving Kabul soon, then."

"As soon as the merchants complete their business," the havildar said grimly.

"Where does your route take you?"

"Kerman, Damascus, and Gaza."

Jaufre nodded. "I see. As it happens, havildar, my party wishes to travel west," he said.

"Does it? And how many are in your party?"

"Four."

The havildar scratched his chin, staring off into the middle distance. "I have no wish to be discourteous, young Jaufre of Cambaluc, but in these unsettled times I would be remiss in my duty to the security of the caravan if I did not inquire as to your companions, and your business." The havildar's gaze was steady on his.

"Of course," Jaufre said. "We are merchants, late of the house of Wu Li, also of Cambaluc."

"Wu Li," the havildar said. "I have heard the name."

"My master was not accustomed to travel west beyond Kashgar, but he had a large network that extended as far as Venice," Jaufre said.

"News came down the Road some time back that Wu Li had died." The havildar's tone carried only mild inquiry, but his gaze was intent.

"Sadly, that is so. Early last year." Jaufre thought the wound scabbed over but something in his expression made the other man look away.

"My condolences on the death of so worthy a master," the havildar said, bowing, more deeply this time in respect of Wu Li's memory.

Rambahadur Raj made fresh tea and renewed their cups. "There was mention of a daughter," he said meditatively. "Is she one of your party?"

Jaufre unclenched the teeth that had snapped shut. "We left Cambaluc together. Of necessity, we took different routes on the Road. The intent is to meet again in Gaza."

"Hmm," the havildar said. "I can't seem to recall the name of Wu Li's agent in Kabul..."

"Grigori the Tatar," Jaufre said, and pointed. "He lives on the edge of the market, near the Grand Mosque."

"I am acquainted with Grigori," the havildar said. "The others in your party?"

"You have already met Félicien," Jaufre said.

"And what is it you do, young man?"

"I am a scholar, and a seeker after truth," Félicien said, not without pride.

The havildar grunted. "A full-time occupation these days. I wish you luck with it. Who else?" he said to Jaufre.

"Shu Shao, a healer and Wu Li's adopted daughter."

"Another healer is always useful," the havildar said, nodding his head. "That's three. You said you were four?"

"The fourth is..." Jaufre couldn't help making a face. "Hari of India. He is...chughi." At Rambahadur Raj's quizzical glance, he added, reluctantly, "A priest."

"A priest?" the havildar said, thoughtfully. "A proselytizer?"

"No," Jaufre said firmly, repressing the memory of Hari being beaten before the gates of Kashgar for practicing religion without a license. "He is, as is young Félicien here, a seeker after truth."

"So long as he doesn't seek after one truth to the exclusion of all others," the havildar said drily.

"He does not," Jaufre said, still firmly, and resolved to make the matter plain to Hari before they set out. "And the fee?"

"You will mount yourselves?"

"We will."

"Provide your own food and fodder?"

"Yes."

The havildar mentioned a sum, Jaufre reacted in horror, and after fifteen minutes they had agreed on a sum that Rambahadur Raj thought was too low and Jaufre of Cambaluc thought too high. A good bargain, sealed by a handshake.

"Consider you have been given the usual warnings against fire and quarreling with your neighbors," the havildar said.

"Of course," Jaufre said.

"As to our departure, as I said before. We leave the instant my merchants have sold their last sack of rice, their last bale of cotton, and their last slave." The havildar raised his voice. "Alaric!"

One of the guards, taller than the rest, detached himself from a group of men setting up tents. "Havildar."

"Meet Jaufre of Cambaluc. His party of four will be joining us when we depart Kabul. Jaufre of Cambaluc, meet Alaric the Templar, my second in command."

"Not a Templar, havildar," the man said in a long-suffering tone.

He was dressed in the ankle-length, belted coat and baggy pants with the gathered hems of the Persian, and at first that was what Jaufre mistook him for. As he approached, though, Jaufre saw that his face was long and his nose thin, and when he raised a hand in casual salute of the havildar his sleeve fell back and Jaufre saw a flash of paler skin and realized that the color of his face came from long exposure to the sun.

Most interesting of all, the sword that hung at Alaric's side could have been the twin of Jaufre's own.

· Five ·

Spring, 1323 A.D.
Talikan

⊢——⊣

"Y ou cannot be serious," Johanna said. She was ignored, and in spite of the clear warning in Firas' eyes she went so far as to lay a hand on Farhad's sleeve as he brushed past her. "Farhad, if you fight Ogodei, he will kill you, he will kill every single one of your people and he will raze Talikan to the ground. To the ground, Farhad!"

That morning, upon the discovery of the bodies, Johanna had sent Tarik back for the sheik, who had sent his son. Farhad had looked at the remains of his scouts and returned them all inside the walls of the city at once. The sheik had dispatched other scouts to confirm the story, and the men who came back all too quickly bore first-hand-reports of an approaching army infiltrating the valleys between the surrounding hills and laying waste to everything and everyone in its path.

"How soon will they get here?" the sheik said.

The first scout exchanged a glance with his peers. "An hour, my lord," he said. "Perhaps two. No more."

The sheik and his son, aided by a circle of grim-faced counselors, began immediately to lay plans for a siege. Now, an hour and a half later, they stood on the wall next to the great eastern gate now, watching Ogodei's army spill from the hills onto the verdant plain between the hills and the city. Columns of smoke rose from farm buildings and villages.

Johanna wasn't supposed to be there at all, but she had taken advantage of the panic and confusion of the first moments of discovery to follow Farhad to his father's side. So far, everyone had been too busy to notice, or if they had, too distracted to order her back to the harem. "Look!" she said now, pointing. The Mongol army seemed to move forward like lightning, in horizontal bolts that covered terrifying amounts of ground in thrusts and forays. "They will be on the city in minutes!"

Farhad cast a casual glance over his shoulder and gave her an indulgent smile. "Calm yourself, Nazirah. Remember, we have seen this Ogodei. A bully, merely, who like all bullies backs down at the first challenge."

"A bully with a hundred thousand men, Farhad," she said. "And they are Mongols. It hasn't been that long since Genghis Khan laid waste to the Persian empire. You must have heard the stories." She thought of Halim the dyer, and of Alma and Hayat, and of Ishan the stable master. What Ogodei's men would do to them and their families would make death seem like a blessing. She tried to speak in conciliatory tones that would reach beyond the pride that formed such a strong barrier between Farhad and any reasonable viewpoint. "A bully, perhaps, as you say, but a bully with siege engines, and poisoned arrows, and fire bombs, and Ogodei alone knows what other horrors."

"I would match our walls against a hundred hundred thousand such men. We have withstood sieges before, Nazirah. There is nothing to fear."

His father was standing a few paces away and before Farhad could stop her she stepped in front of him, dropping to her knees to touch her forehead to the floor. "Sheik Mohammed, I beg you, for the life of your city and the lives of all its citizens, I beg you to hear me."

There was a sudden stillness in their immediate surroundings. No one in Talikan had ever seen Johanna offer anything but defiance to anyone within its walls, and her obeisance shocked them all into momentary silence.

The stillness gave her hope. "Lord, you have observed Ogodei with your own eyes. He was known as an ambitious man in Cambaluc, it was the reason he was posted to the West when he was named to his hundred thousand. He is a great admirer of the Great Khan, Genghis himself. It was suspected in Cambaluc that he views himself as a stronger ruler than any vying for power in Everything Under the Heavens." She was speaking rapidly, afraid that she would lose the sheik's attention. "He was a friend of my father's, who knew him well. From the words of my father, the honorable Wu Li, whose voice was respected from Cambaluc to Kashgar, I believe I divine Ogodei's thought. I believe that he wishes to build his own empire on the back of your own, and with that empire at his back to bring even Everything Under the Heavens itself under his rule. Perhaps even to challenge Oz Beg Khan in the north."

She raised her eyes and somewhat to her astonishment found the sheik looking directly at her. Encouraged, she said, "Lord, I beg you, I beg you on behalf of all the people of Talikan to treat with Ogodei. If you submit to his rule, he will spare you and your city." She swallowed. "If you defy him, he will destroy it, and every citizen in it."

He opened his mouth as if to reply, and then shut it again. "When they come," she said quickly, "the front troops will consist of every man, woman and child from surrounding towns in villages, as well as soldiers defeated in other battles whom they have taken prisoner. They will drive these before their own troops, forcing you to waste your arrows and bolts before Ogodei's own troops arrive at your gates with siege engines."

"We have no report of siege engines in the infidel's train," the sheik said.

"They will build them," she said. "Even now their engineers are razing the villages and towns they have captured for materials."

"Father," Farhad said, "she can't know any of this. And why would you listen to a woman who dares to speak in your presence of war anyway?" He seemed to recall where they were. "She should not be here. She out of her place. Send her back to the harem."

It felt as if they were standing at the center of a large storm, surrounded by a whirlwind of frantic effort and only nearly contained panic. Johanna was conscious of Firas standing behind her, of Farhad one pace to left, and of the sheik, tall and still in his white robes, the white band of his headdress casting shadow over his deep set eyes. She hadn't seen him in over a month. He had lost weight. He looked pale and tired and she got the impression that he stood erect beneath the weight of his robe only with great effort.

He stirred. "My son has a point. How is it you know so much of the war tactics of the Mongols? Your father must have been foolish indeed to allow it."

"Lord, what does it matter!" she cried. "They are Mongols! Remember Baghdad! Remember Kiev! They have made an art of warfare! If you resist, they will destroy you, and Talikan, and every living soul inside its walls!"

The sheik listened as the echo of her words was devoured by the thunder of the approaching army.

In an agony of apprehension, she could only imagine what was going on inside his head. The Persians were a proud race, even now, hundreds of years after the fall of the empire that had once laid claim to everything from Khotan to Zaranj to Toprak Kala. Broken now into many separate pieces, walled cities and oasis towns separated by vast stretches of steppe and desert and truncated and isolated by mountain ranges, it was every community for itself. No leader of any community, no Persian and certainly no follower of Allah would find it easy to bend the knee to a barbarian horde out of the East.

But this man must, she thought desperately. He must.

He raised his contemplative eyes from her face and looked at his son standing behind her. "Perhaps it would do no harm to speak to them," he said.

Something seized her braid and she cried out in surprise and pain as she was yanked from her knees to her back. Farhad dragged her across the rough stone and dropped her in an unceremonious heap out of his way.

"You are old, father," Farhad said, "with an old man's ideas." And before anyone could say anything else, before his father could move out of the way, Farhad drew his scimitar and thrust it deep into his father's breast.

Johanna watched numbly as blood welled from around the blade and stained the front of his robes. His legs buckled and he crumbled to his knees before his son, in a parody of the Muslim observance of prayer.

Farhad withdrew his sword from his father's chest and flicked the blood from the blade. Johanna felt warm splatters on her face. "We shall not kneel before this infidel horde and beg for mercy," he shouted. "We will fight!" There was a ragged cheer, although there were more than enough older men who did not cheer, who had heard Johanna's words, even if those words had been spoken by a woman. They were older men, she noticed with the part of her mind that was still functioning. The younger men looked excited and all of them had their swords out and raised in salute to Farhad. "And we will not just fight, we will destroy them utterly!"

He raised his scimitar over his head. A last drop of blood ran down the silver blade. "Allahu Akbar!"

"Allahu Akbar!" This time the response was larger and louder and longer.

"Allahu Akbar! God is great! Allahu Akbar!"

And with that, the transition of power was complete. Farhad began snapping out orders. Men leapt to obey.

Johanna tore her gaze away from the still face of the late Sheik Mohammed and got to her feet. "You are a fool, Farhad," she said fiercely, "and my only consolation is that you will know just how big a fool before Ogodei kills you!"

He looked over her head. "You, Firas, isn't it? See the Lady Nazirah safely back to the harem."

"Lord." Firas took her arm and force-marched her away. "You do our cause no good by calling him foolish in front of his men," he said in a fierce undertone.

"I would call him more than that!"

He gave her a hard shake. "Be still! This may be our chance."

Her vision, occluded by rage and fear, cleared at once. "To get away?"

"Yes, but we will have to do it before the city is surrounded."

"They will flank it," she said. "Ogodei knows me for Wu Li's daughter, he will know North Wind, could we not ride out to meet him and beg for the city's life?"

The glance he gave her was pitying. "Nothing you said to Farhad was untrue, young miss. If the city fights, it and all the people in it are forfeit. It is known that Ogodei has done the same to other cities ever since he came down from the Terak. He is building his own empire, and he will brook no interference. Besides, you have forgotten."

She looked at him.

"Gokudo," he said.

She halted at the top of the steps, and a sliver of unease shivered down her spine. "Gokudo," she said, although it sounded to Firas more like a hiss, and then they were both nearly knocked from their feet by a deafening roar of challenge that they could feel through the very stone of the walls of Talikan itself. As one, they turned and raced to peer over the side of the wall.

As far as the eye could see the plain was covered with men on horseback, mirrored armor glittering in the morning sun. Spears beat against shields and the shouts of a hundred thousand warriors joined in a deafening wave of sound. They were laughing, shouting, gesticulating obscenely at the men on the wall and above the gate. As more and more of them poured from the hills into the plain, Johanna saw more than one defender of Talikan grow momentarily still and pale beneath the sinking realization that there would be no defeating this massive army. Most of them had very probably never seen a hundred thousand men in one place before. Ogodei's force filled the plain in a broad wedge from canal on the right to river on the left, which left Talikan surrounded on every side they weren't bordered by water.

A ragged hail of arrows sailed over the walls and struck at Ogodei's front lines, filled with unarmed men, women and children who looked like farmers and their families. They fell, pierced by Talikan's arrows, and more were shoved forward to take their place. It was a plan designed to take the heart out of the fiercest defender, their own arrows killing their own people, and it did not fail of effect. An order was shouted, Farhad's voice, she thought dazedly, and another flight of arrows hurled themselves from behind the walls, striving for farther targets, most of them failing to find them.

"They are wasting ammunition," she said, her voice lost in the cacophony. Who knew that war was so loud?

She looked then for Ogodei, and picked out an unarmed man riding bareback, moving swiftly from the front of the force to a knot of men on a small rise well out of bowshot. The rider would be a courier, and she followed him as he bowed to the figure at the center of the knot. She pointed, and Firas pulled her hand back when an arrow sailed over her head too close for comfort. The Mongols were shooting back, but not in any concentrated way. They were saving their arrows, she thought. Farhad, if he had a brain in his head, would notice and act accordingly.

She had no hope that he would.

Firas put his mouth to her ear. "We must go!"

But then her eyes found Gokudo.

He was forcing his way through the throng gathering around the great wooden gates, which inside had four sets of massive wooden bars dropped into heavy brackets embedded into the walls. They looked formidable from where Johanna stood, until she looked again at the force on the other side of them.

Gokudo, the dull black of his quilted armor set apart from the sewed skins of the Mongols, looked more so, especially with the tall black spear with the curved blade held at his side.

Being told that he was alive when she had left him for dead so many leagues and months ago was one thing. To seem him resurrected before her was like a body blow, and she bent at the waist, gasping for breath. Firas grasped her arm and drew her upright, preparing to pull her from the wall by force if he had to.

By some malign chance Gokudo chose that moment to look up. He saw her immediately, and there fell one of those odd, fleeting moments of stillness that come in the middle of even the bloodiest of battles. The world fell away, and there were only the two of them left, she staring down at him, he staring back up at her.

"Hah," he said, she could swear softly, although how could she have heard him if he hadn't shouted it at the top of his voice she would never know. "Wu Li's daughter," he said, and smiled when her white face flushed with gathering rage.

He made an odd bow in her direction and looked around him. As she watched, he handed off the naginata to pull a woman from those being held in front of the Mongol warriors. She was more of a girl, Johanna saw, she couldn't have been fifteen years of age. Gokudo forced her to her knees in front of him, pushed his thumbs into her cheeks to open her mouth, and used her thus, all the while his eyes never left Johanna's. The girl struggled and choked, her hands clawing ineffectually at his. He finished, wiped himself on her hair and threw her behind him, where she was fallen on by more of his men, shouting and laughing as they held her down and fell on her one at a time. This led to an orgy of rape at the front of the force facing the city, many of the women used a dozen, two dozen times, until they died of it, or had their necks snapped and their corpses left where they lay.

This, too, she thought dimly, was part of a deliberate plan, to instill disgust and hatred and above all terror into the defenders, to see Persian women so used and so dishonored by Mongols, to stir them to do something reckless and careless and misjudged, to allow ungoverned rage to open a breach in their own defenses through which Ogodei's forces could then pour. They had done it before. It always worked.

Gokudo was still watching her, oblivious to the arrows raining down all around him, none of them coming close enough even to wound, let alone kill. He seemed to be wearing an invisible cloak that protected him from all harm. She saw his lips move, and thought numbly that she could hear the words he spoke as clearly as if they were standing back in the courtyard of her father's house in Cambaluc. "I look forward to our next meeting, Wu Li's daughter," he said, and bowed again, and laughed.

"I told you to get her back to the harem!" Farhad said, and cuffed Firas across the face and was gone again. The evil spell cast by Gokudo that had held them frozen in place was broken. Without more ado Firas hustled for the stairs, Johanna's arm clutched in his as she stumbled behind him.

They had passed through the door into the garden when she again realized where they were. "Give me a weapon," she said. At his look she said, "There are no weapons in the harem other than those worn by the guards. Give me a dagger, something."

His hand went first to the serviceable dagger at his waist, and then from somewhere produced one smaller and slimmer knife in a thin leather sheath with straps. "This can be fastened beneath your clothes."

She slid the blade out. It was a narrow piece of steel that looked deadly even at rest. "Firas. What happens to the harem when the sheik dies?" When the news of the sheik's illness has reached the harem there had been rumors, of course, but Firas, a Persian man, would know.

They had reached the door between the garden and the courtyard that led into the harem. Firas spoke rapidly, in a low voice, one eye on the door. "It depends on the sheik's will, and on how much attention the sheik's heirs pay to his will."

Farhad was his heir, Johanna thought, and he had already told her his intentions.

"They can be provided for for life. They can be sold to other masters." He met her eyes. "They could all be tied into sacks and thrown into the river."

"They could be given to Ogodei's men for toys," she said, the horror of the scene at the east gate heavy upon her.

"So long as they lived," he said, and by the expression in his eyes she knew he was thinking of it, too.

They heard the twang of bows and the exuberant ululation of Farhad's warriors. "The fools," she said bitterly.

"Soon to be dead fools," he said. "I will be at the harem door just after twilight."

"I won't leave without North Wind."

Firas, a dignified man, would never do anything so obvious as roll his eyes. "Of course. I will saddle him before I come for you. And—the black?"

She shook her head. "The gray. He's smaller but he has almost beaten North Wind a few times." She hesitated.

"What?" he said with foreboding.

"If they will come, I will be bringing two others with me," she said.

Firas looked thoroughly exasperated. "Young miss! It will be difficult enough to get the two us safely away!"

Johanna thought of the girl Gokudo had used before the gate. "I will not leave without them. Unless it is their will to stay, "

"Can they ride?"

"I don't know. Probably not."

"Young miss!"

"We'll tie them on if we have to, Firas. Saddle two more horses."

Muttering imprecations, he reached for the latch on the door. She stopped him with a gesture. "What now?" he said.

"Halim. The dyer."

"What of him?"

"No. Just...warn him." Her eyes were pleading. "He is a friend to everyone in the harem. He smuggles drugs in when they are needed. Warn him. Please, Firas?"

He was relieved she didn't want to bring the dyer along, too. "I will do so, young miss."

"Thank you, Firas." There was another outcry beyond the walls, nearer this time, and deep enough for them to feel the vibrations in their feet.

"At dusk, young miss."

"We will be there, Firas."

He marched her up to the harem door, every bit the efficient, impersonal guard, and exchanged nods with the two standing before it. They both looked distinctly uneasy, which proved they weren't as stupid as Johanna had always assumed they were, and they broke protocol enough to say to Firas, "What is that sound?"

"It's an army, come to assault the city," Firas said, and then added without looking at Johanna, "A very large army."

"The sheik?"

"Is on the walls," Firas said, without specifying which sheik.

The guard brightened. "We will fight! Allahu Akbar!"

The second guard looked less enthusiastic but echoed, "Yes, we will fight, Allahu Akbar."

"Allahu Akbar," Firas said gravely in response, and nodded at the door.

The first guard recollected his duties and restrained his martial fervor enough to hammer on the door as the second guard drew back the outside bolts.

There was no response from inside. The guards exchanged a look, and hammered again. A third time produced the desired result. The inside bolts were drawn back and the door swung open the merest crack.

Johanna, who had an idea as to what must have happened, pushed past the guards and stepped inside the door, closing it firmly behind her and drawing the useless filigreed bolt across.

Hayat was standing there with an anxious look on her face.

"Where is Kadar?" Johanna said in a low voice.

"I don't know," Hayat said. "I was getting some tea when I heard the knocking. When I came out, there was no one on the door."

"He knows," Johanna said.

"Knows what?"

"Come with me," Johanna said, and towed Hayat through the harem rooms to the little common room in back that Hayat and Alma had made their own. The other occupants of the harem were clustered in small groups, looking frightened. The sounds of battle were softened but not stifled in here.

"Nazirah!" one, braver than the rest, said. "What news from outside?"

"Talikan is under attack," Johanna said. "The sheik is preparing to fight." Like Firas, she did not specify which sheik.

There was an excited buzz and a few shrill screams and more questions but Johanna didn't stop. In Hayat's room, Alma had heard them coming and had risen to her feet. Her eyes were wide and her face was pale and she saw Hayat with relief. Hayat ran to her side and pulled her into a reassuring embrace. "It's all right, love, it's all right. Johanna is back, and all will be well."

Johanna wished she had Hayat's confidence. She beckoned both women closer, and dropped her voice to the merest whisper, conscious of listening ears clustering outside the open door. "Sheik Mohammed is dead. Farhad killed him." When they would have exclaimed she held a finger to her lips. "The city of Talikan is under attack by a force much too large for them to withstand. I know the man at the head of that force. He is a Mongol." Both women gasped. They had heard the stories, as indeed had everyone heard them, with the possible exception of that idiot Farhad.

She looked at the two women, her only two friends in the harem, the only two people she even marginally trusted within the walls of Talikan, and her heart sank. Alma was the daughter of a king and had been married to Sheik Mohammed as a means of ensuring a treaty. Hayat had been the daughter of a poor family who had sold her into slavery as a means of feeding the rest of their children. Neither had known anything in their adult lives but the useless luxury of the harem. "Can either of you ride?"

Alma looked scandalized, Hayat worried. Both shook their heads. Johanna took a shaky breath. "Do I have to explain to you what will happen when the Mongols attack the city?"

"No, Nazirah," Hayat said soberly. "No, you don't have to tell us." Alma shook her head, white to the lips.

"It may be that I can get you out," Johanna said, and held her finger to her lips when the other women would have exclaimed. "Dress in your warmest clothes." She surveyed the gauzy vests and pants of the two women and said, "Dress in all your clothes. Have you anything better to put on your feet than those slippers?"

"No."

No help for it. "Then wear what you have, as many pairs as you can fit over your feet. We'll try to find something better later." If there was a later for any of them.

"Where will we go?" Hayat said.

"We'll worry about that if we manage to get out of Talikan alive," Johanna said.

"What about—" Hayat said.

"The others?" Johanna said, and set her jaw. "I can't save them all. I might be able to save you. Will you come with me?"

The two women looked at each other for a long moment, and turned to face Johanna as one. "We will," Hayat said firmly. Alma, still pale, only nodded.

"It is well." Or she hoped with all her heart that it would be. "If we are caught, by either side—"

"We will come with you, Nazirah," Hayat said firmly.

"All right. Say nothing, nothing, do you understand, nothing at all to anyone else. If you do they will panic and likely cause a riot and we will never get out of here." There was a noise like a thunderbolt far off, followed a few seconds later by a crashing boom somewhere in the city. Johanna thought she could hear the screams even through the thick walls of the palace. Judging by the cries in the harem, she wasn't the only one. "It has begun. Dress. Take nothing you have to carry, nothing that you can't fit into your pockets. You'll need your hands to hang on to your mounts. We will leave at dusk."

"What about Kadar?" Alma said. "The guards?"

Johanna's lip curled. "I am certain that Kadar is at present currying favor with Farhad," she said. Only one thing would absent Kadar from his office and that was his determination to keep it for himself no matter what the change of regime. "And we have a friend on the outside. I promise you, the guards will be otherwise occupied."

She left them rummaging through their belongings, speaking to each other in fierce whispers, and went back to her room. The first thing she did was pull the knife Firas had given her from inside her tunic and strap it to her forearm. She practiced pulling it a dozen times. It felt good in her hand, friendly, and deadly. She immediately felt much better dressed.

She stood still for a moment, staring hard at the walls that had been her prison for too many months now. She had the knife. She had her wits. She had Firas. She had soft boxing, which she had continued to practice each morning before the harem woke and each evening after it had gone to sleep, but it would be effective only in situations where there was ideally one enemy, two at most. Also an asset was the fact that she was a woman, a being perceived as incapable of fighting.

It would have to be enough. She would make it be enough.

Food, she thought, and water, and then rejected out of hand the notion of trying to find and pack anything. It would only draw attention, and they couldn't afford that. They would have to forage on the Road.

The stables should be deserted if everyone was fighting on the walls, and she had a fair idea of the average speed of Sheik Mohammed's horses. Firas could be depended on to choose the best and the fastest ones. If only Hayat and Alma could manage to stay on them.

She went through all of her belongings. She was already wearing her tunic and trousers. She stripped out of them and donned two vests scratchy with embroidery and two pairs of the gauzy harem trousers, then pulled her real clothes on over them. As always, she felt for the lumps in her hems, and wondered if she should remove two or three for bribes, just in case. She discarded that idea, too. Speed and surprise were all that would save them now.

She rolled some slippers and tucked them into her pockets, and wound several of the long, diaphanous veils around her throat, tucking the ends inside her tunic.

She looked around. The harem was a place singularly unsuited for preparing for long trips. A movement in the silvered mirror on the wall caught her eye and when she looked around she was astonished to find that she was smiling. Although there might be too many teeth to call it a smile. A snarl, perhaps.

Time to go.

It required every ounce of self control she had to wait in her room as the light faded from the sky. The sounds of battle didn't help. Ogodei's siege engines would now be at their destructive, deadly work. She'd only ever seen models and heard stories. It felt somehow as if she were in one of the stories now, as if she were one step removed from real life.

Muted sobbing could be heard from frightened women in rooms all over the harem. She set her jaw. There was nothing she could do for them. There was nothing they could do for themselves. From what Firas said, even if by some miracle Farhad did manage to beat off Ogodei's forces, with the death of Sheik Mohammed, their owner and master, their future was tenuous in the extreme.

The afternoon crept on, minute by agonizing minute. She tried to nap, but every time she closed her eyes she saw the girl at the gate, and she couldn't shut out the sounds of worried whispers and frightened cries at every distant boom and crash of the battle. None of them had as yet sounded so near as to cause her to fear for the disruption of her plans. Ogodei's catapults, it seemed, had yet to get the range of the palace. Certainly it would be a prime target when they did, and yet, was it her imagination or did the crashing sounds and screams seem to be moving away?

At long, long last, when her nerves had been stretched to the shrieking point, the shadows began to lengthen along the floor. A whisper of silk on tile, and Hayat and Alma drifted silently into the room. Johanna got to her feet and held out her hands. Hayat's hand was dry, her grip fierce. Alma's was damp and trembling. They held on to each other for a long moment, taking and giving courage. The two women were wearing multiple layers of clothes as she'd suggested, and, Johanna saw approvingly, had wound many scarves around their waists and throats and crossed them across their torsos.

Johanna led the way, slipping out of her room and down the corridor, seeking the shadows. Everywhere she looked clumps of women clung together, cowered in corners, huddled together in darkening rooms. If their passage was seen, no one had the courage to say so. Johanna's heart was wrung with pity for them, but she moved steadily forward.

The carved wooden door loomed up out of the shadows, its bronze fittings gleaming. Kadar was still nowhere to be seen. There were no eunuch guards on this side of the door, or anywhere else in the harem that she could see. If the fighting was going badly, every man with a weapon would have been conscripted to the walls and the gates.

Johanna laid hands on the bolt and drew it softly back. The door swung open.

She stepped forward into the courtyard, and her heart sank.

Farhad smiled at her. "Nazirah. How lovely to see you. Although you could be rather better dressed for the occasion."

He looked and sound supremely confident. He had brought only two guards with him. One held Firas' arms behind him and a blade to his throat.

Firas barely glanced at her. He looked less threatened than patient, and she took heart from that. Hayat and Alma had the sense to keep to the shadows behind her. "And what occasion is that?" she said, facing Farhad and trying to show no fear, although her knees had a tendency to tremble. So close, so close.

"Listen," Farhad said, holding a hand to his ear. They listened, and the sounds of war did seem to be diminishing. "We have beat them back, Nazirah, as I told you we would. My men are even now in pursuit." His eyes glittered as they passed possessively over her body. "I would celebrate my victory."

"You pursued them?" Johanna said. "After they fell back? Your forces are outside the city walls?"

He strolled forward and put a caressing hand beneath her chin. He raised it to look her over in an appraising manner. "Of course. They have caused much damage and many deaths. They will pay for it. All of it."

"You fool," she said in a low, intense voice. "You fool, Farhad!"

There was a large whistling sound overhead, approaching nearer and nearer and while Johanna had never experienced anything like it she knew intuitively what it was. She opened her mouth to scream at Hayat and Alma to—

—and the projectile crashed through the roof. In the very brief moment granted to her for observation, Johanna saw that it was a large, heavy urn, stoppered with a round wood cover pierced with small holes and sealed with wax. And then it smashed into the floor and splintered into shards and slivers.

Inside there were snakes. Many snakes, of different kinds, with, Johanna saw at a glance, only one thing in common: they were all of them deadly. Time seemed to slow down. Johanna saw a cobra rear up and extend its hood, and strike seemingly at nothing. A knot of purple snakes with pure white heads uncoiled themselves and slithered in half a dozen different directions. Smaller adders with distinctive zigzag patterns flowed over each other and seemed to pull darkness with them as they slipped away.

Screams behind her said that members of the harem had been enticed into the entryway by the opening of the door, screams of fright and then screams of pain as they were bitten.

"You fool, Farhad!" Johanna said. "They have flanked the city!"

Farhad gaped at her and she leapt on his moment of surprise and inattention, pulling her knife and slashing it across his face. He flinched, but her blade caught his uplifted arm and left a growing red stain, and she knew a fierce satisfaction. He stumbled backward, tripped over a viper and went down to the floor.

She whirled. Firas had disarmed his captor, who was on the floor choking on his own blood. A man screamed and she whirled again, to see Alma with an adder held just behind its head, pulling its fangs from the second guard's throat and throwing it to one side. Their eyes met for a brief moment and Alma's face split in a feral smile.

A second missile crashed through the roof, another urn, this one filled with smaller pottery balls that burst into flame on impact. One burst at the feet of a woman whose flimsy clothes exploded into an instantaneous fiery veil. She screamed and ran, only fanning the flames and setting draperies and two other women alight. It was a horrifying sight, and Alma and Hayat were mesmerized.

"Go!" Johanna shouted. "Go, go, go!"

The four of them ran for the door to the garden, leaping over snakes and flames alike. The guards were gone and it was unlocked, and they charged through into the stable yards.

Ishan, the stable master, met them at the door. "Lady! What are you doing!"

"Get out of my way, Ishan!"

Instant comprehension flashed across his face. "You are leaving."

She pushed past him. "North Wind!"

The great white stallion already had his head over his stall door and he whinnied in response to the sound of her voice. She slipped the latch and he shouldered out, nosing her and nickering. Firas had succeeded in saddling him before he was taken. She tried to get her foot in the stirrup but North Wind kept moving. She hopped after him, clutching at the edge of the saddle.

"Here, lady." She looked around to find Ishan cupping his hand. She stepped into it and he threw her up on North Wind's back. She froze, staring down at him.

He held her gaze for a long moment, before telling Firas, "The gray, yes, and the little mare, but not the black. He will not carry you far, he has no stamina, no endurance."

He pulled saddle and bridle from the black and replaced them on a rangy chestnut who stepped nervously but delicately in place. Alma was put up on the mare, Hayat on the chestnut, and Firas mounted the grey gelding.

They all hesitated inside the door of the stable, looking at Ishan. "Come with us," Johanna said.

He bowed to her. "I am honored, lady, by your invitation. But my wives, my children…" A vague wave indicated the city's interior. "I must go to them."

Johanna bit her lip. "Get out then, Ishan, get yourselves out of Talikan as soon as you possibly can."

He bowed to her with his hand on his forehead. "Peace be upon you, lady."

"And upon you, Ishan," Johanna said. Impulsively, she held out her hand.

He took it in a firm, brief clasp, and smiled up at her. "Keep my horses safe."

They had never been the sheik's horses, not to Ishan. Johanna's throat was tight and her eyes burned.

The stable master went ahead of them to stand by the doors to the track that Johanna took every day, that at the end of which only this morning, only hours before, Johanna and Firas had found the bodies of the scouts. "Are you sure?" she said to Firas.

"As sure as I can be, young miss," he said, gathering his reins. "If Ogodei runs true to Mongol tactics, he is at present bringing in two flanks of his troops to engulf the Talikan pursuers."

"I know," Johanna said.

He nodded curtly, leaning forward to check bridle, saddle and stirrups, and then moving to Hayat and Alma to check theirs. "Ogodei's troops are fully occupied at the main gate, which is almost directly opposite this one. This is our best chance."

Our only chance, Johanna thought. North Wind snorted and sidled beneath her. He didn't like the sounds he was hearing. The tension on the reins told her that he had the bit between his teeth. But then he was always ready to run, in peace or in war. "Alma, Hayat? Don't. Fall. Off."

Their faces turned to hers, Hayat's grim with determination, Alma's white with fear. But Alma had been the one to snatch up a venomous snake and use it as a weapon, and effectively, too. "Don't fall off. Just don't. We won't have time to stop to help you if you fall. Do you understand?"

They nodded mutely. Ishan had fastened their feet to the stirrups with quick lashings of what looked like spare reins. Their vests and pantaloons and scarves would be no protection and if they survived Johanna hated to think what the insides of their thighs would feel like.

Dana Stabenow

"Keep your balance." She attempted a smile that she feared was more of a grimace. "It's just like dancing."

Again they nodded, far too trustfully for her liking.

"All right," Johanna said. "Ishan, add to your goodness and open the doors to the track?"

He unlatched the doors and dragged them back. No invading force immediately poured in, which Johanna took to be a good sign. "God be with you and your family, friend Ishan!"

"Allah keep you and yours, lady!" she heard him say.

She bent low over North Wind's neck and kicked him sharply in the sides, and he went from a standstill to a full gallop in one pace. She heard the faint sound of hoofbeats behind her. Before her, the moon was near full on the horizon, vying with the last light of the setting sun opposite. The white sand of the track was easy to follow in the dusk. Behind them she heard yells and the sound of additional hoofbeats as a counterpoint to the thunder and smash of battle. All seemed to recede almost instantly but she knew better than to trust to that impression. She pulled a little on the reins, slowing him enough so that the other three horses could keep up.

Risking a look around she saw that Alma was being jolted from one side of her mount to the other, but recovering in time to pull herself back up again. Hayat had fallen too far to her left to recover. Johanna checked North Wind, dropped back to reach out, grab Hayat's arm and dump her back in the saddle.

Something whirred by her face, and she looked around to see that their pursuers were a dozen Mongols armed with bows, presumably the guard set on the stable doors. Their ragged steppe ponies were no match for prize racing steeds out of Sheik Mohammed's stables. She turned to face forward and bent low again over North Wind's neck. He passed Hayat's mount and came up to Firas. "Archers behind us!"

"Really, young miss?" Even at full gallop, the wind whistling past their ears in one direction and the arrows past their heads in the other, Firas managed to sound sarcastic. "Thank you for drawing it to my attention. Look!"

He pointed at the canal beside them, and in it Johanna saw scum in it she had not seen that morning. "They've poisoned the canal!"

He didn't bother to answer, only pointed ahead. "We are making for that cleft, there, between those two hills, do you see?"

"I see!"

"There is water there, a small stream, where we can rest the horses." If they managed to lose their pursuers. He didn't say it, but they both thought it.

They didn't dare keep the horses at a full gallop for an extended length of time. She glanced again over her shoulder. The archers were definitely falling behind, and six of them had left the others and were making for the battle, either to apprise their commander of the escapes or not to miss out on their share of the women and the plunder when the city was sacked. Possibly both, and Johanna swallowed back the bile rising in her throat. The city could not hold without a leader, and when last seen that leader had fallen into a seething mass of poisonous serpents. Johanna hoped in passing that three or four of them had bitten him. She had been a prisoner in Talikan, but she had met with kindness from some of its inhabitants, all of whom would all very probably be dead before nightfall. She thought of Halim the dyer, and Ishan the stable master, and the ornamental, useless women of the harem.

They pushed on as long as they dared, a league and a half, before reining in the horses to a walk. North Wind was sweating but only lightly, the other three horses more, but none of them had thrown shoes or picked up rocks in their hooves. Alma and Hayat both had tear-streaked faces, but no one mentioned that, or much of anything else. The rest of their pursuers had vanished, very probably now at the gates of the city with the rest of the Mongol forces.

They rode for another league, not speaking, before nudging the horses into a canter. They passed burned-out farms and mills, villages with no whole houses left standing, the bodies of men, women and children brutalized and butchered and left where they lay. With this fast-slow-fast pace, it was midnight before they achieved the notch between the two hills Firas had pointed out. They reined in to the incongruous sound of running water, a cheerful chuckle as it tumbled down in a series of rocky pools. Johanna slid from North Wind's back. He drank from the creek while she loosened his cinch and wiped him down with an armful of dry grass. She led him away before he drank too much and tethered him to a nearby tree.

Firas had loosened the ties that bound Alma and Hayat's feet to their stirrups and helped them down. Neither woman could stand upright at first, and they limped splay-legged to the creek, there to drop to their knees and drink deeply. Firas came behind with their horses and the chestnut gelding. Like Johanna, he didn't let them drink too much before leading them to a wizened tamarisk and tethering them to its lower branches.

They knelt next to Alma and Hayat and drank deep of the clean, fresh water, and then drank more, and rested for a few moments.

Johanna rose to her feet.

"Where are you going?" The restrained terror in Alma's voice caused Hayat to reach for her hand.

"To the top of that knoll. We should be able to see what is happening in Talikan from there."

Alma rose waveringly to her feet and pulled Hayat, protesting, up with her. Unaccustomed to drinking from creeks, they were both wet to their waists. "I want to see, too."

Firas joined them, following Johanna up over the small knoll. It was overgrown with some low-growing herb that emitted a cloud of fragrance with every footstep. Lavender, perhaps. She got to the top a pace in front and stood, catching her breath, as she looked across the long plain over which they had fled.

So far as she could tell by the moon's pale light, they were still not pursued, and it was plain as to why. At this distance, about five leagues, the sounds of human terror and agony could only be imagined, and she was grateful for that, but in a queer way it only more clearly defined what was happening there in her imagination.

Talikan lay in the bend of a wide river of the same name, the canal paralleling the path having been dug to irrigate of the farms that filled the valley. The river lay at the city's back, the main gate at its front, and it was at the front gate that Ogodei had concentrated his attack. Two wooden towers on wheels stood near the walls, but not so near that the defenders could pour oil on them and light them off with flaming arrows. The catapults mounted on the towers continued to load and swing and hurl deadly projectiles inside the city's walls.

The great gates were burning, as were the walls on either side, the heat of the flames no doubt driving the defenders from the gate. "What is that?" she said.

"A ram," Firas said, as it crashed into the gates.

She nodded, numb.

Before the walls, two wide curves of mounted men rode toward each other, enclosing a comparatively pitiful force between them, the third force of Mongol riders closing the last arc of the circle. Talikan's defeat was nearly complete. She wondered if any city had ever fallen in less than a day before. She thought again of Halim, and Ishan, and the harem. "Do you think Ogodei gave the city a chance to surrender?" she said.

"I don't know," Firas said. "Given how soon he began the attack upon his arrival, it would seem unlikely."

"Why wouldn't he? My father said that Genghis Khan always gave cities a choice."

"Ogodei isn't Genghis Khan." She felt rather than saw him shrug. "Perhaps his men are hungry. Mongol armies are foragers, they feed themselves on the march. If that is the case, an outright defeat means less time between his men and the city's storehouses than negotiating a surrender. And a surrender presupposes that enough stores would be left to feed the city's people, which would be that much less for Ogodei's men." He sighed. "I don't know, young miss."

"How did they catch you?"

He shrugged. "We were not quite as discreet as we might have hoped, young miss. Tarik saw us talking and followed me to the stables. He saw me saddle the horses and sent for Farhad. They took me when I was on my way to the harem."

She nodded. "We were fortunate that Farhad thought he was safe with only two guards."

He almost smiled. "Yes," he said.

They watched as flame leapt from beyond the gates. It was impossible at this distance, but Johanna felt that she could hear it crackle, could feel its heat, could see the ravenous flames eat up everything in the city. "How do you bury that many people?" she said at last, her voice barely above a whisper.

"You don't," Firas said, and stirred. "Young miss. We must go."

"Yes," she said. "We must."

She turned her back on Talikan for the last time and the four of them slipped and slid back down the knoll to the little glen with its life-saving creek, where they surprised a massive striped cat who had come to the spring to drink. North Wind had broken the branch of the tree he had been tethered to and was pawing the ground, preparing to give battle. The tiger snarled at all of them impartially and slunk away into the night.

Hayat seemed frozen in place, until Alma burst into sobs. Hayat relaxed enough to put her arms around the other woman.

"I'll need a bow and arrows as soon as possible," Johanna said, and hoped no one else noticed how shaken her voice was. She was probably as frightened as Alma and Hayat, but the accumulated shocks of the day seemed to have left her temporarily numb to any new experience no matter how life-threatening.

Firas let out a long sigh. "We were lucky he wasn't hungry. He could have taken down any one of our horses. Or all of them."

Johanna looked at North Wind, still vastly annoyed at this disruption of his well-earned rest. No, not all of them.

"Here," Firas said, "this will make you feel better." He handed around bits of dried goat's meat. He had managed to pack a saddlebag, Johanna saw, and one water skin. "Chew it slowly. It has to last us for a while."

"We'll need food," she said, teeth working at the dried meat, which was very dry indeed. "And more water skins, and better clothing for them." She nodded at Alma and Hayat, who still stood together with their arms around each other, Alma's face buried in Hayat's shoulder, Hayat's own shoulders shaking. The tiger had been merely the last horror in a day filled with them.

"What do you intend to do with them, young miss?" Firas said in a low voice.

"That's up to them," she said in a hard voice that warned him away from further discussion of the topic. "Did you come this way when you came to Talikan? Is that how you knew of this spring?"

He shook his head. "I came roundabout, from the west. I am of Alamut, and so I said, and Alamut is west of here. But I asked questions in the guard house, and looked at maps, and listened to stories. Among these hills, higher up, is a small village that may be out of the way enough to have escaped Ogodei's attention."

"How much farther?"

"Ten leagues, twelve." He shrugged. "We should reach it before sunset tomorrow if we keep up this pace."

She thought. "You will occasion less comment if you go in alone."

He almost smiled. "And what will they say when I ask for women's clothing?"

"Don't ask for women's clothing, ask for men's," Johanna said. "Tunics and trousers and boots and cheches, if they have them. Tell them you were in the employ of the Sheik Mohammed, that you escaped the sack of the city and that you and your three men are running for your lives. They've lived this long this close to Talikan, if they still live, they will honor the relationship they had with the sheik. And they will be grateful for news."

She hoped.

⋆ Six ⋆

Spring, 1323 A.D.
Kabul

⊢——⊣

"Lapis lazuli," Jaufre said.

"Emeralds," Shasha said. She hesitated. "Copper? I've never seen so much copper for sale in one place as I have here in Kabul."

"Heavy," Jaufre said. "Depends on how much copper and how far we have to carry it. We should take counsel of Grigori the Tatar."

"One camel can carry five hundredweight," Félicien said. "The profit on that much copper ought to pay for the camel's feed with more than enough left over to make such a venture worthwhile."

The other three looked at him in some surprise. He reddened beneath their scrutiny. "I have been traveling with you for over a year," he said with asperity. "Even an idiot would have picked up a little knowledge by now."

Jaufre gave him a buffet on the shoulder that nearly knocked the goliard over. "You have fallen in with traders, Félicien. Who knows where it will end?"

Hari caught Félicien and helped him regain an upright position. "I have been speaking to the teacher in the madrasa," he said. "He knows of a man with a great store of maps, some old, some new."

Jaufre laughed. "Even the priest has succumbed to our wicked influence," he said, winking at Félicien, who reddened again. "I would look at these maps, Hari. Maps, old and new, are always valuable to someone. And light in weight." He paused, and exchanged a look with Shasha. "You are both continuing with us, then?"

"I am," Félicien said. "I have been five years in the East, and I would see the shores of the Middle Sea again."

"Hari?" Jaufre said.

"By all means, young sir," Hari said, bowing. "The Nestorian patriarch here in Kabul has told me that no seeker after truth can cease from looking until he sees Jerusalem."

"We're only going to Gaza," Jaufre said. "But Jerusalem, I'm told, isn't even twenty leagues away." He stood up, aware that Shasha's healer's eye was upon him and determined to betray by neither wince nor flinch that he was still very shaky on his feet. "Very well, then. I will go to the market and see what I can find in the way of a few decent camels."

Shasha rose, too. "I'll come with you. I want to see what the current prices are for lapis."

He held up an admonitory finger. "Don't buy until we know how many camels I can find. There could be nothing on the market but fifty-year old nags suffering from advanced blister." He felt for the purse at his waist. It was plump enough. He patted it and raised an eyebrow in Shasha's direction.

"If I am forbidden to buy," Shasha said tartly, "I have more than enough to see out our stay."

She'd been testy with him since he'd woken up that morning, and he had sense enough to realize that she was as worried about Johanna as he was, however determined they both were to keep it to themselves. Rambahadur Raj's news that Ogodei was moving south in what might be first Johanna's direction and then theirs was unwelcome and unsettling. "I have no right to forbid you to buy, Shasha," he said mildly. "I advise only caution in what we spend of our available funds. We have a long way to go, and I prefer food in my belly at regular intervals."

Félicien and Hari pretended not to hear either their squabbling or the subject matter, Félicien because he paid his own way with songs and stories and Hari because Jaufre was convinced he had no notion of the concept of money. Still, he had the knack of making friends, a good asset anywhere on the Road. Jaufre thought of Hari enthroned on a pile of carpets, deep in philosophical discussion with Ogodei on the plateau of Terak, and quashed the memory immediately. Johanna had still been with them then, and the farther he kept Johanna from his thoughts the better off they would all be. He fixed his thoughts instead on Gaza where they would meet again. Admittedly his mental wanderings overlay the prospect with a golden haze involving the two of them alone and with most of their clothes off. It was a vision enticing enough to move him forward.

But she would be there, with her clothes or without them. He would not, could not admit of any other possibility.

"I'll walk in with you as far as the storyteller's café," Félicien said, falling beside him. "There is a man from Turgesh who tells the most delightful tales of a Nasredden Hoja."

"Increasing your repertoire, young scholar?" Hari stood. "And I will return to the madrasa, to inquire after the man of maps. Young sir, is there a date for our departure?"

"Rambahadur Raj gave me to understand that we will be off at the earliest possible moment," Jaufre said. "There are…" He glanced at Shasha. "The times are unsettled," he said. "Rambahadur Raj wishes to outpace them."

They departed for the city in a body, separating at the Grand Mosque. Out of sight of the others, Jaufre allowed his pace to slow and silently cursed again his physical inability to walk even a league without having to mop the sweat from his face. He wondered gloomily if he would have to be roped to his mount on the Road, and made a mental vow that he would do no such thing, if he slid from the back of his camel and was trampled beneath the hooves of the entire caravan for it.

He sought out the camel yard and looked over the stock. The camel dealer singled him out as a young man of little experience and made his best effort to show him every sway-backed camel, horse and donkey with infected hooves and spavined knees he had in stock, most of which also exhibited bronchial coughs that splattered everything with yellow phlegm, including the dealer, whose robe showed signs of having endured the assault numerous times before.

Jaufre's acerbic comments on the kind and condition of what was on offer cast the situation in a different light, and the dealer led him round the back where animals in better condition waited in varying degrees of patience for purchase by their new owners. Jaufre found six camels whose teeth were not yet yellow with age, whose coats were thick enough to withstand both heat and cold, and who moved as if all their feet and the legs attached to them were healthy enough to last the distance to

Gaza, or at least to the next city large enough to support a camel yard, where the sick, lame and lazy could be replaced.

They adjourned to the dealer's office and bargained over mint tea. An hour later Jaufre emerged feeling better than he had since he woke up, weak and enfeebled and bedridden. With the single camel Firas and Shasha had managed to liberate from the sheik's men, that meant they had seven head of freight stock, capable of transporting forty-two hundredweight of goods.

He next sought out the offices of Grigori the Tatar, who was a swarthy, stocky, taciturn man who said very little but whose sharp eyes saw everything. "Young sir," he said, rising to his feet. "The foster son of Wu Li honors me again with his presence."

"I thank you, Grigori the Tatar," Jaufre said, and tried not to fall onto the carpet-covered bench Wu Li's agent waved him to. Grigori sent for the inevitable mint tea and cakes, and Jaufre regained his composure and commanded himself not to think of his trembling legs.

Grigori offered brief commiseration again over the death of Wu Li, which Jaufre accepted with what he hoped was dignity, and wondered how to ask his next question. "Have you," he said, "had any messages from any other members of the house of Wu since last we spoke?" The thought of Wu Li's widow extending her clawed reach this far was unlikely but not impossible. It was lucky for them that she had not had time before Wu Li's death to gather all the reins of Wu Li's business into her hands. He thought of the tiny woman with the painted face and the gilded fingernails as long as her forearms, a being of infinite forethought and malice, brooding in Cambaluc on the wrongs she had suffered at Johanna's hands, and had to repress a sudden smile. And it had been lucky for them, too, that Johanna was such an accomplished thief.

"None," Grigori said. "Only yourself and Wu Li's foster daughter, young sir."

Jaufre nodded in acknowledgement, hoping his relief didn't show. "I went to the camel dealer you recommended," he said after the refreshments had been delivered. "When the camels are delivered and accepted, he will bring you a piece of paper with Wu Li's bao and an amount inscribed upon it." He handed over a pouch. "Of your kindness, please give him this as payment in full, less your commission, of course."

Grigori accepted the pouch and caused it to disappear somewhere about his person. "Young sir," he said. "You are lately come from the east. Is the news true? Are the Mongols once again on the march?"

"I believe it to be true, Grigori," Jaufre said. He hesitated. "If a much younger and less worldly man may presume to advise his elder in years and experience…" A minute nod gave him permission. "I know that the mountain passes between here and Persia are filled with fierce tribes who gave pause to Alexander and even Genghis Khan himself. And perhaps, even if Ogodei does make it this far, your city leaders will be wise enough to yield to him."

Not a muscle moved in Grigori's face but Jaufre got the distinct impression that his host had little faith in the wisdom of Kabul's leaders.

"My advice to my elder would be to look to his own," Jaufre said. "And to do so sooner, rather than later." He paused, and stretched his back. The wound ached much less now, more of a phantom pain than a real one. As with Rambahadur Raj, he was not about to admit that he himself knew Ogodei. Absent proof, there was no reason for the Tatar to take his words as other than youthful braggadocio, and even if he was believed, he had no wish to become known as an authority. However, as a member of the family of Wu Li, he owed a duty to a retainer in that family's service. "The havildar of the caravan recently arrived in Kabul?"

"Rambahadur Raj," Grigori said. "He is well known as an able and prudent man."

"He is determined to leave Kabul at his earliest opportunity."

Grigori said nothing for a moment, and when he did speak again it was to talk of lesser things.

Jaufre made his farewells and went next to the caravansary on the outskirts of the city, where he found Rambahadur Raj overseeing the beating of an unfortunate man who, Rambahadur Raj said, had had the temerity to try to steal a horse that belonged to one of the merchants. His back was bloody when he was finally released, but he could stagger off under his own power and at least he still had both of his hands. Commonly the sentence for thievery had the right one lopped off. "But have you seen how many one-handed men there are in this city, Jaufre of Cambaluc?" said Rambahadur Raj. "I would not add to the city's burden of men who cannot work for their living. Not that this one did, but perhaps his sore back will remind him that there are less painful ways to earn one's keep." The havildar waved Jaufre to a seat before his yurt and sent for refreshments.

When they came, mint tea of course, Rambahadur Raj cocked an eyebrow. "You have news, young sir?"

"I do, havildar. My party will join you with three donkeys, six horses, and seven camels. If we can find reliable help, we will bring two and possibly three men to help with the livestock."

"A cook?"

"We have our own." At another quirk of an eyebrow, Jaufre added, "The healer, of whom I spoke before."

Both of Rambahadur Raj's eyebrows went up. "A healer and a cook," he said. "I would meet this paragon."

"You will, havildar. When do we leave?"

"In three days' time," the havildar said promptly. "Is that agreeable to you?"

"It is," Jaufre said. He hesitated. "I noticed when I was last with you," he said finally, "that you had a slaver in your train."

"I did."

"Will he be traveling with us?"

"No. He passes south, on through the mountains to Punjab." The havildar raised an eyebrow. "Do I understand you to have some objection to traveling with slavers, young sir?"

"My mother was captured and sold into slavery," Jaufre said bluntly, too exhausted to dissemble. "I would speak with him to see if he has heard of her."

"I see," the havildar said. "My sympathies, Jaufre of Cambaluc."

"I thank you, Rambahadur Raj. May I have the slaver's name and direction?"

"Ibn Battuta is his name. He is a Berber from Maroc, and a very young man to be such a successful trader, in my estimation. He had fully three hundred in stock when he joined us in Balkh."

"Three hundred!"

"As many," Rambahadur Raj said, nodding. "Although he did suffer some attrition through the mountain passes. Those Afghans." He shook his head, and observed Jaufre with a sapient eye. "You are prepared to defend yourselves, Jaufre of Cambaluc?"

"We are, havildar."

"Well, well, I doubt it will come to that." The havildar grinned. "Or what are you paying me for?"

Jaufre followed the havildar's directions and found Ibn Battuta established in a large house with an enclosed courtyard near the slave market. He begged an audience of the doorman, an enormous Nubian who looked as if he could pick Jaufre up and break him in half with very little effort. Jaufre tried not to be envious of the man's obvious strength and excellent health.

He had used the name of Rambahadur Raj to gain entrance and so was not very surprised to be granted an audience. Ibn Battuta was indeed a young man, not very much older than Jaufre himself. Tall, slim, richly dressed, his manner was grave and somewhat avuncular, as if he feared his youthful appearance would cause people to take him less seriously and so was determined to make up the difference by assuming the manner of a man three times his age.

He was surrounded by pen and ink and pieces of parchment, but he set these to one side upon Jaufre's entrance and sent for refreshments. Jaufre already felt awash in mint tea, but he minded his manners and made no demur. Presently it was delivered by a slender girl dressed in the briefest of clothing, who fluttered her eyelashes at Jaufre.

"You like?" Ibn Battuta said, noting his interest. "A good price can be arranged."

Jaufre had a sudden vision of his mother in just such a situation and knew an instantaneous, consuming fury. It took him a moment to muster up a civil tone. "I am not in the market for a slave at present, effendi," he said, and waited until the girl had left the room to come to the point. "Effendi, my mother had the misfortune to be traveling in a caravan that was attacked by bandits. She was captured and sold into slavery."

"Unfortunate," Ibn Battuta said. As an owner and a seller of slaves and a successful one if these surroundings were any indication, he could hardly offer his condolences.

"Yes," said Jaufre. "She was Greek, with dark hair and eyes. Her name was Agalia. It may be that she was given the name of the Lycian Lotus when she was sold."

"When was this?" the slave trader asked.

Jaufre swallowed. "Seven years ago."

Ibn Battuta stared at him, startled out of his assumed stolidity. "Seven years! My dear young sir!" He strove to regain his composure. "I sympathize with your loss, but the thing is impossible. Surely you see that." He gestured with a hand that had never seen labor. "Do you have the name of the buyer?"

Jaufre shook his head. "I know only that he was a sheik out of the west."

"There are many such sheiks," Ibn Battuta said, not unkindly.

"I know," Jaufre said. "No such woman has passed through your hands, effendi? Or been offered you for sale? Dark, slender but well-formed. She would now be forty-one years of age. Agalia, or the Lycian Lotus."

Ibn Battuta shook his head. "I am very sorry, young sir."

Jaufre stayed just long enough not to be rude, and left.

He was exhausted by the time he got home. He stopped at the fountain to wash and drink long of the cool, refreshing water, and sat for a time on the edge of the fountain, gazing unseeingly into the water.

He had been asking after his mother in every slave market between here and Cambaluc, and the answer had always been the same. Seven years ago, the Road had swallowed his mother up and left nothing of her behind for him to find. She was lost to him.

Oh, he would keep asking as they traveled farther into the west. He didn't think he could stop himself, but he had to begin to accept the possibility that he would never find her. He hoped with all his heart that the man she had been sold to in the Kashgar slave market was a good master, and kind to her. She had been fortunate in her beauty and her intelligence. Certainly the price she had reportedly brought meant that she would be highly valued by whomever paid it.

He closed his eyes and let himself remember the sound of her voice in his ears, the feel of her arms around him, the laughter of his parents together.

He opened his eyes and blinked away tears. What was the name of Rambahadur Raj's second in command? Alaric? Alaric the Templar, the havildar had called him, seemingly in jest and definitely to the other man's displeasure.

Jaufre's father had been a Templar. And he had had a sword like Alaric's, the one now hanging from the wall inside.

He got up and went to stand before it, looking at it as if for the first time. He knew the names of the various parts of it now, as he had not as a child when it was all he had managed to save from the men who killed his father three days from Kashgar. A large pommel, set with precious stones. A metal grip covered in sharkskin, much less ornamental. An abbreviated guard. The blade itself, made of something very near but not quite Damascus steel, or so he'd been told by every smith he'd taken it to. The edge kept sharp for longer than any other blade he'd ever owned. He'd cut himself on it enough times.

Yes, Alaric's sword was very like this one.

And if his employer was to be believed, he was or had been a Templar. Jaufre did not know exactly what a Templar was, but he did know from his childhood memories that his father had been one too, before he had met and married his mother. Perhaps Alaric had known of him.

Perhaps he had known him.

If he had lost his mother, perhaps he could at least find out more about his father. Perhaps he had other family to be found, somewhere in the west.

Suddenly and thoroughly exhausted, he stretched out on his cot. He was instantly asleep.

Muted voices and the smell of roasting meat woke him at twilight. He blinked his eyes and found Félicien stirring something in a copper pan under Shasha's direction, and Hari in a corner with his legs folded beneath him, chanting his oms.

Jaufre pushed himself to a sitting position. Shasha looked over her shoulder. "Ah. You wake, just in time for dinner. Well timed."

He rose to his feet, yawning hugely, and stumbled outside to use the necessary. Dinner was being served on his return, browned root vegetables baked in cabbage leaves and a skewer of goat's meat, this latter for all but Hari, who ate no meat. More of last year's apples followed.

It might have been the best meal Jaufre had ever eaten. It was amazing what a little forward motion did to improve one's appetite. He cleaned their few dishes and tidied their cooking utensils away and they gathered outside their door around a ring of small rocks in which a fire had been kindled. Smoke rose from similar fires in the little enclave of mud-brick buildings that constituted their neighborhood. The stars were winking into existence overhead and a three-quarter moon was cresting the peak of an eastern mountain.

"I found camels," Jaufre said. "Six of them."

"Six," Shasha said. "I did not think you would find half so many."

By her expression he could tell that she was mentally adding up all the goods she had found in the market that day and dividing them into seven loads. "I spoke with Rambahadur Raj, too. We leave in three days."

Félicien scratched with vigor. "Good. I don't believe I have stayed in a more pest-ridden place in my life."

"Did you find your man of maps, Hari?"

"I did, young sir, I did." Hari hitched his yellow drapery about himself, one shoulder bare as always. He seemed impervious to cold and heat alike. "He lives in a small room he rents from the mullah's sister. I went there, and what I found was curious, most curious indeed."

"He has maps?"

"He does, and all manner of other curiosities. He showed me a very old memoir, almost assuredly a copy, of a treatise written by a Christian in Sinai. It is called The Geography of Christ, I believe he said, or something very like. It is written in a tongue foreign to me but he translated some of it. This writer claims there are only four seas, the Middle Sea, the Persian Sea, the Arabian Sea and the Caspian Sea. Even more strangely, he claims there are only four nations, the Indians in the east, the Celts in the west, the Scythians in the north and the Ethiops in the south."

Jaufre looked at Shasha. "He wasn't a Christian, Hari, he was Muslim. His name was Cosmas, and he was of Alexandria."

Hari looked surprised. "You have heard of this man?"

"We have. Our uncle told us of him, before we left Everything Under the Heavens. Cosmas constructed a box, he said, with a map of the world in it. His world. It evidently left out quite a bit. Or it was a very small box."

Hari meditated on this information for a moment. "The man of the many maps, his name is Ibn Shad, he says that the author of the book signs himself a Christian. And that he apparently was no scholar, as he has the shape of the world flat, longer by two than it is wide, and founded on their god. By which I took to mean held by him."

"Like Atlas," Jaufre said.

"Atlas?"

"A Greek god of whom my mother told me. I can't remembered the full tale, but he misbehaved somehow and was condemned to hold the entire world on his shoulders for all eternity."

"A round world or a flat world?" Shasha said.

"Be cautious," Félicien said unexpectedly. "Especially after we arrive in the west."

They looked at him. "Cautious?" Shasha said. "But why?"

Félicien poked at the fire with a stick while they waited. "The god of the West, the god of my country, is a jealous god. Very jealous," he said, emphasizing his point with a vicious jab that made the sparks fly upward. "Philosophy exists only as it relevant to faith. Therefore faith, in particular the Christian faith, dictates all philosophy, and only religious men can be scholars." Another poke, more sparks. "Map-making, for example, is not respected, and any western map I have ever seen is dictated by the texts of the Christian Bible."

Hari looked intrigued. "The Bible?"

"It is like the Koran, or the Upanishads, for Christians." Félicien's smile was crooked. "I believe I can even quote to you the exact verse that inspired Cosmas to his view of the world. 'Thou shalt make a table also of setim wood: of two cubits in length, and a cubit in breadth, and cubit and a half in height.' Exodus, chapter 25, verse 23." He said the words first in Latin, and then translated for them, adding, "The church frowns upon travel, too."

"Travel?" Jaufre and Shasha spoke as a chorus of disbelief.

Félicien's smile was wry. The shadows cast by the flickering flames fined down his features, making them appear almost delicate. "I quote from the blessed St. Augustine himself, now. 'And men go abroad to admire the heights of mountains, the mighty waves of the sea, the broad tides of rivers, the compass of the ocean, and the circuits of the stars, yet pass over the mystery of themselves without a thought.'"

"But—but—" Jaufre was spluttering.

"We are meant to stay at home, then?" Shasha said skeptically.

Félicien nodded. "So as to better contemplate the glory of god."

"Is god not in the mountains, and the waves, and the rivers, and the circuits of the stars, then?" Hari said.

Félicien sighed. "So I thought, when I left home, Hari."

"Do you no longer think so, young scholar?" Hari said.

Félicien raised his head, his eyes filled with fire. "Even more now than I did before, Hari. I left because what I wanted to study was forbidden me, and," he laughed a little, "because I had seen a text even older than your Cosmas' memoir, by a man called Solinus. He wrote two or three hundred years after Christ, and the text had these marvelous illustrations of all manner of creatures, the dog-men in Ethiopia, in Tartary dolphins that can leap the masts of ships, the dread Basilisk of the Syrtis whose breath is fatal." He laughed again. "I found none of them, of course. But I found other things even more wonderful, built by the hand of god, and of man." He looked around the circle. "And I found friends."

"But—but—travel?" Jaufre said. "How are goods moved, then? Do they make everything they need themselves?"

"Oh, they trade," Félicien said, "every chance they get, and traders, perforce, travel. They are not much respected. Of course many of them are Jews, which makes it easier for the Christians to despise the profession."

"I have heard of Jews," Hari said, "but I have never met one. Tell me of them, young scholar."

"That," Félicien said, "is a far too long an explanation to go into this evening. I will reserve it to while away the long hours on the Road between here and Gaza, good Hari."

"But—travel?" Jaufre said again.

Shasha poked him in the side. "Remember what Uncle Cheng said," she said. "We will do well to adopt the prevalent faith of whatever culture we happen to find ourselves in."

"Wise words," Félicien said, nodding.

"We don't go to mosque," Jaufre said. "And Hari says his prayers wherever we go."

"He says them in private," Shasha said, "and we don't shop on Fridays." She changed the subject pointedly. "I found a merchant who deals exclusively in good quality lapis, if his samples are anything to go by. It was very expensive, until I mentioned Grigori the Tatar. He then cut his prices in half, but I think they are still too high. I found a trader who deals in gemstones, too, but he would not speak with a woman. I think we should employ Grigori in both of these negotiations."

"Copper?"

She shook her head. "The prices are very high, I think because the mines close in the winter and the stocks are subsequently low in the spring."

"Well, we have seven camels. One is already loaded with spices—"

"Not as loaded as it once was," Shasha said. "I have traded perhaps half already."

"Why didn't you—"

She let her eyes flick down to their hems and back to his face. "I thought it would be best if it we were not known to have...special resources."

"We'll have to use them sometime, Shasha."

"To pay for our passage across the Middle Sea," Shasha said lightly. "We'll let Johanna decide, when she deigns to rejoin us in Gaza."

"You seem very sure that she will," Félicien said.

Shasha looked at him in surprise, but he was looking at Jaufre.

"Of course," Jaufre said, and there was that simple certainty in his voice that stopped any further comment Félicien might have made. He bit his lip and looked away.

Villagers began to appear in twos and threes, old women, young men, children up past their bedtime who had learned that song and story were to be found around the fire of the feranji. They brought naan freshbaked that morning, and cool pomegranate juice in pails, and pieces of precious gaz, covered in spun sugar that whitened their fingers and mouths. Félicien got out his lute and struck up a lively tune that had evidently been acquired locally because everyone joined in on the chorus, and the rest of the evening was spent agreeably in song and story.

The next day Jaufre took delivery of the camels. Two days later they loaded ten hundredweight of first quality rough cut, jewel grade lapis, five hundredweights of dried fruit, another of almonds in the shell, a quantity of well-made copper pots and pans that Shasha had found at a bargain price at the last minute, and a small bag of emeralds that no one knew about except for Shasha and Jaufre and which never left the pouch Shasha wore next to her skin beneath her tunic. She had wanted to buy some of the famous pomegranates of Kandahar but reluctantly agreed when Jaufre pointed out that they would only spoil. Their store of spices was augmented by mint (of course), saffron and cardamom.

There was also a pack of twenty-five old and new maps rolled into a calfskin, as well as half a dozen bound manuscripts folded between sheets of parchment scraps, including Cosmas of Alexandria's *Topographia Christiana*, and that geographical flight of fancy by one Gaius Julius Solinus called *Collecteana rerum memorabilia*, which Félicien had mentioned and upon which the old man had assured Jaufre most of Cosmas' even more fanciful account was based. They were both copies, of course, and both in Latin. While Jaufre remembered very little of that language as laboriously schooled into him by Father John so many years before, since they were headed for a land of Latin speakers he was determined to learn it again so as not to be at a disadvantage when he got there.

He had exited the old man of the maps' lodging only to encounter Ibn Battuta on his way in. The slave trader regarded Jaufre's full arms with a sour expression Jaufre recognized as part envy and part annoyance. He brushed by Jaufre without a greeting, and Jaufre walked home with a step made lighter by having beaten the slave trader to the preferred pieces of the old scholar's stock.

The afternoon before they would depart they moved down to the caravansary, accompanied by a gratifyingly universal bewailing on the part of their neighborhood. They pitched a new yurt near Rambahadur Raj's and settled in. Félicien, with his unquenchable curiosity, struck out immediately to see who would be traveling with them. Hari went with him to see who worshipped at which altar.

No sooner had they left than a voice called from the other side of the flap, and Jaufre stepped outside to find Alaric the Templar waiting for him. "Well met, Jaufre of Cambaluc," he said.

"Well met," Jaufre said, unsure of how to address the man, since he had protested at Rambahadur Raj's introduction. Jaufre was wearing his father's sword, being able to bear its weight again, barely, and Alaric's eyes went to it immediately.

"A fine sword," he said.

"My father's," Jaufre said.

"Do you mind?"

Jaufre drew it forth and presented it, hilt first.

Alaric, like Firas, handled the sword as if it were an extension of his arm, but he studied it with an intensity that seemed out of proportion to its existence.

"It is a style very like your own," Jaufre said.

Alaric glanced down at the sword at his side. "It is." He made a few passes with it before handing it back. "Are you a soldier?"

"I'm a trader," Jaufre said. "It is, alas, a profession that requires the occasional fight. I was studying with a sword master on the Road, before we became separated."

Alaric smiled, an expression that momentarily changed his long, sad face into something charming and attractive. "We practice, the men and I, at sunrise each day."

Jaufre wondered if all masters of the sword considered getting up before dawn as a requirement for a successful training program. "I would join you," he said. He hesitated. He didn't want to make excuses, but he didn't want Alaric and his men to think they would be seeing Jaufre's best effort on the morrow. Indeed, he knew a lively hope that raising his sword in a beginning parry would not leave him flat on his face. "I have been ill," he said at last, "and I am not yet entirely recovered. I'm afraid I won't provide much competition for you or any of your men."

"We'll take it easy on you at first." Alaric said. "But only at first."

Jaufre laughed, and other man smiled again and then grew serious. "We will need every sword, Jaufre of Cambaluc," he said. "The mountain tribes that live along the pass between Kabul and Faryab are fierce and predatory. We fought off three attacks by bandits on our way here."

"And the times are unsettled," Jaufre said, "with the Mongols abroad again. Every strong man in every community is out to acquire as much as he can before the Mongols come take it all away."

"So young and yet so wise," Alaric said dryly.

"It is only common sense," Jaufre said, "and besides, haven't we all seen it before?"

Alaric's face resettled itself into its customary melancholic lines. "Indeed we have."

He paused for a moment to look long into Jaufre's face, long enough for the younger man to become restive beneath his gaze, and then abruptly bid him goodnight and strode off into the twilight.

Jaufre looked after him with a thoughtful gaze. There had been a certain pained recognition in Alaric's eyes when he looked at Jaufre's sword, and even more so when he looked into Jaufre's face, though Jaufre was certain that he had never met the other man in his life.

Had he seen Robert de Beauville in Jaufre's face, and Robert de Beauville's sword hanging at Jaufre's side?

Jaufre slipped from the tent before sunrise the next morning, moving stealthily so as not to wake Shasha, who would have woken the entire caravan with her protests. He found the practice yard. Of course there was a wooden post. Firas' practice field had had one just like it. He sighed, and waited for Alaric and the rest to arrive. One of them was sure to have a practice sword.

An hour later, on legs that would barely hold him up, he returned to their site of their yurt to find it, mercifully, struck and packed away, along with their bedrolls. Shasha eyed him smolderingly but said nothing, while Félicien slipped him some naan and dried fruit. Hari was omming from his usual cross-legged position facing the rising sun. His eyes were closed but one of them opened to give Jaufre a quick head-to-toe survey before closing again. "Life is suffering," he intoned. "Blessed be the way."

Jaufre measured the distance between the tip of his boot and Hari's behind, but he didn't have the requisite energy.

All around the caravanserai, men were shouting and camels were groaning as the caravan came slowly to life. Rambahadur Raj was everywhere, checking a girth, smacking the behind of a boy who wasn't moving fast enough with a pack, consulting with first one traveler and then another. He strode up to Jaufre and ran an approving eye over their livestock, their packs, and them. "Yes!" he said. "Someone who knows how to balance a load so it won't slip and pull the cursed camel off the trail!"

Jaufre gave a tired grin. "I was well trained."

"You were indeed, young sir," the havildar said. "Ready?" His quick eye had noticed the sweat drying on Jaufre's brow. He probably already knew the reason for it. There were no secrets in a caravan.

"Ready, havildar," Jaufre said. No excuses, for whatever reason, for this man.

"Good!" Rambahadur Raj said again, and turned to bellow, "Mount up! Mount up! Mount up!"

Jaufre swung his leg over the saddle and settled himself down. His camel was a male, about fifteen, with a thick coat that would do much to keep Jaufre warm on the trail, at least through the mountains. When they reached the desert, that would be another matter, but that was for tomorrow. Today, if felt good to be on the move at last.

Shasha was astride and her camel already on his feet, and as he watched she turned her head and looked toward the north.

Johanna, he thought with a pang. His camel came to its feet and he nudged it next to Shasha's. "Gaza," he said. "We will all meet again in Gaza."

"All of us?" she said.

He didn't know what she meant. "Yes, you, me and Johanna. All of us."

She shot him a glare that took him aback. "That isn't all of us, Jaufre," she said, and kicked her camel into a walk.

He stared after her, agape. Félicien came up beside him on his donkey, looking up into his face. "She sent Firas after Johanna, Jaufre," he said. "He may not have survived the attempt."

"Firas?" he said. "And Shasha?" His head swiveled around and he stared at the back of Shasha's unyielding head.

Félicien sighed and kicked his donkey into motion.

The camels picked up stride and became a long, undulating line that snaked slowly out of the city and up into the foothills. He looked at the line of mountains, crowned with the remnants of a hard winter's snow and ice. Johanna was somewhere on the other side of them.

It wasn't the first time Jaufre had been on the back of a camel, going in the opposite direction of a woman he loved. Then he had been ten years old. Now he was recovering from wound and illness and evidently even more helpless than he had been then. His heart in his breast ached as much as his whole body.

Hari rose to his feet in a single fluid movement, shook the dust from his yellow robes, and mounted his donkey. "Do not dwell in the past, do not dream of the future," he said. "Concentrate the mind on the present moment, young Jaufre."

Jaufre would have glared at him, but he didn't have the energy for that, either.

◆ Seven ◆

Summer, 1323 A.D.
Balkh

├────┤

Three days and fifty hard leagues later, the refugees camped near a city mostly in ruins called Balkh—yet another city leveled by Mongols—and Firas prepared to go inside the city walls, such as they were, to find food and clothing for Hayat and Alma.

"You'll need money," Johanna said, and sat down on a tree stump and prepared to draw upon the Bank of Lundi for the first time.

"Wait," Hayat said, and unwound a veil to reveal a row of gold bangles that spanned her arm from wrist to elbow.

For the first time since they had fled Talikan, when all her attention was focused on flight, Johanna noticed that beneath the veils they had wound about their persons that Alma and Hayat both were nearly dripping with gold and gems, around their arms, their necks, in their hair, tied to their waists in more veils. Alma produced a pair of opal earrings in an elaborate gold setting and handed them to Firas along with Hayat's bangles.

She looked up and smiled at Johanna's expression. "A woman's jewels are her own, Nazirah, even in the harem."

"So you needn't have hidden yours in your hems," Hayat said with a trace of her old mischievousness. At Johanna's expression, she said, "Oh yes, we knew. We all knew, Nazirah, the moment you would not allow the servants to wash your clothes. There are no secrets in the harem."

None in a caravan, either, Johanna thought.

All three women began to laugh, a little tremulously, and Firas collected the jewelry and vacated the area at once, before the laughter became hysteria. He was a perspicacious man. The moment he was gone, Alma's laughter changed to sobs. At Alma's first sob Hayat burst into tears herself. Johanna, more out of fear that she might join in than because the display of grief and relief made her uncomfortable, left them to hike up the rise that hid the little creek they had stopped beside.

Balkh sat near the open, west-facing end of a river valley between two arms of the Hindu Kush. They'd ridden hard and long over the northern arm, stopping to rest only infrequently, and Johanna thought that it was a good thing that Hayat and Alma had been tied to their mounts because the rough mountain trails were so narrow and so steep there would have been nothing to recover but the body if one of them had fallen off. Fear had carried them from Talikan to here, but both women were now paying for the hard ride, neither of them able to do much more than hobble once out of the saddle. Physical pain was probably one of the reasons they were both crying now.

She lowered her eyes from the mountains to the valley beneath, where a long, blue line indicated a river paralleling the course of the valley. On their side of the river, against the green of the valley she could see a small village or town. Opposite it, in the hollows of the hills behind, lay the ruined city of Balkh, whose proud history could be intuited from the amount of rubble left behind. Here and there small, habitable buildings that had obviously been built from materials harvested from the ruins showed signs of life in hanging clothing and wisps of smoke. She could just make out the tiny figure of Firas's mount picking his way between a tumble of white stone blocks that had once been part of a wall, and fragments of what might have been a gatehouse. He passed within, unchallenged.

She raised her eyes again and looked at the mountains they had crossed. It had been a nightmarish journey, as they had not dared to stop for anything but a snatched meal or a quick watering of the horses. They had slept by day and traveled by night, at considerable risk to both themselves and the horses. Ogodei and Gokudo could not have missed their escape, and they would have both have known North Wind on sight, even at a distance, and known that only she could be riding him. Would they follow? She could not guess, but neither could she take chances with her life and the lives of Firas, Hayat, and Alma.

A scream from the hollow below spun her around. She leapt down the loose scree of the knoll and slid into camp in a scatter of loose gravel, barely managing to stay upright. There she found Hayat and Alma clinging to each other as they watched two young men, ragged and dirty, close in on their three mounts, which were cropping peacefully at a patch of grass next to the little stream.

The two men whirled at Joanna's dramatic entrance, and then relaxed. "Only another woman," one said, grinning. He affected a bow toward her and said, "Pretty lady, we mean you no harm. We only have need of your horses." The expression on the second man's face said otherwise as he appraised first her, and then Hayat, and then Alma.

"This great white stallion," the first man said. "Surely he would prefer to be ridden by a man?"

"I'm sure he would," Johanna said, her amiable reply hiding the fact that her heart was pounding in her ears. She waved a negligent hand. "Go ahead. Take him."

The first man laughed, excited, and tugged at the sleeve of his friend, turning his attention from the negligible women to the much more important horses. He caught at North Wind's bridle.

What followed wasn't pretty but it was certainly efficient. When it was over Alma helped Johanna bury the bodies and Hayat helped her to clean a still indignant North Wind's legs and hooves. Alma would always be more comfortable with dead men than live horses.

When Firas returned at sunset they didn't mention the incident, mostly because they were too tired to move camp. Firas had done well in the city, having acquired a complete outfit of clothes for both women, including sturdy leather boots that could be made to fit if they wrapped their feet in veils, and more importantly a bundle of naan, half a lamb, a sack of pomegranates, and dried meat, dried fruit and shelled nuts in enough quantity to sustain them on the Road for several days, or until they reached the next community with food for sale, no questions asked. He rigged a spit and they ate every scrap of the lamb without thinking twice about the bodies beneath the rocks not so very far away.

Johanna was secretly amazed at Alma and Hayat's acceptance of the presence of dead bodies so near their persons. By neither word nor deed did either woman betray any regret at their chosen path. They retired into a clump of trees to change into their new clothes, and proved adept at cobbling them to fit when the pants proved too long and the tunics too baggy. They needed help with their cheches, and the sight of Firas by firelight soberly winding material and tying intricate knots around both women's heads, and then instructing them in how he had done so, would stay with Johanna for many a day.

Firas had bought saddle bags and bedrolls as well, along with two small, belted daggers and one small sword, also belted, which he handed to Johanna. "Am I right to believe that you can be trusted not to cut yourself open with this?"

She smiled and accepted it. "You are. Although I am better with a bow. And better still at soft boxing."

He nodded. He had observed her and Jaufre practicing every morning. "Still, taking on two men alone is one thing."

She looked up from the blade, surprised.

"I can read sign, young miss," he said, casting an expressive look around the campsite. "The bodies are buried around that corner of rock, yes?"

"Uh, yes," Johanna said. They had moved away from the fire and were speaking in low tones. Hayat and Alma had taken two of the bedrolls and retired to a rocky alcove out of the light of the fire.

"Good," he said. "It will keep the carrion birds away, which will keep them in turn from drawing attention to anyone who might come looking for them."

She shook her head. "They didn't look as if they were members of a tribe or village. Outcasts, perhaps, or—" she sighed "—perhaps more of the dispossessed from Ogodei's incursion into the west."

"There will be more," Firas said.

"Yes," she said grimly. "Hundreds more. If not thousands." She braced herself. "Tell me about Jaufre."

He answered immediately, as if he'd known the question was coming. "His wound was not as bad as it looked, but despite Shu Shao's best efforts it became infected. We took shelter in a village which came down with typhus while he was still recovering."

"He got typhus?" she said faintly.

"Yes, but he got over it," he said, "although he then contracted a case of what Shu Shao believed was ague." He told her the rest.

She could feel the fine trembling of her limbs and stilled it with an effort. "Why Kabul?"

He sighed. "I had traveled there before, I speak the dialect and I have friends among the tribes, so I was fairly certain of safe passage. Kabul is a large city where we would be able to find a doctor who didn't rely on astrology and camel urine to heal his patients. And..." He paused. "And Ogodei did not appear to me like a man who would stop at Terak. If he didn't, if he really is bent on conquest, he will come to Kabul regardless, but the mountains and the Afghans will slow him down, perhaps long enough for Jaufre to recover enough to stay on a camel. It was not the easiest route for someone in your foster-brother's condition, true, but I deemed it to be the safest."

"And did Shasha find a doctor?"

"Yes," he said. "I believe a good one. Your Jaufre was still alive when I left them, young miss." He let her absorb his news for a few moments, until he judged it time to direct her attention back to their present circumstances. "In the town today—"

Her head came up like North Wind on the scent of an enemy. "Yes?"

"There is another town across the river, where many of the residents of Balkh resettled when their city was destroyed, and where their descendants live today."

Johanna nodded. "I saw it from the top of the rise."

"There is some visiting and trading back and forth between the two communities, naturally—"

Johanna wondered what the old Balkh had that could possibly interest the new.

"—and I heard talk in the marketplace of a troop of men, arriving today across the river."

She stared at him, and spoke through dry lips. "It can't be. Not so soon. Not at the pace we have been maintaining. And we would have seen them coming!"

He raised his hand in a calming gesture, glancing in the direction of the other two women to see if they had heard. "Quietly, I beg you, young miss. We would not, in fact, have seen them coming. We traveled by night, if you recall, North Wind by day being a beacon bright enough to set the entire world aflame and have all of it running after us."

She thought he almost smiled. It steadied her, and she lowered her voice. "Did they say in the market who they were, this troop?"

"No," he said. He hesitated, and her heart sank. "But they said that one of them wears black armor and carries a spear curved at the head."

"Gokudo," she said, her voice the barest whisper. At first she could feel nothing but shock, but when she looked for it, she could see the tiny flickers of building anger gathering around the edges of that shock.

"There was no cover for us when we escaped, and we know at least six of the guards saw us the instant we escaped Talikan." He hesitated again, and said gently, "It is in my mind that Ogodei would have been very pleased with the quick destruction of Talikan, and that afterward he would have been willing to grant his captain any wish he desired."

"Including coming after me," she said.

"Even that," he said, nodding.

She stood where she was, staring into the darkness. "We should separate, Firas," she said.

"No," he said.

"Firas—"

"No," he said more firmly. "I gave Shu Shao my word I would bring you back safely. I will not return to her without you."

"You can't do that if you are killed," she said tartly, "which you very may well be if you stay in my company."

"Even so," he said.

She took in a deep breath and let it out, thinking. "If that dog-fucking, frog-humping, son of a whore and a monkey is so determined to pursue us…"

He didn't so much as blink at her language. "Yes?"

She smiled, little more than a baring of teeth. "Then perhaps we should lead him where we want him to go."

"Yes?" he said again.

"It may be that I have a notion of how to rid ourselves of Gokudo once and for all. It would require going back into the mountains." She looked at the dark shadow where Hayat and Alma had hidden themselves. "Should we ride on tonight?"

He followed her gaze. "I don't think they can."

She agreed with him, and a rest for herself and North Wind and the other horses was necessary, too. Still, "They would if we told them they had to."

"They would. They have heart."

She was aware that this was high praise from Firas. "Tomorrow, then?"

He shook his head. "We still don't dare travel by day."

"Tomorrow night, then?"

"Tomorrow night," he said, and waited.

"I know how tired you must be," she said.

"How tired must I be to refuse to do what you are about to ask me?"

She looked up, startled, and his white teeth flashed in his black beard in the first full grin she had seen on his face. "Can you?" she said. "Cross the river and find out if it really is Gokudo, and exactly how many men he has with him?"

"I can," he said, "and I will. You will stand watch against my return?"

She nodded. "If we are not to travel until tomorrow night, we can sleep through the day." She looked again in the direction of the two women. "They need it."

He regarded her for a moment. "I ask again. What are you going to do with them?"

Her mouth quirked up in a half-smile. "And I answer again, that is up to them."

"Will you bring them all the way to Gaza?"

She shrugged. "If that's where they want to go."

"What kind of life will they have, two women on their own?"

"Well," she said, "they are more resourceful and have more stamina than I thought they would. And they certainly aren't penniless."

He didn't point out what Johanna already knew, that the two of them could travel much faster on their own. He didn't believe in wasting his breath. Instead, he melted into the night, and Johanna went to sit beside the small fire, pulling the blade Firas had given her from its sheath. It was rusty with disuse, and she found a whetstone and oil and a rag in Firas' pack and went work.

"Nazirah?"

She looked up to find Alma standing before her. "My true name is Johanna," she said. "It would please me to be called that."

"Jo-han-na," Alma said. "Johanna. A difficult name to pronounce."

"Then it suits its owner," Hayat said, coming into the reach of the firelight. "My true name is Miriam, which my family gave me before they sold me into slavery. I will remain Hayat."

"Mine," Alma said, "was always Alma."

The two women ranged themselves on the other side of the fire from Johanna. Both had taken the opportunity of running water to wash and tidy themselves, and neither one of them appeared weighted down by the scene at the campsite that afternoon. If anything, the cautious and hesitant manner that was the norm in the harem, where for one's continued safety and good health every word was presumed to have been overheard by those who did not wish you well, had disappeared. They spoke now in voices not loud but not hushed, either, and with the certainty that only the person they were talking to was listening. In spite of herself, in spite of her fears for Jaufre and her longing to see him and Shasha again, Johanna felt a corresponding lift in her own spirits. Those stifling months locked away from the world had worn on her more than she had known. Here, she was free, to speak, to ride, to travel to destinations of her own choice.

To fight.

"We heard you and Firas talking," Hayat said.

Of course they had. "Do not concern yourselves," Johanna said, returning to her blade. "This is something personal, to do only with me, and Firas."

"Of course we will concern ourselves," Alma said sharply. "This man—Gokudo?—he wishes to kill you?"

"Afterward," Johanna said. She hesitated, and then told them of Gokudo and the girl at the gate.

A pregnant silence.

"I see," Alma said at last, and exchanged a look with Hayat.

"We would be dead now if not for you, Jo-han-na," Hayat said. "After what I imagine would have been a very long and painful time. We owe you our lives."

Alma looked up at a sky covered with stars. They lit her face with reflected glory. "And our freedom." She looked back at Johanna. "How can we help?"

· Eight ·

Summer, 1323 A.D.
East of Balkh, north of Kabul, somewhere in the Hindu Kush

⊢——⊣

Afull month since Talikan, most of it spent traversing rough, precarious mountain trails, made all the more dangerous by traversing them at night, and Alma and Hayat were sitting much more securely in their saddles. Their skin was chapped and their hands were calloused and they were both much thinner and they'd probably never smelled quite so badly in either of their lives, but Johanna was more impressed every day by their strength and resilience. Neither of them had wavered in their determination to win their mutual savior free of her pursuer, and Firas and Johanna had yet to hear a complaint from either of them over hard beds or short rations.

They had camped the previous morning beneath a rocky outcropping that sheltered them somewhat from the day's rain. Firas had taken advantage of the storm to scout out their pursuers, and had returned at daybreak with the news that they were a day behind them. "A day, no more," he said, looking at Johanna.

She frowned. "I thought they would be nearer."

Firas removed his cheche, wrung it out and rewound it about his head, tucking in the wet ends neatly. "I'm sure they would be desolated to hear that you were disappointed in them, young miss."

Hayat laughed, her unquenchable dimples still in evidence, grime notwithstanding.

"Still Gokudo and his twenty?"

"Yes, young miss." Firas sounded regretfully respectful. "None have dropped out."

Johanna nodded. "Do they know we are watching them?"

"No," Firas said, very firmly.

"You're sure?"

"I am sure, young miss. I have been very careful."

"Very well, then." Johanna reviewed their plans.

They had had considerable difficulty in finding exactly the right village to help them. Many were too small, without enough men. Others weren't poor enough, having staked out the only arable land in a day's walk and therefore capable of feeding themselves and their families without resorting to too much robbery. Some were simply apathetic from hunger suffered for too long, disinterested by malnutrition to any exertion.

She had begun to think that the fierce reputation of the Afghan hill tribes had been greatly exaggerated when they happened upon Aab, a small village at the confluence of two trickles of water contaminated by the effluent from the lapis mine at the head of one of them. "The mine is played out, young miss," Firas said, "and they are wondering if they should abandon their village to look for another."

A slow smile had spread across Johanna's face. "Were they thinking they would have to walk out?"

"They were, young miss, until I explained matters to them, and suggested our plan."

"And?"

"And the village elders would be pleased to assist us," Firas had said demurely.

"And us? Will they leave us alone afterward?"

"They can always attempt to take North Wind by force," Firas said.

After the village of Aab had agreed to join forces with them, they had had to backtrack two days to allow Gokudo and his men to pick up their trail again. Now they sheltered beneath this rock overhang, damp, shivering and content. The steep sides of the narrow canyon they were in were thickly covered in stunted cedars and junipers, twisted from wind and lack of sun. The stream that had carved it was narrow and deep and filled with boulders that had broken free of the cliffs above, and it was running very high from all the rain.

"Today, then?" Johanna said.

Firas gave no quick answer. The decision was too important to be made without thought.

"You said they were using the cover of the rain to advance," Johanna said. "They think to surprise us in our wet and cold misery." Her grin was fierce.

If she could be brought to admit it, which she never would, Johanna would have said that she had thoroughly enjoyed this month in the mountains. She had seen Gokudo, oh yes, but he had not seen her, and would not unless she meant him to.

"Today," Firas said. He looked down the narrow canyon. "We'll never find a better place."

They rose to their feet, and the three women stood patiently while Firas personally checked to see that all their weapons drew freely and that each had at least one edge that could cut. After which Johanna led their horses away and Alma and Hayat began to rummage in their packs for their harem clothing.

Gokudo and his troop of twenty men, none of them known to him before Terak Pass, had been chasing a rumor of their objective for thirty days. Their diet had been hard rations, their beds, when they were allowed them, hard and rocky and cold and often damp, if not wet. The men vaguely remembered Johanna—they remembered North Wind much more clearly—and the others with her they neither knew of nor cared. They were with Gokudo because Ogodei, their ruler in all things, had ordered them to be.

Thus far, following Ogodei's orders had led to riches beyond imagining, their pick of beautiful women, treasure in the form of anything they fancied from any of the cities that had fallen beneath their swords, full bellies and whatever soft noble's bed they chose each night, so long as they hadn't burned down the noble's house first. But the last month had been a long, hard slog with no reward. They had been subsisting on wild game, ibex and urial and boar when they could find them, marmots and weasels and lizards when they could not, supplemented by wild fruits and nuts and fish from the mountain streams, which were not plentiful, the local villagers having cleaned them out when times were hard. And times in these mountains were almost always hard.

They had no thought of rebellion because they would follow Ogodei unto death, and anyone he named unto death as well. There was no thought of mutiny, and as yet none of them had questioned Gokudo's authority, not even out of his hearing. But they were cold, and tired, and hungry, a little annoyed that none of the mountain villages they had stumbled across in their peregrinations had anything to plunder. They were perhaps even a little impatient with the single-minded obsession of this foreign captain, which was to purse his quarry to what appeared to be the ends of the earth, no matter how long the journey, how remote the destination or how uncomfortable the weather.

It was in this mood that they turned a rocky corner of this narrow canyon and found a small stretch of smooth gravel next to the stream. Two women were kneeling next to the water, washing clothes.

It occurred to none of Gokudo's men to wonder why two very attractive women were washing clothes next to an isolated mountain stream, without male supervision, in the rain, or why in this weather and these rough surroundings they were dressed in the flimsy vest and baggy pants of the harem, which had dampened enough to cling enticingly to their curves. They were here, they were within reach, they promised some relief from the hard days past, and what fool would question such a gift?

Since rape was not best accomplished from the back of a horse, and since it was obvious that the canyon ended not much further on and that it appeared the people their captain had had them chasing for the last month had finally run out of places to run, half of them naturally dismounted. The two women dropped their wash, screamed convincingly and ran to the nearest cliff and began to scramble up, grabbing at stunted bushes, their frantic feet causing tiny avalanches of loose rock. Gokudo's men laughed and exchanged ribald comments as they started after them. There was no hurry.

"Gokudo!"

Their captain's head snapped up, eyes fierce. A feral grin curled one corner of his mouth.

Johanna sat on North Wind's back at the head of the narrow little canyon. Her bronze-streaked hair was loose around her head and curling damply in the rain. She wore her black raw silk tunic and trousers, the last clothing she would ever have from material that had been traded for by her father. At her waist she wore a sash made from the gauzy silk of a harem veil, blood red in color. Over it she wore a belt and scabbard.

Johanna had her blade out, and she'd choked up on North Wind's reins enough so that he danced impatiently in place. He was wet and hungry and tired, too, and disinclined to take any correction to his manners, which were wearing thin as it was. This mountain travel was all very well, especially as he had his favorite person on his back, but he was more accustomed to flat racecourses and the adulation of the crowds and the sooner he returned to them, the better.

"Did you want me, Gokudo?" Johanna said. She worked hard to put a bit of a quaver in her voice, which wasn't difficult because she was terrified on behalf of Alma and Hayat, now engaged in pulling down half the cliff face in their manifestly desperate attempt to escape the attentions of Gokudo's men. "You certainly have been trying hard enough to find me!" She waved her sword with all the expertise of a ten-year old issuing a challenge to a playmate of equal years and experience. She was no threat to Gokudo and she was demonstrating it as blatantly as possible. "Because you have certainly been persistent in following me."

"And now I have you, Wu Li's daughter," Gokudo said, his voice coming out in a growling purr.

"Not yet, you don't!" she cried, brandishing her blade again even more clumsily.

Gokudo sat astride a steppe pony, the same animal that mounted his troop. "Come!" he said in his broken Mongol, raising his naginata. "We have them now!"

He kicked the sides of his mount and it began to pick its way up the side of the stream, avoiding rocks and holes with nimble sureness. Those of his men who were still astride, perhaps ten of them, followed.

Johanna wheeled North Wind and appeared to vanish around the corner of granite at her back. Gokudo urged his shaggy pony into as fast a gait as the terrain allowed.

He heard the sound of hooves plunking through water, and North Wind whinnied, high and loud. When he rounded the corner Johanna and North Wind were standing at the end of the canyon, boxed in on three sides by steep walls and the mass of green undergrowth hanging from them. The headwaters of the narrow creek cascaded down the rock face behind her in a small waterfall, where it splashed to earth to form the stream that rushed between them.

The rain was easing. Finally, things were going his way. "Yield, Wu Li's daughter," he said, his voice thick with anticipation. "Yield to me, and I will not kill you." Or not immediately, he thought. Not until Dai Fang insisted that he must, long after he bore this impudent, thieving bitch back to Cambaluc in triumph.

He slowed the pace of his pony, allowing it to pick its way without haste. Behind him the last of his men rounded the corner. The move effectively split his force in two, which he didn't realize until too late.

The hand of some fickle god parted the clouds at just that moment, and a slender ray of sunshine slipped through and fell in a golden shower on the girl and the horse, illuminating them against the green and gray background. It was so unexpected and the subsequent vision so striking that it halted Gokudo for a moment in something like awe.

It was just long enough, although it wasn't necessary. From their cover in the dense green growth, the men of Aab rose in a body, drew bowstrings and let fly. One of Gokudo's men was killed instantly by an arrow through the eye. Three fell from the saddle, clutching at arrows in their sides. One man took the measure of their hopeless situation at a glance and pulled his mount around to head back downstream and out of range as fast as his pony could carry him, riding right over one of his wounded comrades. In his haste his sleeve caught the edge of the rock corner and unhorsed him. When he landed he was immediately skewered with arrows. He screamed and groaned, and went still.

After the first volley, the men of Aab scrambled nimbly down the canyon wall, more arrows already fitted to their bows. Gokudo's men, in the act of reaching for the bow slung on their own backs, raised their hands in surrender. They were capable and knowledgeable warriors, veterans of many battles. If they had chosen to fight they knew they could have inflicted much damage on the men of Aab, but they could not have won the day. Ogodei had not commanded them to follow Gokudo into a situation that was certain suicide for them all.

Those that remained mounted were pulled summarily to the ground, including Gokudo. Some of the men of Aab began to lead the captured steppe ponies away at once, while others relieved the men of their weapons and, wounded and hale alike, kicked them stumbling downstream in the direction from which they had come. Half a dozen others grouped around Gokudo, arrows nocked and ready. He stood with his mouth half open in disbelief. From one second to the next, he had moved from a position where he had all the power, where he finally had Johanna in his hands to do with as he pleased, to a position where he had none and was entirely at her mercy. The change of fortune was impossible for him to immediately comprehend.

Nor did she intend to give him time to fully understand it. Beyond the corner Johanna heard shouts and screams and the clash of arms and the thrum of arrows even now diminishing.

She nudged North Wind into motion, and he picked his way down to where Gokudo stood. His naginata slipped easily from his slack grasp to hers, and she rested the butt on her foot. It felt heavy and cold and alien in her hand. "Bring him," she said over her shoulder, and she and North Wind continued down the little canyon.

Behind her, she heard a muffled grunt and the stumble of feet.

Around the corner, only two of Gokudo's remaining men were left standing and were being efficiently divested of their weapons. Like their fellows upstream, they did not resist. Firas was flicking blood from his sword, others were dispatching the wounded. Her eyes searched feverishly for Hayat and Alma, and found them just then rising from a crouch in a thick patch of brush halfway up the side of the cliff. "All well?" she said.

Their smiles were shaky. "All well," Hayat said.

Johanna nodded. The troop's horses had been attached to two leading reins and were being led downstream by two young boys. The men of Aab waited in a circle, exchanging contemptuous remarks on the caliber of soldier that had pursued their benefactors into the mountains. One of them laughed and said something to Firas, who wiped his blade clean and sheathed it again, and replied with a comment Johanna didn't hear. They all laughed this time. Gokudo's men, some of whom must have understood what was being said, stood with blank faces, motionless beneath the strung arrows.

All but one. "Bitch!" one of Gokudo's men said. "Cunt! Daughter and granddaughter of pimps and whores, may God curse them all! May you suffer in sixty thousand hells for all eternity!"

Johanna looked at him, puzzled at first, and then on an indrawn breath recognized the contorted features beneath the filth. "Farhad," she said.

Firas turned to follow her gaze. "Why, so it is."

There was little remaining of the elegant sheik's son. He wore a torn and tattered coat that looked from the stains as if it had been taken off a dead man who had taken a long time to die. His beard, once neatly barbered, was now a wild bush, and his hair hung greasily down from beneath a rolled cap that looked as if it harbored a healthy population of vermin. Two of the men of Aab were advancing with knives drawn, while Farhad's companions were trying to restrain him. He struggled, maddened, as he called more curses down upon her head.

Her head remained remarkably unbowed. "Not dead of snake bite after all, I see," she said pleasantly. "What a pity. How did you convince Ogodei to let you live, I wonder?" She paused and let her gaze wander over him insultingly. "Or maybe I don't. You used to be almost attractive." She smiled. "And Ogodei is known to be…liberal, in his tastes."

He was nearly sobbing and his eyes were wild. He struggled futilely against the hands holding him. "Daughter of pigs! May you give birth only to more!"

Firas walked up to Johanna, who brought her leg over the saddle to slide from North Wind's back. "The men of Aab want to know what they should do with the living."

She shrugged, indifferent. "As they wish."

"They don't want them among their own," Firas said.

"Well," Johanna said, "if they are inclined to set them free, Ogodei's men can return to their master. If they think he'll take them back after this."

"May you never know the father of your child!"

Her smile didn't reach her eyes. "But they'll have to walk."

Farhad was almost weeping. "Bitch," he said, "cunt that has seen a thousand cocks!"

"Come, Farhad," she said in a silken voice, "surely the prospect isn't so bad as that."

And with that echo of his own words in his ears, his companions dragged him away from her, shrieking more and worse imprecations to the sky.

"What are you going to do with that?" Firas said, indicating the naginata she still held.

"Which one is the headman of Aab?" she said.

Firas beckoned one of the men forward. He was older than the rest but still very fit, and he kept a wary eye on the curved blade of the naginata as he inclined his head in salute. He said something in a dialect Johanna hadn't had time to pick up. It was almost Persian, but not quite.

"Jibran complimented me on the success of my plan," Firas said. "I told him it was your plan. He offers you his compliments."

"Tell him it would not have succeeded without the courageous and able men of Aab," she said, and held up the naginata. "Tell him I would give this to him as a personal gift, in gratitude."

The headman's eyes widened and he replied vociferously, at extensive length and with sweeping gestures to an approving murmur from his men.

"He accepts," Firas said.

"I am pleased to hear it," she said. "Tell him it has one more task to accomplish before it passes into his hands. I would ask him, as leader of his tribe, to bear witness to that task."

Firas translated. Jibran squared his shoulders and replied with a long and complicated sentence that went on for five minutes, ending it with a bow and a flourish. All of his men bowed, too.

"He is honored," Firas said.

She turned and looked at Gokudo. He was on his knees in the middle of the stream, his hands bound behind his back. He was muttering to himself in his own tongue. Johanna had been to Cipangu with her father and while she was by no means fluent in Gokudo's tongue, she had spent enough time on the docks to realize that his insults were by an order of magnitude even more insulting than Farhad's.

"Not here," Johanna said. "I don't want to get my feet wet. Or foul the water."

They hauled him up on the little gravel shoal where Hayat and Alma had been washing their clothes only minutes before.

She stood before him. "You dishonored my father with his second wife," she said in Mandarin, "and then you tried to kill him by cutting the girth on his saddle. When he didn't die quickly enough, at Dai Fang's order you smothered him in his own sick bed."

His muttering died away, and he blinked up at her as if he had just realized she was there. Behind her, she could hear Firas translating her works for Jibran and his men.

"My only mistake was in leaving justice for my father in other hands. Today, I rectify that mistake."

Johanna took a few practice swings with the naginata. Watching from behind and to her left, Firas motioned everyone farther back, which may have been an unusually superfluous gesture. Though she tried to hide it, it was obvious she found the staff heavy and the blade weighting its end heavier still.

He saw her set her jaw and square her shoulders. She choked up a little on the staff, but only a little. She readjusted her stance, moving her feet farther apart, bending her knees slightly, and adjusted the height of the blade to where it looked to Firas like she was aiming for the level of Gokudo's ear. Her torso twisted so that if she had pulled the naginata any more to her left she would have broken her spine off at the base and commenced the swing. Its own weight brought the blade down to the height of Gokudo's neck just as the edge touched his skin. Her momentum and the weight and acute sharpness of the blade did the rest.

Gokudo's head bounced once with a meaty thud and rolled a few feet away, his face still looking a little puzzled. His eyes blinked rapidly six or seven times. His body crumpled into a disorderly heap. Blood at first fountained from his severed neck, then flowed, then streamed, then trickled, and then stopped.

The swing of the naginata pulled Johanna around almost as far to her right as she had begun it to her left, Firas noticed with profession detachment, so far as to pull her left heel from the ground. She let it, probably so it would look as if it was her idea, until the naginata's swing slowed and she was able to regain her authority over it.

She neatly reversed its waning momentum to bring it back level in front of her, and let it lay flat against her palms as she presented it to Jibran with a slight bow, the blade still wet with Gokudo's blood. Firas believed that only he saw the fine tremble in her arms.

Jibran looked at Johanna in silence for a long moment, and then bowed once more, deeply, respectfully, profoundly. As one, the men of Aab bowed with him. He accepted the naginata with due reverence and respect, and then he and his men began to melt rapidly down the canyon in the wake of the boys who had taken the horses, leaving Farhad and the other soldiers standing where they were, stupid with fatigue and shock, staring at Gokudo's severed head.

Hayat and Alma came up, having changed back into their traveling clothes and leading their horses. They looked at Gokudo's body. Alma shuddered. Hayat gave Johanna an approving nod. "All done here?"

"All done," Johanna said, and mounted North Wind.

As they passed down the canyon, Farhad lunged for Johanna, again calling down curses on her head and her line and her descendants until the end of time. Displeased, possibly by Farhad's intemperate language, possibly by his uninvited nearness, North Wind exercised the excellent muscles in his right hind leg to plant his hoof squarely in Farhad's belly. Farhad flew backwards and landed in the stream with a magnificent splash, where he lay gasping for breath.

Johanna gave North Wind's neck an extra pat. He gave his ears a nonchalant flick. They walked around the next curve of the canyon without a backward glance.

· Nine ·

Summer, 1323 A.D.
On the Road

├────┤

"Tell me about the Templars," Jaufre said.
Alaric sighed. To Jaufre's ears it sounded a little theatrical. "First, I beg you, please rid yourself of the habit of calling me Alaric the Templar," the older man said. "Ram will have his little joke, but the farther west we travel, the more dangerous it gets."

"Why?"

"Because our order has been proscribed, by church and state."

"What church? Which state?"

"All of them," Alaric said gloomily.

"Since when?"

"That depends," Alaric said, and launched into a disjointed history frequently interrupted by strong personal opinions and bitter asides that lasted, on and off, for four days. They had come out of the foothills and were well launched upon the eastern edge of the aptly-named Emptiness Desert, and Rambahadur Raj had switched travel time from days to nights. Traveling across the great salt waste with the stars painting the sky overhead lent an otherworldly element to the tale, which might have been partially responsible for leaving Jaufre inclined to believe less than half of what he heard. It was all so very improbable.

The short version seemed to be that the Knights of the Temple was an order of warrior monks first established a little over two hundred years before by a Frankish knight named Hugues.

"De Payens," Félicien said, who kept close by during the entirety of the long nights of the tale of the Templars and evidently felt empowered to correct anything he felt Alaric got wrong.

Alaric, who had taken an inexplicable dislike to his fellow Frank at first sight, harrumphed and continued. "He went on crusade to the Holy Land—"

"Crusade?" Jaufre said. "Oh, I know, I remember my father talking about it. There's a shrine or, no, a city. Something near the western shore of the Middle Sea that—Christians, isn't it?—regard as belonging to their religion." Father John had spoken of it, he remembered. "Where your Christ was born," he said out loud.

"Everyone's Christ," Alaric said in a shocked voice, and this time Jaufre thought of Uncle Cheng. "His birthplace has fallen into the hands of the infidels. It is a holy cause to regain it."

"It was that," Félicien said, as if admitting an unpalatable truth. "But it was also driven by the need to re-open trade routes to the East." Jaufre couldn't see the goliard's lip curling but he could hear it in his voice. "Our noble rulers can't do without their nutmeg."

"It was a quest to reclaim the holy places where our Lord and Savior once walked and preached the Gospel," Alaric said frostily.

"It also gave the knights of Europe a new target to fight, instead of each other."

Alaric reared back so violently that his camel stumbled and protested. "My dear young student, as you say you are, you would do well to listen if you wish to learn."

"And Hugues de Payens…?" Jaufre said.

Alaric, very erect, said, "The evil Saracens—"

"Also known as the Seljuk empire," Félicien said to Jaufre. "Mostly Turkics."

"—were robbing and murdering pilgrims—pious, unarmed travelers to the holy places of Jerusalem, where—"

"—once our Lord and Savior walked and preached," Félicien said in a sing-song voice, and grinned at Alaric's fulminating look, unrepentant. "And you say I don't listen."

Alaric harrumphed again. "The Holy Father on his throne in Rome—"

"Pope Urban II in 1096."

"—responded to these outrages—"

"As well as to a request from the emperor of Byzantium," Félicien said, "who was worried about the Seljuks knocking at his front door, and his back door, too, for that matter."

"—by preaching the First Crusade at the Council of Clermont."

"And Hugues de Payens…?" Jaufre said.

"Yes, yes," Alaric said testily, "that came later."

"How much later?"

"About a hundred years later," Félicien said, and he and Alaric fell into another wrangle about just when the Knights of the Temple had been officially established. As near as Jaufre could make out, the Templars were a volunteer force from when Hugues de Payens and his companions offered their services to King Baldwin of Jerusalem in 1113, but they weren't officially an arm of the Christian church until fifteen years later.

"So," Jaufre said, making a mental effort to sort all this into a timeline, "they protected pilgrims on the road to Jerusalem."

Alaric straightened. "It was our calling."

Félicien snorted.

"I beg your pardon?" Alaric said, the frost back in his voice.

"They were bankers," the goliard said. "And some of the richest landowners in Europe. And that is exactly why they no longer exist." Except as superannuated old fidgets like this one, his silence added.

"But—"

"They became too powerful, too rich," the goliard said. "It created a great deal of jealousy. Philip of France had borrowed heavily from them, and he didn't want to pay it back. And—"

Someone called for a guard and Alaric spurred away, gladly, Jaufre thought.

He saw Félicien's head turn as he watched the older man move down the line of the caravan. "And?" he said.

"And they lost," Félicien said. "They lost Jerusalem to Saladin in 1187. In 1291, they lost Acre, the last Christian outpost in the Holy Land. Eleven years later, they lost Ruad Island, most of the Templars who were there dying in its defense. In the end, they lost everything the Crusades had gained." He paused. "Well," he said, "at least everything they gained in the first Crusade. None of the rest of the crusades amounted to much."

"And when they lost the Holy Land, everyone turned against them?"

"How do you think the Crusades were paid for, Jaufre?"

"Oh," he said, after a moment.

"Yes," the goliard said, "taxes. The Christian world paid and paid and paid again to regain the Holy Land for those of their faith. Lords great and small from Italy to Spain to France to England bankrupted their estates financing this holy effort. A wasted effort, in blood and in treasure. I'm surprised the Templars lasted as long after the fall of Acre as they did."

Jaufre subtracted. "Twenty-one years."

"Fifteen," Félicien said grimly. "Philip the Fair arrested as many as he could lay hands on in 1307. Pope Clement held out as long as he could but Philip finally forced his hand at the head of an army. In 1314, with full papal approval, Philip burned the last Templar Grand Master at the stake in Paris, and it was all over."

Jaufre wondered where his father had been in all this. Alaric had given him to understand that Templars were monks and that they did not marry, but Jaufre himself had been born in 1306, four years after the fall of Ruad, a year before the first arrests and eight full years before the head of his order had been executed. "You don't seem all that fond of Philip the Fair," he said cautiously. "He was your king."

"He was my father's king," Félicien said, his voice devoid of his usual mockery. "De Molay, the Grand Master, cursed them both from his pyre. Pope Clement and King Philip, both. They both died within the year, and there hasn't been a king able to keep the throne of France beneath his ass for more than a few years at a time since then."

"And you think the curse had something to do with that?"

"You don't find the juxtaposition of events persuasive?" The customary mocking tone was back in the light voice.

"I'm not a superstitious man," Jaufre said.

He heard the shrug in Félicien's voice. "As you wish. They're still dead."

So are the Templars, Jaufre thought, but refrained from saying so. There was that in the goliard's voice that spoke of much unsaid, something personal, if he had to guess. Was there a Templar in Félicien's family, perhaps? Or a family bankrupted by taxes raised for a Crusade?

At dawn, when they set up camp to sleep through the heat of the day, Jaufre took his sword to the guards' practice ground and whaled away stoically at the wooden post set up there. The men had at first teased him over his weakness and ineptitude, but his determination had eventually silenced them, and now when he was done they came forward to offer one-on-one practice. Slowly, too slowly, he was building his stamina and his skill back to where he might be able to beat a ten-year old child, if said child were armed only with a dinner knife.

He staggered back to collapse next to their campfire, and drank the entire bowl of soup Shasha handed him in one gulp, chunks of goat meat and all. She refilled it and handed it back without comment.

And so the days on the Road progressed, unchanging, monotonous, seemingly without end. The desert continued flat and salt, and Rambahadur Raj delayed their start a little longer each evening to allow the ground to cool before they set out across it. They had no trouble with raiders in this first leg of their journey. There weren't many people of any kind, the oasis towns few and far between, and the people of the caravan looked forward to Kerman in eager anticipation. Kerman was a storied city famous for carpets and turquoise and must certainly support a caravansary worthy of the name, with running water and public baths.

In this they were proven right, thankfully. Two mountainous ridges capped with late-melting snow hid the city from view until they were right on it, and at last they beheld the sprawl of red brick buildings, a vast expanse of peaked and arched and domed roofs rising up to a central fortress whose size awed them all into momentary silence.

"It's bigger even than the palace at Cambaluc," Shasha said.

"By half again," Jaufre said.

"It's not as tall as Chartres," Félicien said, and kicked his donkey into motion again.

The caravansary was large and spacious, with a fully functioning fountain and indoor plumbing. The stables were vast and the lush personal accommodations were better than Kashgar's. Jaufre and Shasha agreed to splurge on a suite of two rooms that opened onto a balcony over the central court, and they drew back the shutters so that the sound of water trickling out of the fountain would sweeten their sleep all night long.

Félicien leaned out the window and inhaled deeply of the scent of roses growing riotously beneath. "How long do we stay here?"

"Rambahadur Raj said his merchants want to spend a few days in trade," Jaufre said. "I wouldn't mind a look around the market myself." He looked at Shasha. "Should we buy some carpets?"

She answered his question with another. "I wonder what the going rate is here for lapis?"

"Did Wu Li have an agent in Kerman?"

She shook her head. "I think he bought most of his carpet stock through Tashkent."

"Wouldn't hurt to ask around," Jaufre said, and did so that afternoon, making the rounds of the market, which featured piles of carpets taller than he was arranged in long, straight corridors interrupted by spaces for the merchants to entertain opening offers.

"Wu Li of Cambaluc?" they said, doubtful. "I may have heard the name, young sir, but just sit here for a moment while I try to remember. My assistant will show you some of my finer carpets while you wait." A wink. "Very rare and fine, two hundreds of knots per finger, I assure you, you may count for yourself."

It would be an hour or more before he got away, and by the time he did there would be three or four other merchants clamoring for his attention. It was no wonder that he didn't notice the small, dark nondescript man who detached himself from a shadow near his fourth stop, and followed.

In the end they sold half of their lapis and could have sold it all but that Shasha wanted to see what the price was in Damascus. "Greedy," Jaufre said, and Shasha made a face at him while Félicien and Hari laughed. The copper pots went, all of them, at a twenty percent markup that was so easily swallowed that they were sorry he hadn't marked them up by half again.

Still, they had freed up loads on two of their pack camels and made serious inroads on a third. "I shall go down to the carpet bazaar," Shasha said the next morning, in the manner of Alexander announcing his descent on India, and she stalked off with Félicien in tow. The goliard would probably write a song about it.

"There is a Zoroastrian community here I wish to explore," Hari said in the manner of one anticipating the sight of a herd of exotic beasts, and he too was off.

Jaufre, on his own, went up to get as close a look at the fortress as he could without offending its guards, who were each large men, well armed, and looked very capable. He noticed towers rising up from the edifice, tall ones with perforations. Surveying the city, he saw many more, tall and short, rising up from buildings large and small everywhere. He bought a glass of fresh fruit juice from the cart of a friendly-looking vendor, who gave him a quizzical look in answer to his question. "Towers? Ah, you mean the bâdgir, the wind catchers."

Without further ado the vendor closed up his cart and ushered Jaufre around his city, displaying wind catcher after wind catcher and lecturing his new young friend extensively on Persian architecture, desert weather and prevailing wind dynamics throughout the year. He concluded the tour by bringing Jaufre to his favorite café and introducing him to all of his friends, who included an architect, two builders, and a philosopher of astrology who insisted on having Jaufre's birthday and birth place and who grew very sorrowful when Jaufre could provide him only with the former. Jaufre suspected there was something in the astrologer's glass besides tea, but no one said anything, alcohol being forbidden by Islam and all of his companions being good, observant Muslims.

He still hadn't noticed the small, dark man, who might have been made to order to blend into the woodwork, who sat at the back of the café and nursed the same carafe of pomegranate juice for three hours, impervious to the black looks of the waiter.

Jaufre and his new friends drank oceans of mint tea late into the night, swore eternal friendship, and everyone went home, Jaufre boring everyone back at the caravansary with an enthusiastic recitation of all he had learned that day. Balked of sharing by his companions' determination to sleep soundly off the ground for the last time for what would undoubtedly be many weeks, if not months, he attempted to enlighten the ignorance of his sparring partners the following morning at practice, and was soundly spanked for his pains.

Over breakfast, Shasha informed them that they had acquired a load of carpets and that she would need help loading them that afternoon.

"I have found a man of books," Félicien said. "He has so many he wishes to sell some of them to make room for more." He smiled. "Reluctantly."

"I don't know," Jaufre said, looking at Shasha. "Are they bound or scrolls? Bound books are bulky and heavy."

"They are also more valuable, pound for pound," Shasha said. "It can't hurt to look."

"In the souk they speak of a blacksmith who turns out fine knives," Hari said.

"Do you have his name and direction?" Jaufre said, and Shasha threw up her hands. "I'll go with you," she said to Hari, but raised an admonitory finger. "You must all be back in time to help pack!"

At the home of the man of books, Jaufre was surprised to find Alaric sitting cross-legged on the floor, mooning over an illustrated manuscript with brilliantly colored drawings of fantastical beasts, unicorns and dragons, and "Look, here, a parandrus. It is an animal that can take any shape, and so trick its enemies by becoming them, until they learn it too late to save themselves."

It was written in Latin and weighed as much as Jaufre's sword, scabbard and all. "What did you say it was called?"

"A bestiary," Alaric said, in the tone of someone better describing a catalogue of heaven itself.

"So I see," Jaufre said untruthfully.

"Look," Alaric said, displaying a particularly magnificent illustration glittering with gilt, "a dragon! Have you ever seen such a dragon before, young sir?"

"About a million of them," Jaufre said truthfully, and when Alaric gaped at him he said, "Carved from ivory and jade of every color, painted on lacquered boxes and jars and vases, embroidered on tunics and tablecloths and robes of state. There are dragons on practically every flat surface of Cambaluc."

It was only a slight exaggeration, at that. He and Félicien stepped around Alaric for the next hour as they inspected the personal library of a man who, judged on its contents, had as much money as he needed to buy any book he wanted, and evidently he had wanted every book he ever saw. Jaufre found a manuscript called "Historia Calamitatum" by someone named Abelard, bound together with letters between him and a woman named Eloise. What he liked best about it was that it was written in Latin on the left-hand page with what Félicien told him was a French translation on the right-hand page. He could improve his Latin and learn French at the same time from this book, and he set it to one side, wondering briefly how it had wandered so far from its country of origin.

Alaric bought his bestiary and they bought half a dozen other manuscripts, Félicien falling in love with a collection of cansos by someone called Bernart de Ventadorn, who the goliard said was a famous singer a century before. Jaufre peered over his shoulder, saw text shaped like poetry, and retreated in a hurry. He had found a travel guide to Persia, illustrated, and a couple of scrolls that weren't quite ragged enough to substantiate the owner's claims that they dated from ancient Rome and were by the hand of Virgil himself, telling the story of Antony and Cleopatra. This said with a wink and a nudge, both of which mystified Jaufre, but he bought them, if for rather less than the seller wished to accept.

They were about to leave when Jaufre caught sight of another manuscript tucked at the back of a high shelf. He fished it out. The covers were calfskin stretched over wooden boards and it was bound together with five lengths of thin leather straps. Opening it, he realized that the binding was much newer than the manuscript, which was tattered and torn and had pages missing, some of them probably harvested for their illustrations. The text, neatly copied, was arranged in two columns.

He flipped through it and discovered that the remaining illustrations, though somewhat faded and with most of the gilt flaked off, were still perfectly legible. More than a few were stunning, faded or not.

He turned back to the beginning. "'Il Milione,'" he said, sounding out the words. His eyes dropped farther down the page, and he almost dropped the book.

The Travels of Marco Polo. He couldn't read Italian but he was certainly able to puzzle out that much.

He heard a snort. "Marco Milione."

Jaufre looked around to see Alaric reading over his shoulder. "You're familiar with this book?"

"Who isn't?" Alaric snorted again, with contempt even more vast than he had the first time. "Marco Milione, that's what they call him," he said. "A liar and a braggart. If even a quarter of what he says is true, the world is a marvelous place, indeed." His tone indicated that he highly doubted it.

In a daze, Jaufre dickered only briefly over the price, although he would gladly have ripped out one of the rubies secreted in the hem of his trousers to meet any price the old bookseller set.

As they turned from the alley leading to the house, the small, dark man who had been following Jaufre ever since his morning among the rug merchants slipped from the shadows, knocked, and was admitted to the bookseller's house.

Back at the caravansary Jaufre drew Shasha to one side and showed her the book by Marco Polo. Like Jaufre and Johanna, the victim of sporadic tutoring in the romance languages by a Franciscan friar who had been more interested in converting the heathen than in educating them, she recognized the name and little else. She paged through the book, pausing here and there. "Could there be more than one Marco Polo, do you think?"

"Who traveled from Venice to Cambaluc, and spent twenty years in service to Kublai Khan?" he said. "I doubt it."

She gave an absent nod. "Wait till Johanna sees this. She'll be thrilled."

"I wonder…"

"What?"

"If he writes about Shu Lin. And Shu Ming."

The answer to his question would have to wait until they learned to read Italian. Jaufre bundled his purchases away, and he and Félicien departed immediately again for the armorer Hari had spoken of, where they found eating knives, skinning knives, fighting daggers, and the curved swords of the Persians, like the one Firas wore. They were nothing fancy, but they were well crafted and looked like they would hold an edge, so Jaufre bought a dozen of the eating knives and Félicien, a little to Jaufre's surprise, bought a long knife somewhere between a dagger and a sword, encased in a plain leather sheath. "Are you expecting trouble?"

"No," Félicien said, buckling the blade around his waist, "but that is when trouble always comes."

They returned to the caravansary, the sun low in the sky, to find everyone in an uproar of packing and cursing men and whinnying horses and braying donkeys and groaning camels protesting beneath their loads.

A little after dark, they set off. Félicien had his lute slung across his shoulder and as the city dropped behind them he began to play. Soon they were all singing along, or humming as in the case of Hari.

They sounded good, Jaufre thought, but not as good as if Johanna was with them.

The caravan had been increased by one rug merchant and a dozen camels. Among the handlers of the new camels was a small, dark, nondescript man who had demonstrated an ability with pack animals. He said so little that no one else with the caravan, if asked, could have said who he was or where he came from, or even what his name was, or what he was doing, other than traveling west.

· Ten ·

Summer, 1323 A.D.
Between the Hindu Kush and Baghdad

⊢——⊣

The morning after Gokudo's execution, Johanna said, "Will you teach me the ways of the blade?"

Startled, Firas said, "Of the sword, do you mean?"

"Knife, dagger," she said. "Perhaps not the sword, or not your sword. I was not able to lift Jaufre's sword for any length of time, much less swing or thrust it." She swallowed, and added with difficulty, "I could barely raise Gokudo's naginata to do what needed to be done."

"You managed, nonetheless," Firas said, very dry.

"I wish to do more than manage," she said. "Yes, I practice form every morning, as I have most of my life, and it will serve to defend myself against unarmed attackers, so long as there are only one or two. I do well enough with a bow. But I have very little skill with the blade. The Road is a dangerous place, and the more ways I have to protect myself, the safer I will be."

Firas the Assassin, man of Alamut and master of the sword, inclined his head. "A worthy ambition," he said, somewhat to Johanna's surprise, because as a Persian Firas should have appalled at the very notion of teaching such a thing to a woman.

The lessons commenced the following morning. At first Alma and Hayat only watched. After a few days, Alma came to Johanna and said simply, "Hayat and I would like to learn to use a blade, too."

Firas shook his head but he didn't say no, and doubled the practice times to mornings and evenings. Johanna began to teach the other two women soft boxing. One evening, watching the sun sink down below the horizon as she stood post, Johanna became aware that Firas had joined them. Nothing was said, then or later, but from then on he joined them. He seemed to catch on quicker than either of the two women, but one day he heard Johanna say, "You don't have to pretend to be less able at this than he is, Alma."

"But he is a man," Alma said. "And our protector."

"The point is to be able to protect ourselves," Johanna said.

"From someone like Ogodei, or Gokudo?" Hayat said, skeptical and rightfully so.

"No one can protect themselves from an all-out assault by a full army," Johanna said grimly. "In that situation, the only recourse is to run, and we did. Or to conspire, which we also did. But one on one, there should be no reason—there will be no reason for us not to be able to defend ourselves from the harm that men would do to women when they are alone."

After that, Alma became much more difficult to confound at Four Ladies Work at Shuttles, of all the thirty movements of soft boxing the hardest to master. Hayat was left-handed—"Always an advantage in a right-handed world," Firas said—and proved to be quick and sure with a knife. When they passed a small town, Firas went into the market with a heavily veiled Johanna and found a slender, double-edged knife in a small belted sheath which he showed Hayat how to fasten to her forearm. Thereafter, he made her practice continually, until she perfected a draw so swift it was almost as if the knife sprouted from her hand.

Johanna was no match for Firas in upper body strength, but he made her practice with a heavy wooden practice sword for a month before he found a small sword in another market which weighed half of what the practice sword did. She discarded the first rusty blade he had bought in Balkh and blocked his first parry at their next practice with skill and quickness and even some ability. Her surprise and pleasure was evident, as was a beginning sense of pride.

He dropped his sword and stepped back. She dropped her guard. He leapt forward and with one circular pass disarmed her. Her sword flew from her hand and landed several feet away and a moment later the point of his blade pressed into the vein pulsing in her throat.

"Unless you are facing another woman armed with a sword, a highly unlikely circumstance, you will be facing armed men. They will not be Jibran, who is a man not so bound by Islam that he cannot recognize strength when he sees it, no matter the vessel. Nature has made men stronger than women. We will always have the advantage in strength, and most of the time in training as well." He dropped his blade and stood back.

She picked up the small sword and regarded it with a glum expression. "Then what is the point of all this practice?"

He could have pointed out that she had been the one to ask him to teach her. "Surprise will be your biggest advantage," he said. "No man will expect to face a woman with a blade. Even when they do, they will very probably laugh."

Her eyes flashed.

"Yes," he said. "Use their ignorance. It will be infinitely more powerful than any other weapon you could possible possess."

She looked from her small sword to his scimitar, which was twice as long and outweighed it by half.

"Don't allow the size of a weapon to intimidate you," he said. "The fact that you will be able to raise a weapon in your own defense will make them pause in sheer astonishment. Use that moment to your best advantage. Take time to think first, then act. Remember, your best weapon is up here." He tapped his head.

He looked at the three of them, weapons in hand, intent looks on their faces. They were committing his words to memory, and for a moment his heart failed at the thought of these women in a fight with real weapons against real opponents. An experienced soldier, an Assassin like himself or one of Ogodei's Mongols, one with years of training and the experience of many battles, could dispatch any or all of the three at one blow. Two, at the most. "Don't fight if you can possibly avoid fighting," he said. "But if you have to fight, win by whatever means necessary."

They were keeping to the less-frequented routes across central Persia. Some were so seldom traveled that they had to find elaborately circuitous ways around rockslides and fallen trees that had come down since last it had been used. The terrain was a continuous expanse of desert interrupted intermittently by low mountain ranges that ran more or less north and south. The narrow passes that led through these ranges required careful negotiation, populated as they were by tribes who regarded them as natural traps set by a providential god. Any travelers who attempted to negotiate them were regarded as fair game and their persons and their belongings as rightful winnings.

The women got their first chance to practice their newly-learned art against a band of men who leapt out from behind a heap of boulders that crowded a steep, narrow path with few trees and no water. The fact that their party was in a hurry to find the next stream or village with a well, whichever came first may have accounted for them not paying as much attention as they should have, because their attackers were not particular stealthy. North Wind bellowed outrage and reared and plunged but the trail was so narrow that he was as much hindrance as help, and the men cascading down the rocks seemed like sixty instead of only six. Alma kept her composure, waited until one of the grinning men got close enough, and leapt from her saddle to land right on his chest, knocking him flat on his back. He let out a roar of triumph and started to tear at her clothes, but the roar ended in a surprised gurgle when her blade efficiently located the narrow space between his first and second ribs and slid easily straight on into his heart. He died staring into her eyes, a look of astonishment on his face.

Hayat let another of the raiders grab her leg and pull her from the saddle. She used his own strength to turn the motion into a somersault that vaulted her right over his head and came up standing with her knife in hand, which she sank in the back of a third man who was gaping at Johanna, fighting to stay on North Wind's rearing back. Hayat spun back to face her first attacker, who stared at her with his eyes goggling unable to recover from his astonishment fast enough to live much longer than that.

When North Wind reared again Johanna slid down his back and over his tail, landing neatly on both feet, her blade out and her cloak looped around her left arm to form a felted shield. One of the attackers recovered his senses enough to slice at her with his dagger and she ducked beneath his arm and thrust her sword up into his belly, dodging back out of the way so his blood and guts would spill onto the ground and not on her.

The surprise of facing four warriors instead of one man with one sword and three helpless women worked, as Firas had predicted to Johanna, very much in their favor. He put his foot on the belly of the last man who had been standing and pulled out his sword, wiping it free of blood on the downed man's robes. When he turned, Hayat and Alma were rifling the dead men's purses and collecting swords and knives. "What are you going to do with those?" he said, indicating the weapons.

Hayat spared him a brief glance. "Throw them over the first cliff we come to. Johanna says so their relatives will have to find new weapons with which to ambush the next travelers through this pass."

North Wind, scenting blood he hadn't himself shed and annoyed about it, stamped and snorted his disapproval until Hayat's mount whinnied his own dismay and North Wind nipped him firmly on the haunch in reproof. The only one allowed to complain was him.

"You knew they were there," Johanna said.

Hayat and Alma looked up. "What?"

"You knew they were there, Firas," Johanna said. "You didn't raise your blade until that last man was about to stab Alma in the back. You knew they were there."

"You will never learn to defend yourselves if you never have a chance to, young miss," Firas said, entirely without apology. "And if you had been paying better attention, you would have heard them from that stand of spruce trees a quarter of league back. They displayed all the subtlety of North Wind at a gallop."

Johanna looked at Alma and Hayat. They looked back at her with sober expressions. She wanted to be angry at Firas, but he was right.

They remounted and went on their way, negotiating the rest of the pass with care and unmolested. Scouting ahead, Firas found a village among a few terraced fields, with a well, but Johanna said, "If it's the nearest village to the pass, the men who attacked us probably came from there. Let's go on."

Firas, who had been about to say the same thing, repressed a smile. They did, and as their reward found a small stream trickling over a rock shelf as they reached the bottom of the pass. Their horses gathered around the tiny pool, heads down as they lapped at the water, and Johanna shared out trail rations for her companions and hard grain biscuits for the horses.

Over the next few weeks Firas let Johanna take the lead more and more, stepping in with a quietly suggestive comment now and then when it seemed merited. Hayat and Alma, with a lifetime's training in deferring to the male, took longer to assert themselves, but soon began to contribute the occasional opinion as well. None of their comments were at first very useful, as their experience in both travel and survival was limited, but they were slowly progressing from merely doing what they were told. Firas revised his private estimate of their ability to survive on their own from zero to perhaps ten percent.

When a gang of thieves attacked on the other side of another pass, who were far more professional than the opportunistic villagers who had previously ambushed them, Firas fell back to monitor the fight, taking an active part only when one of his students became hopelessly outnumbered. The three women prevailed, although Alma received a wound in her knife arm and Johanna took an elbow to the face that left her with one eye swollen completely shut and both bruised in a steady progression of spectacular colors over the next week. Hayat was unscathed and smug about it, even as she tended to the other two women's injuries.

As a graduation exercise, it was definitive. Firas revised his estimate sharply upward.

The next morning he woke before dawn to find Johanna's bedroll empty. Their camp was in a rocky hollow beneath an encircling ridge, next to a clear mountain stream that gave off a peaceful chuckle that had lulled them all to sleep the night before. He found her on the ridge above, watching the lightening edge of the eastern sky, and took a seat beside her.

After a while she said, "I never killed anyone before."

He watched the horizon in silence. She wasn't speaking of the men she had killed in the two ambushes.

Presently, she said, "I wondered if I would be able to. I hated Gokudo for what he did, but this life, Firas, whatever Hari says, I believe this life is all we have. Even though I know, none better, what I would have suffered if I had fallen into his hands, his life was all Gokudo had. I took it from him."

He waited. There would be more.

The line of line on the horizon turned from dark blue to pale mauve. "I feel no remorse," she said, watching it. "I have had no bad dreams. I rubbed him out of this realm with a firm hand, and I didn't even worry about his blood on my trousers." She looked down at them, the raw black silk worn but holding up well to the rigors of the Road. "And now there are others to add beneath his name. And there will be more."

"And you want to know if you are a monster," Firas said.

She swallowed hard. "Yes," she said in a very small voice.

"You are not," he said.

Her spine seemed to stiffen a little from his matter-of-fact tone. "I want to believe that," she said.

"You can," he said firmly. "Regard this man. He acted to kill your father, not once, but twice, and was successful the second time. Affection and honor both called for his death. More, he professed his intent to harm your own person. You have the right to defend yourself from harm. Thirdly, there is the matter of justice." He considered. "In the fifth surah, it is written the life for the life, and the eye for the eye, and the nose for the nose, and the ear for the ear, and the tooth for the tooth, and for wounds retaliation."

She digested this. Organized faith had not been a part of her raising. She and Jaufre had taken some classes with Father John, a Franciscan friar who had made his way to the khan's court, who did his stern best to convince them in between Latin lessons that they were born sinners condemned to a fiery hell and that their only recourse was to adopt his faith, confess their every sin both real and imagined, and be redeemed in the eyes of what seemed to them to be a very vengeful and judgmental god. They had, at Wu Li's instigation, taken other classes with a Confucian scholar who was given to the pipe and who lectured them on the importance of family and education from the interior prospect of a rosy opium dream that admitted gods only as distant, cloudy outlines to be respected but not worshipped.

This regimen, overall, had been more productive of a healthy skepticism than blind faith. With a sudden shock of realization Johanna now realized that that might have been her father's purpose all along.

Whatever Wu Li's motivation, neither teacher had encouraged them to belief in an afterlife, and a life lived on the Road, at risk of lethal diseases, avaricious raiders, natural disasters and political upheavals, where your best help was an ear attuned to the most recent news, a lively sense of self-preservation and a fast mount, bred less dependence on faith and more on one's own competence and intelligence and ability to make friends. Doubtless many blameless citizens had fallen to their knees and implored God for salvation that awful day in Talikan. Equally doubtless none of them had received it. She remembered the scene she had watched from the wall and repressed a shudder. No, she could not conceive of a faith that forgave behavior so wicked, so evil.

But this man, this warrior come so lately into their company, he had proved more than worthy of her respect and trust, and besides, she liked what his god was telling her, so she sat still and listened.

He turned to look directly at her. "It is written later in that same verse whoso forgoeth vengeance, it shall be expiation for him." She didn't like that as much, and Firas raised a hand. "Gently, young miss, gently. Here, I believe the Prophet revealed enough to merit this man's death. If you had shown mercy and let him live, would he have let you live, unharmed, as well? I think not, as I judge the words out of his own mouth. How many leagues did he pursue you over the trackless wastes of desert and rough trails of mountain? He would not have stopped. He could not." He sighed. "It was, young miss, truly, you or Gokudo. One would live. The other would not." He gave a faint smile. "Inshallah."

"If God wills?" she said.

"You are here," Firas said. "He must have willed it so."

She was silent again until the first sliver of gold lit the distant line of desert. She rose to her feet. "The others will be awake and ready for practice." She hesitated. "Does it show?" she said in a low voice. "On my face?"

Gravely, he inspected her countenance for traces of rabid killer set loose upon the world. "No," he said. "It does not."

Although, over the next weeks, he decided that perhaps it did show in some subtle ways. Not the act of slicing off Gokudo's head itself, no, she was not bent or haggard from guilt and certainly showed no signs of grief. But there was an added assurance in her stride, in the lift of her head and the straight set of her shoulders that he had not noticed before. It was as if she had discovered of what she was capable at need, and of surviving it, not easily, but with body and soul intact.

As they neared Baghdad they saw the ruins of the famous canals, pulled apart by Hulegu's forces sixty-five years before, leaving little but dusty ditches behind.

"Once canals encircled the city, filled with water from the Tigris and Euphrates Rivers," Alma said, very much in the manner of a scholar instructing the ignorant. "They were used for irrigation and some were even large enough for transportation. Some had to be crossed on bridges."

She gazed around at the barren and bridgeless landscape, crossed by more dust-filled ditches that seemed to parallel themselves outward from the city growing larger on the horizon. She sounded disappointed. "I don't see why the Mongols had to destroy them. They could have used them themselves, couldn't they?"

"Hulegu was uninterested in occupation, mistress," Firas said, at his driest.

Like Ogodei and Talikan, Johanna thought, gazing at what was left of what surely had been a highly advanced system for the delivery and recovery of water. What makes some men build, and others destroy?

She was unaware that she had said the words out loud until Hayat answered her. "Men will always tear down what they didn't build themselves."

"What a waste," Johanna said.

They moved on.

It was four altogether different travelers from the ones who had escaped the sack of Talikan who trotted beneath the east gate of Baghdad one bright and dusty afternoon. They commanded the best rooms in the best inn nearest the gate and the best stabling for their horses. North Wind attracted much attention, as did the others, the sheik's racing bloodline having held up well over the leagues. North Wind had acquired a few scars on his legs but he seemed somehow bigger even than he had before, larger in stature, grander in manner, much more imperious in attitude. As long as they were in Baghdad, Johanna spent the hour after each morning's practice just brushing his coat, which North Wind took very much as his just due. His ego had not noticeably diminished during the long journey, either.

There were baths nearby and that was their third order of business, after rooms and new clothes for all four of them. Alma and Hayat had to be very nearly forcibly removed from the bathhouse, hot water having been in short supply on the Road. They reassembled at dinner, scrubbed and shining, around a table they had neither to set nor to clear, loaded with dishes not cooked by their own hand over an open fire, nor killed and cleaned by them, either, for that matter. It was a nice change.

As their attendant brought a tray of sweets and a samovar of hot tea, Johanna sat back and took stock. Firas looked the same as ever, stoic, calm, fit, dangerous. He had taken advantage of the bath barber and his beard was newly trimmed and dark against the white wool of his jellaba.

Alma and Hayat, by comparison, were vastly changed from the women they had been. Gone was the pale, soft skin and plump forms so desired in the harem, replaced now by golden tanned skin and a fine ripple of muscle and sinew. The elaborate hairstyles had been replaced by single braids in imitation of Johanna's, the colorful, diaphanous costumes by hardworking linens and wools in creams and browns. Instead of falling instantly into studied poses of languor and invitation, both women sat comfortably erect, alert to what was going on around them. Their first response to a man in their midst would once have been instantly to seduce him. That reaction now was more a cool, measuring glance, mentally locating weak spots and formulating a plan of attack.

The word "seductress" did not instantly come to mind. Neither did "victim." Johanna wondered what they saw when they looked at her.

"How long do we wish to stay here in Baghdad, young miss?" Firas said, sipping his tea.

Johanna sipped her own tea and took her time answering. "It's been a long, hard summer," she said at last. "Let's take a few days to soak the dust of the trail completely out of our hair, and to gather the news and tour the souk." She smiled. "Who knows? We might find something there to interest the merchants of Gaza."

Firas stroked his beard. "I see no fault in this plan. The soldier is always better for rest and relaxation between campaigns."

"I have inquired after Wu Li's factor in Baghdad but I am told Basil the Frank no longer resides here," Johanna said. "Could you ask around—discreetly, of course—for the more honest jewel merchants in the city?"

Firas inclined his head. "It shall be so, young miss. I myself would like a look at the local armories, and, as you say, to hear the news." He stopped himself from saying more, but Johanna knew what was in his mind. Ogodei could well be turning his attention westward, and if that were so—and even if it were not—rumors of his approach would be rife in the marketplace. The oasis towns of Persia had for hundreds of years been an attractive target for avaricious warlords bent on plunder and acquisition, and the last time Mongols had arrived on Baghdad's doorstep it had not ended well for the city.

"I would like to see Baghdad," Alma said with a sparkle in her eye.

"It is not what it was since Hulegu sacked the city," Firas said.

"Even to stand in the ashes of the House of Wisdom would be a privilege," Alma said reverently. Behind Alma's back, Hayat rolled her eyes.

"Hayat?" Johanna said.

"I no longer smell and my clothes are no longer in tatters," the younger woman said with her dimpled smile. "I don't know that I have any right to ask for more."

And we are alive, her eyes said when she looked at Johanna. Yes, there was that, too.

While Alma toured the monuments of pre-Mongol yesteryear and communed with the spirits of philosophers past, Hayat in amused if a trifle bored attendance, Johanna plunged into the souk, which was something of a revelation. Until then Kashgar had set her standard for markets, but Bagdad's market was larger by half and much better organized and maintained. The streets were wide and clean, the booths were of a uniform size and shape, and the signage was large, easy to spot, and marked in pictures instead of words. Sometimes the signs bore actual items, a mortar and pestle for the apothecaries, a stool for the joiners, a scrap of damask for the weavers. The moneychangers were at the center, forming the heart of the market and the hub of the streets, although Johanna raised her eyebrows at the interest rates chalked on boards outside the various booths. There wasn't much to choose between them, which led her to suspect that rates were settled on well before the market opened in the morning.

But in the market itself, oh, there were all the goods here she had ever seen before and more, many more that she had not, or certainly not in these amounts. Where she had been used to seeing goods only of the East, now here they were interlarded with goods of the West. A tall, heavyset man with graying blond hair and a taciturn expression held down a corner of the weavers' market with heaping piles of a heavy wool fabric with a thick nap that would surely protect the wearer from the hardest winter. In the spice market she found a root with no aroma, until it was peeled and grated, when it made her eyes water and induced a fit of sneezing, but was delicious with beef, or so the merchant selling it claimed. In the next stall she was introduced to a green herb that when the leaves were bruised smelled sweet and spicy at once, and when served in a sauce over a bit of lamb made a small explosion in her mouth that rivaled the taste of the curries of India. Every mineral from alum, for the fixing of dyes to zinc, which mixed with copper made brass was displayed for sale. Sandalwood, whose fragrance was so sought after by the ladies of Cambaluc and whose oil was so useful in the treating of wounds. Spices of all kinds from everywhere displayed whole in sacks and in their milled forms on round trays heaped into pyramids of yellow and red and orange and brown, dizzying passersby with their commingled aromas. Drugs and their every component part, wax, camphor, gum arabic, myrrh, and a selection of herbs that would have driven Shasha mad with avarice. Fruits fresh and dried, including grapes both red and white. Precious metals, especially gold and silver, in dust, coins, ingots and bars.

Her merchant's nose twitched.

There were chests made of a medium dark wood whose careful finish displayed a beautiful grain that she was informed resisted the teeth of insects of any kind or amount, a safe repository for her most precious clothes and draperies. She found no paper merchant worthy of the name, however, just a series of stalls selling the same vellum and parchment she had seen in every market after the Pass. One merchant glumly displayed an attempt at something made from wood pulp, and Johanna, amusement held at bay behind an expression of polite interest, wondered what the message would look like that would of necessity have to be written around the bits of wood embedded in it. There were some decent pens, but the ink was nothing like what she was accustomed to, thick, runny and indelible on skin, as she discovered when a drop fell on her hand. It would be days of repeated washings before it would disappear.

The silk she found overpriced, even if she had thought their selection was various and adequate, which she did not. Most of it, she was told, came not from Cambaluc but from Merv.

There were also gemstones from semi-precious to the rarer diamonds, although she saw no rubies as fine as the ones stitched into the hems of her traveling clothes. She found small round beads made of a forest green stone striated from dark to light, suitable for jewelry or embellishing clothing. The color reminded her of certain jades, although it was opaque rather than transparent. They were sold by the pound, sewn carefully into unbleached muslin bags.

Those beads were available in the stock of only one dealer in the entire Baghdad market, and he knew it. She made him an offer and he reacted in horror. He was a Muslim and told her candidly that he was surprised to see a woman trading like any man, but displayed no dismay at her presence and no reluctance to strike a bargain with her. He ordered tea and they settled down to it. An hour later they had agreed on a price for a tenweight, but discovered a further problem. The merchant would take only bezants, and Johanna had only taels and drachmas. She secured the merchant's word against a small coin acquired along the Road whose provenance they neither of them recognized but which was indubitably gold, and ranged forth in search of suitable currency.

Down the way there was a baker peeling fresh rounds of bread from his oven. She stepped up and paid for one in drachmas and received florins in change. She paid extra for a brush of oil infused with garlic and crushed herbs and devoured it on the spot, and waited for the next batch to come out of the oven to buy a second, less because she was still hungry and more because doing so was in some odd way homage to Ahmed, the market baker in Kashgar, and Malala his wife, and Fatima, their daughter and Johanna's lifelong friend. And Azar, Fatima's betrothed, who was so carelessly murdered by Gokudo in his attempt to kidnap Johanna on the Terak.

She felt anger well up inside her again, and willed it away. Gokudo was dead now, at her connivance and by her own hand. He had paid in full for the deaths of Azar and Wu Li.

Father, she thought with a pang.

She willed away the tears and plunged back into the crowded byways of the Baghdad marketplace in search of bezants. Bezants, as it happened, were hard to come by in Baghdad, for whatever reason, and her choice was either to go to the money lenders, despite their high fees, or lose her gold coin to the gem merchant. Instead, after some thought, she bought a length of brightly patterned silk that almost looked as if it could have been woven in Chang'an. Elsewhere she found a spool of gilt cord, and returned to the gem merchant in triumph.

The gem merchant, whose name was Mesut, regarded her purchases with a quizzical expression. "These look not like bezants, young miss," he said, stroking his beard. "Although I am old and I admit my sight is not what it once was, so I could be mistaken."

Encouraged by the twinkle in his eye, she said gravely, "You are correct, effendi, these are not bezants, but I believe you will find what you can do with them even more valuable." She indicated his stock, which was laid out on flat tables, the beads threaded into strings and the loose stones in wooden trays. "I see you also sell lovely pearls, as from the waters of Cipangu." She didn't mention that she herself at been to Cipangu, had dived with the pearl fishers there and could plainly see that his pearls were from another ocean entirely.

"I do," said Mesut."

"So, I see, does Karim, two booths down the way, and, if this unworthy one may say so without giving offense, his pearls look to be of much the same quality."

The twinkle became more pronounced. "One may," Mesut said. "Karim and I buy from the same wholesaler."

She nodded. "I see here also some trade beads, from Nubia, I would judge."

He nodded, curious now.

"But on the next street over Hafizah effendi also has Nubian trade beads, which look very much like your own."

"That is so."

She shook her head sadly. "And he is selling them at very much the same price."

Mesut smiled. "I suppose I could run back and forth between our stalls to make sure my beads are priced at less than his, but I confess the prospect does not appeal to me." He smacked his substantial belly with both hands, and in spite of herself Johanna grinned.

"No, indeed," she said. "Why waste your energy jumping about like a squirrel when there is a way to better entice the customer to your stall?"

"And what way would this be, young miss?"

She raised her brows and looked around, as several interested parties were loitering within earshot. Mesut followed her gaze, and said smoothly, "But we should step inside, out of the sun, young miss. I will send my daughter for tea."

"That would be most welcome, effendi."

She followed him inside to take a cushion next to the low table that occupied the back of his shop. After the tea came and they had refreshed themselves, Johanna cleared the table and produced the length of silk and the spool of cord. With her belt knife she sliced the silk into small squares and pooled strings from Mesut's stock of semi-precious stones, pearls and trade beads in the centers of them. These she folded over and tied with one of the elaborate knots she had learned from Halim the dyer in Talikan, what seemed now like a lifetime before. Baghdad's sophisticated marketplace required something grander than Halim's bright scraps of cotton, and so the silk. Halim was not here to hand-dye lengths of jute, and so the gilt cord. Halim the dyer, almost certainly dead, along with all of his family, and friends, and the entire population of his city with him.

With steady hands, she pulled the triple bow into equal loops, and presented it to Mesut cradled in both hands.

He examined the bright, sparkling little package and cocked an eyebrow. "But how are my customers to see what is in the package?"

"Two ways, effendi," she said, "that choice being yours, of course. The first is that you, or perhaps your daughter—" this earned her a smile from the girl with the flashing eyes who had watched all this very intently from her father's side "—could learn this style of wrapping and wrap each sale as it is made."

"And the other?"

"Have the merchandise wrapped in individual packages before it is sold, but leave one string out for people to examine."

"Why should anyone assume that each package contains what is on display?"

"Why the name of Mesut, surely, effendi," she said demurely

He laughed outright. "And so they should, young miss." He looked at his daughter. "What do you say, Rashidah? Are you willing to learn to tie string?" His belly shook as he laughed.

Johanna spent the rest of the afternoon teaching an eager Rashidah various ties and bows, and inventing a few on the spot. Rashidah came up with a design of her own that vaguely resembled the openwork crown on a minaret, and had the inspiration to thread one of the stones on the gilt thread so that it not only decorated the package, it alerted the interested as to what was inside.

After the heat of the day had passed, they brought out a few of the packages and placed them on display. If a crowd did not immediately gather, the gaily wrapped packages did disappear in gratifyingly rapid fashion, and before very long Hafizah effendi was seen to be loitering in the background. He wasn't quite gnashing his teeth but he was chewing on his beard, which Mesut said was a sure sign of agitation, and which Mesut seemed to find vastly entertaining.

Mesut was suitably grateful, discounting the price of Johanna's beads and accepting florins instead of bezants. He sent for more tea and cakes this time to cement the deal, and Rashidah joined them. Father and daughter were obviously fond of one another and Mesut treated Rashidah very much as an equal partner in the business. Again, Johanna missed Wu Li with a ferocity that almost occluded their next comments, but she surfaced in time to hear Rashidah's teasing remark about Mesut backing as good a horse in the next race. Miraculously, Johanna's vision cleared, and she cleared her throat. "Race?" she said delicately, fixing Mesut with what she hoped was merely a polite and not very interested eye.

Rashidah rolled her eyes. "Oh please, young miss, don't encourage him," she said, but she was smiling. "Sometimes I think he should have been a horse trader." She laughed. "There was news recently of some big white bruiser of a stallion new come to the city, and there was nothing for it but for Father to ferret out its provenance."

Johanna looked at Mesut, who returned a glance limpid with innocence.

Rashidah looked from one to the other. "Father, didn't you say that the white stallion was ridden by a woman?"

Mesut sipped tea.

Johanna put her head back and laughed out loud.

And so it was, ten days hence, that Johanna found herself on North Wind's back as he ambled in his best unconcerned fashion onto the large oval racetrack outside the city walls. It was by far the most splendid track this side of Cambaluc Johanna had yet seen, laid with meticulously swept sand and lined with sturdy railings to keep the large and eager crowd from falling beneath the leaders' hooves and interfering with the proper running of a race. Vendors hawked fruit juice and pastries, and touts on makeshift stands shouted the odds to long lines of bettors.

It was a glorious day, not a cloud in the sky, and the temperature was mild. There had been four races before North Wind's, which was the last and evidently the biggest race of the day, and judging by the crowd's reaction possibly the year. The shouting reached near hysteria and the wall of sound caused even North Wind's ears to flick, one time.

Johanna took note of their competition. A fiery gelding on the inside nearly equaled North Wind in size, and judging from the crowd's cheers was the clear favorite. There were three other geldings, two more stallions and a roan mare, very small and dainty, her tail held at a coquettish angle, who was bridling and stamping and tossing her head. North Wind was placed squarely in the middle and right next to the mare. Johanna wondered how close the mare was to coming into heat. She could tell by the alert look of North Wind's ears that he was wondering the same thing.

There was no point in protesting to the race officials. Johanna was new to the racetrack and a woman beside. Mesut, their official sponsor, while a professional merchant of long standing and impeccable reputation, had no standing in Baghdad's horse world. The best she could hope for was that the mare's owner had misjudged the mare's condition.

The mare's rider looked at her and grinned. He didn't think so. Johanna returned a look of bland indifference and the grin faded. The riders of the other two stallions wouldn't meet her gaze. So. North Wind was meant to be distracted by the mare and by competing stallions while the favorite ran away with the race.

The gelding's rider was necessarily focused on controlling his plunging, sidling, rolling-eyed mount, who apparently couldn't wait to get out on the course. Johanna nudged North Wind with her knees and he clopped forward until his front hooves were planted precisely behind the starting rope and, as per usual, gave all the appearance of a horse who fallen completely and soundly asleep.

There was a wooden stand to their right, holding a gaggle of greater and lesser dignitaries. The one who looked like an imam was invoking the smile of Allah upon this race. At least he wasn't calling down His wrath on Johanna's unprotected and female head. Mesut stood to the right of the stand, with Radishah, Firas, Alma and Hayat. Radishah was incandescent, Mesut only slightly less so. Firas looked resigned, as if he'd done everything he could to stop Johanna drawing attention their way in this public and imprudent fashion, and was determined to take his failure with outward composure. Alma was looking around her with an inquiring air, as if she had never seen such a thing as a horse race before in her life, which she very probably hadn't. Hayat had one hand on her dagger and her eye on a shifty-looking fellow who had insinuated himself next to them in the crowd. He saw Hayat looking at him, paled beneath his scruffy beard, and melted discreetly away. Hayat saw Johanna watching and dimpled delightfully.

The imam concluded his prayer. Everyone salaamed, and the imam gave way to the luminary Johanna presumed was the sheik of Baghdad, or whoever the sheik had delegated this chore to. He was a handsome elderly man in a resplendent turban accented by a magnificent sapphire the size of which convinced Johanna that he might actually be the sheik himself after all. He, a consummate politician, welcomed the crowd, praised the horses and their riders, made a joke at which everyone laughed heartily, gave a benign smile and raised a white silk handkerchief. Johanna took another wind of North Wind's reins around her hands and leaned forward, and at the motion felt him go absolutely still beneath her. She almost laughed.

The crowd went silent. There was no sound but the snapping of the decorative pennants in the wind. The white silk handkerchief dropped, and almost at the same moment the rope in front of the line of horses dropped to the track. Johanna kicked North Wind lightly in the ribs, and he exploded from a standing start that if she hadn't been prepared for could have snapped her neck. Within five strides her eyes had teared up and within ten her hair had torn free of its braid. Within fifteen North Wind's speed threatened to strip her from his back. She heard swearing, but only from a steadily increasing distance, until it was swallowed entirely by the thunder of North Wind's hooves. She never heard the roar of the crowd, all her attention on the strip of track she could see between North Wind's ears. The smoothness of his stride was such that he didn't even seem to touch the ground, but that it seemed to pass beneath them while they merely hovered above it.

The next thing she knew they were coming up on the first turn. North Wind moved steadily toward the inside. From the corner of her eye she saw the favorite, or rather the nostril closest to her, which she assumed belonged to the favorite. She was vaguely aware of his rider's arm rising and falling, and she realized that he had to be beating his mount. She felt a moment's brief pity. As if any horse could best North Wind, beaten or not.

North Wind slid in front of the gelding as if he were not even there, and by the second turn his tail was whipping just in front of the other horse's nose. Johanna risked a look over her shoulder and saw that he was North Wind's only real competition. The other three geldings had only reached the first turn. The mare had stopped dead in her tracks just before it, hind legs planted and splayed in traditional equine come-hither fashion. The two other stallions were fighting what looked like a duel to the death nearby, dangerously close to one of their riders, who appeared to have fallen from his saddle and hurt himself sufficiently that he couldn't move out of the way. Johanna tsked reprovingly and faced forward again.

After that it was a glorious, stretched-out, full-throated, league-eating ride, and North Wind didn't slow down when he crossed the finish line, either, but kept going. Johanna, who divined his intention, kicked her feet free of the stirrups in plenty of time and slipped from his back just before North Wind shouldered into the other two stallions, sending them staggering in opposite directions, and mounted the mare without further ado.

The mare braced herself against the onslaught and let out a loud, piercing whinny that sounded a little exasperated to Johanna, as if the mare was saying, "Well, and about time, too!"

Johanna was laughing before her feet hit the ground, and then she realized that everyone in the crowd was laughing, too, and the rest was madness.

Mesut laid on a celebration out of his shop in the souk that evening. The finest delicacies there were to eat and the finest juices and teas and coffees to drink. Everyone in Baghdad came, and Mesut welcomed them all beneath a new turban that grew increasingly askew. Rashidah was kept busy wrapping packages as her father's stock marched out the door as if on legs. Johanna arrived late to the party, waiting patiently until North Wind completed his assignation before leading him off to the stables to feed him and groom him and otherwise settle him down from his various exertions. Johanna did not stint on praise, although he already bore a distinctly satisfied air.

Mesut greeted her with a great welcoming shout that was repeated throughout the crowd. There were immediately a dozen offers to buy North Wind, and later another offer to pay a stud fee, made by a sheepish man Mesut identified as the owner of the mare in that afternoon's race. This offer she accepted.

Tumblers and dancers and singers, attracted by the noise and the prospect of donations to the cause, drifted in and launched into performances. Halfway through the evening a familiar song caught Johanna's ear and on impulse she stepped up and joined in, her mellow soprano filling out the chorus. The bowl that went round after that was overflowing, and Johanna won the head musician's heart when she refused a share. She took the loan of his gitar in payment instead, and sat herself on a stool beside the fire and sang a song about young love, a second about lost love, and a third about a man, his wife and a traveling tinker. She sang Félicien's song about wandering clerks and everyone joined in on the chorus.

She ended with the song about the plum tree, translating the Mandarin to Persian on the fly, and such was the poignant longing in her voice that the crowd was silenced, many of them listening with their eyes closed and more than one hiding sudden, inexplicable tears.

White petals, soft scent
Friend of winter, summoner of spring
You leave us too soon.

She drew out the last note and let it fall, deep, down, into the well of memories that bubbled ever beneath the surface of her bright, impenetrable facade. In that instant she was ten again and back in the caravansary in Kashgar, singing along with Wu Li and Shu Ming and Deshi the Scout, all of them dead now, and Shasha, who lived, she hoped.

And Jaufre, also ten, newly orphaned, hearing the song for the first time, and her watching the expression on his face the moment when he realized that the song was not about a plum tree, not at all.

Alma and Hayat watched in wonder from the sidelines. When Johanna, flushed and smiling, took her bows to a long, sustained applause, Hayat said, "She never sang like that in the harem."

"She never sang at all," Alma said.

"Because she couldn't?" Hayat said doubtfully.

"Because she wouldn't," Firas said, with a certainty that neither woman could gainsay.

The party broke up soon afterward, and no one noticed that the four of them were followed back to their inn by a man of determinedly nondescript appearance, who took up station in the doorway opposite for what remained of the night.

· Eleven ·

Late Summer, 1323 A.D.
On the road to Damascus

⊢——⊣

Ten days out of Kerman their caravan was hit by raiders, a group of some thirty or forty men, a number equal to or out-numbering their own troops of guards. They struck in the hour before dawn, just after Rambahadur Raj had sent out scouts to find them lodging or a campsite for the next day. Almost everyone was dozing in their saddles, not excluding Jaufre, but he woke in a hurry at the sounds of screams and the clash of arms.

He found himself standing on the ground beside his camel, sword in hand, and then running toward the cries of battle. There was no more than a thin band of light on the eastern horizon but his eyes were adjusted to the dark and he saw Alaric's distinctive white tabard almost immediately, surrounded by three men he could smell well before he came into blade's reach. Coming at a run from behind, he sliced into the back of one man's knee and used the force of the upswing from that stroke to thrust into the second man's shoulder. Alaric dispatched the third, who collapsed, screaming, as he tried frantically to stuff a rope of shining entrails back into his belly.

Jaufre saw Alaric's teeth flash in a grin. "Well met, young Jaufre!" which was all they had time for before they were attacked by a new group of assailants.

Their attackers were professionals who lived off of the proceeds of passing caravans, but the disciplined guards led by Rambahadur Raj were their superior. The sun was well up by the time they were delivering killing blows to those wounded so badly there was no recovery for them, friend and foe alike. Afterward, Jaufre went a little way off the trail and was sick.

On his return Alaric handed him a flask without comment, for both of which Jaufre was most grateful. He rinsed his mouth and spat, and tried not to notice the severed fingers scattered in a little fan not an arm's length from his right foot.

The bodies of the raiders were thin, almost skeletal, and dressed in rags. Rambahadur Raj was directing his men to pile the bodies of the dead to the side of the trail, a ferocious scowl on his face. He stopped beside Jaufre and Alaric. "This is my fault," he growled. "I wanted to cut our time to Baghdad, so I took a shortcut. It has much less traffic, and this is the result."

Alaric shrugged. "Not the worst outcome, Ram," he said.

"We lost two men," the havildar said.

"They lost all of theirs," Alaric said. He clapped a hand on Jaufre's shoulder. "And our young friend here has been blooded."

Rambahadur Raj looked at Jaufre. "Is that so, then? Did he give a good account of himself?"

"He earned his feed," Alaric said, and both men laughed, heartlessly, it sounded like to Jaufre. He looked at the bodies being piled into an ever higher mound and thought he might be sick again.

Rambahadur Raj turned somber. "They were hungry."

"Starving," Alaric said, nodding. "Lucky for us. They had numbers, but in their weakened state they couldn't give as good an account of themselves as they otherwise might have. These hill tribes can be fierce when they are well fed."

The havildar said heavily, "I could wish they had chosen any other caravan but mine to ease their hunger."

And Jaufre realized he was not the only one of them to be affected by the growing number of dead in the mound by the side of the trail. Later, he watched as Rambahadur Raj oversaw the construction of a pile of foodstuffs not too near the burning pyre of the dead.

Their women would come, Jaufre thought, and along with their dead men they would find food for their children. He was comforted, a little, but not so much that he did not relive the encounter in his dreams.

They pushed on through that day and the following night to arrive at a small oasis town in a well-tilled valley. There was no caravansary but there was a large campsite with a well, and the members of the caravan were made welcome in the town. When the tale of the raiders was told there was much shaking of heads and sidelong looks. One of them, an elder with wise eyes and a wispy white beard, said, "Ahmed ben Eliazar."

"Ah." Many heads nodded around the circle.

The elder nodded his head, too. "He and his people have been preying on travelers through the high pass ever since we banished him, these ten years and more since."

Jaufre wanted to know why the man had been banished, but he intercepted a fierce look from Rambahadur Raj and subsided. That they didn't volunteer the information said enough. It would only have shamed them to have recounted a story that did not reflect well on one who had once been their own.

The elder looked around at the faces of his family and friends and neighbors. "We should send someone up into the hills for his women and children."

A man was dispatched forthwith.

The elder turned again to the havildar and this time bowed, deeply. "You have solved a problem we were not able to resolve for ourselves, Rambahadur Raj, and we are in your debt. Rest here a while. There will be no fees charged, and our water is your water for man and beast alike." He smiled. "And trade freely, if your merchants have a mind to trade. No taxes will be levied upon your people during your stay."

Already well disposed toward their havildar for his speedy and able defense of themselves and their goods, Rambahadur Raj now soared in the caravan merchants' estimation and Jaufre foresaw a large bonus for him when they reached Damascus. Booths of scavenged poplar limbs and lengths of cloth were set up to form a tiny circular marketplace before the last camel was picketed. Women streamed out of the town and crowded around each vendor, talking and laughing and haggling. Children in high spirits tore around in games of tag and hide-and-seek, so happy and healthy and noisy that after a while Alaric muttered something about strangling them all in their sleep and took himself off. A juice cart appeared, a second cart with rounds of bread on it, a third with stuffed sheep's lungs and other delicacies. Félicien unrolled his rug and produced his lute. After a while a boy appeared with a tambour, and another boy with a flute.

It was a long way from the bloody morning day before yesterday. Jaufre looked on the peaceful scene full of laughing people and to his horror felt tears sting the backs of his eyes.

"Here," he heard Shasha's voice say. "This way."

She led him stumbling to their tent, pushed him inside and shut the flap after him.

He fell on his bedroll and tears were arrested by a heavy sleep that rolled over him like a thick black blanket. If he dreamt he heard the sound of his blade slicing into human flesh, or heard the panicked, pained, disbelieving scream of the first man whose flesh he had sliced into, he did not remember it afterward. Not that first night, at least.

He woke again near dark, and saw that Shasha had left him a change of clean clothes. He took them to the baths in the town, small but adequate and fueled by a natural hot spring that had been brought down from the hills by an ingenious stone trough supported on a series of connected stone arches. He steamed away the rest of his aches and pains, suffered his cheeks to be scraped free of beard, and returned to camp feeling, if not exactly at peace, then once more calm and in control of his emotions.

Shasha met him at their yurt. "Come," she said, "there is food, and drink, and dancing, and song this night." She smiled. "It has been so ordained by the imam, who has taken a great liking to Hari."

"God help us all," Jaufre said piously, and Shasha laughed. She set off and, after tossing his dirty clothing inside the yurt, he followed her.

A large fire had been built in the center of where that day's makeshift market had been, and members of the caravan and citizens of the town intermingled freely. To one side a dignified gentleman in immaculate white robes sat on a rich carpet, in earnest conversation with Hari, who with his thin yellow robe slipping from one shoulder looked distinctly underdressed by comparison. Félicien and his lute were accompanying a tenor with a gitar, the harmony forming a pleasing whole.

"How old do you think he is, anyway?" Jaufre said when Shasha came up with a tray full of lamb and onion kebabs.

Shasha followed his gaze. "Félicien, do you mean?" She arranged the tray and sat down next to him. "Why do you ask?"

"He is yet a beardless boy," he said. "Look at him. He must have left home at the age of ten."

"Some do," Shasha said. She looked at him and smiled. "You and Johanna were late bloomers."

He laughed and chose a kebab. The lamb was crusted on the outside, tender and juicy on the inside. He had never tasted better.

Later in the evening Alaric wandered into the circle of people who had formed around the fire. He had acquired a jug of wine from some illicit source and was very merry in consequence, while the elders of the town looked on with tolerant indulgence. It was not their way, but their way was not everyone's way. It was a very nice sort of town.

"Ho, Jaufre of Cambaluc," Alaric said, squinting. He offered out the jug.

Jaufre waved it away. "I've had wine. I don't like it," he said.

Alaric shrugged. "More for me." He drank, and wandered off again.

They all coped with the aftermath of battle in their different ways.

The conversation continued around them, the city fathers extracting the last bit of news from far and near that Rambahadur Raj had to offer. It wasn't long before one of them said, "Is it true, what we hear? Are the Mongols on the move again?"

The havildar looked grave. "I am very much afraid that it is," he said.

"Where?"

"In Kabul they said he was in Samarkand. In Kerman, they said he was in Kabul." Rambahadur Raj shrugged. "If rumor were truth, the Mongols would be advancing on a dozen Persian cities, all at the same time."

"In this case, perhaps rumor is truth," one of the men said bluntly.

"Even the Mongols don't number that many," another man said.

The first man turned his head and spat. "They settled away to the east, we know that. And we let them, and left them to breed. In a hundred years, who knows how great their forces have become?"

The eldest stirred. "It is said on the desert wind that this Mongol acts on his own for himself."

"Rumor, again."

"Perhaps. If true, however, invasion this time might not involve a horde."

There were muted chuckles at this dry comment. The first man flushed angrily and opened his mouth to speak further. He was elbowed into silence by the man sitting next to him, who said, respectfully, "Eldest, if they are coming, should we not prepare?"

The elder looked at Jaufre. "I am told, young sir, that you are of Cambaluc."

"Sir, I am," Jaufre said, bowing his head in acknowledgement, his heart sinking. He had no wish to be singled out, either as a repository of Mongol wisdom or as a target.

"Is all they say of the Mongol true?"

"Sir," Jaufre said again. He frowned a little, hesitating over an answer that would be both true and satisfactory to his listeners.

It was very quiet now around the fire, Félicien and his accompanists having scented an interesting conversation and downing tools so everyone could hear it.

"It is true," Jaufre said at last, and a sigh ran round the circle. Some looked frightened, others pugnacious. He met the eldest's eyes. "Almost all of what they say is true. If you fight, they will annihilate you to the last man, woman and child. Believe it." He paused. "If you yield—" there was an angry muttering and he raised his voice "—if you yield, yes, you will have to live under Mongol rule. But you will live."

He sighed. "If it comes to that," he said. "Your Bastak is small, and off the main routes. From what I saw in the market, you mine a little copper and a bit of turquoise, is this not so?" Nods. "You grow enough food in your fields to sustain yourselves, but not so much that you have entire grain houses filled to bursting and therefore irresistible targets. And your carpets, while very fine indeed, again are not so fine as to make Bastak the destination for an entire army bent on plunder." He paused again. "In short, eldest, if there is no reason for the Mongol to come here, he will not. He will go around you to find other, richer targets. If, against all logic, he does come…"

"If he does come, surrender, or die?"

Jaufre bent his head again. "I am afraid those are the only options, eldest. You cannot fight, because you cannot win."

There was more conversation after that, of course, the elders now mining Jaufre for every bit of information about Mongols and Mongol soldiers and Mongol strategy and tactics that he had. He did his best to comply, but he was weary before the fire burned low. He left them still in conversation there by the coals.

Most of the camp was asleep by then, and the town, too, but he felt restless. The southeast corner of the city's walls looked like it would have the best view of the valley. At the top of the stairs he found Alaric before him, legs dangling over the edge, jug in hand. "Ho, young Jaufre," he said.

"Alaric," Jaufre said. He saluted the sentry stationed at the corner, who nodded back, and sat down next to the ex-Templar.

The founders of Bastak had chosen their site well, a rise of ground with the western wall of the valley behind them, with a prospect that commanded a view of the valley from north to south. Moonlight limned the narrow peaks on either side and cast a pearly gaze on the irrigated farms that lined the Bastak River, a silver ribbon that wound between them.

"There is a structure made of arches," Jaufre said. "I saw it in the city."

"An aqueduct," Alaric said. "There is a pipe on the top which brings the hot water from the springs into the city."

"It looks very old."

"It should," Alaric said. "It was probably built by the Romans."

"They settled this far east?"

"And farther."

There was a promontory a short distant away, a triangular-shaped wedge of rock formed between the river where it came down out of the western ridge and a smaller tributary, that rose to the height of the walls of Cambaluc. Bordered on all three sides by sheer cliffs, there were what looked like ruins on the top of it.

Alaric followed his eyes. "Ah, yes, young Jaufre," he said. "That is the Bastak that was. Their spring ran dry a hundred years ago. Or maybe it was a thousand." He belched. "And so they moved here." He hooked a thumb over his shoulder. "Young Adab here was telling me the tale."

Jaufre looked over his shoulder at the sentry, and saw a flash of white teeth in a dark beard. "They chose wisely, both times."

"It will do them no good when the Mongol comes," Alaric said.

"It is possible that Ogodei will not bother to come this far," Jaufre said.

"Or the Seljuks from the other side," Alaric said, and belched again. "But peace such as this is only an illusion, young Jaufre. You would do well to remember that. There is no safety, no security from ambitious men who lead their own armies."

Jaufre waited while the other man tipped up his jug. It was empty. Alaric tossed it aside and looked out over the valley with a glum expression. The jug rolled over the edge of the wall and a moment later was heard to shatter on the rocks below.

Jaufre let the silence grow for a few moments. Even the hardest and most cynical heart had to soften at prolonged exposure to this kind of pastoral beauty. Also, he was waiting for the alcohol to take full affect.

After a while he said, almost indifferently, "You recognized my sword when we first met in Kabul, didn't you?"

He felt the other man stiffen next to him.

"And since we have never met before, and since the sword came to me directly from my father, it follows that you might have known him." Silence.

"Or heard of him," Jaufre said. "Robert was his name. Robert de Beauville."

An owl hooted, and was answered by the howl of a far-off wolf. The moon continued its serene passage above, flooding the landscape with light enough to read by.

Perhaps Alaric was inspired by that light, which illuminated so much of the dark places in the valley. Or, perhaps, he had decided that since Jaufre had been blooded and was, perforce, now a man that he was to be admitted to the confidence of other men. "Robert de Beauville," he said, and Jaufre felt the tension that had been coiled around his spine since Kabul relax, just a little.

"Tell me about him," he said. "Please."

"How much do you know?"

"That he was born in an island kingdom far to the west," Jaufre said. "That he was a Knight Templar, sworn to celibacy, but he married my mother. That he was a fine swordsman."

"How did he die?" Alaric's voice cracked on the last word.

Jaufre swallowed, half-forgotten memories of a caravan on a stretch of desert, raiders rising up as if materializing from the very sand. "He was working as a caravan guard, as you are," he said. "We were attacked. There were too many." He paused. "I was the only one who escaped."

"How did you manage to keep Robert's sword?" Alaric said. "That would be prime booty for bandits."

"I was beside him when he fell. He knew he was—He gave me the sword. Told me to bury myself and it in the sand. So I did. I waited until they were gone, and then I buried him." The horror of those moments, of listening to his father die and to his mother and the other women scream as they were dragged off, had never, would never fully leave him.

"Your mother?"

"They took her. All the women and children. We believe she was sold at auction in the Kashgar slave market a week after the attack."

A long silence this time. Alaric had to know how much Jaufre had left unsaid. "How old were you?"

"Ten."

Alaric's eyes closed and he shook his head. "You were lucky."

"Yes," Jaufre said, only now, seven years after the fact, able to admit that it was true. "I was found by a Cambaluc trader three days later. I would have died but for him. He adopted me as his foster son, and raised me as his own."

"You were lucky," Alaric said again. "Many on the Road are not so fortunate."

This time Jaufre waited.

After a while Alaric sighed. "Yes, well, why not. Surely we are far enough away, in space and in time, for the truth to be spoken out loud, here beneath the moon and the stars." He looked up at the sky and began to speak, slowly, even sorrowfully. It felt eerily like a confession.

"Robert de Beauville was born the fourth son of a Norman noble who settled in western England. His father was not wealthy and with three other sons and two daughters to dispose of, Robert was left to find his own way. He took the Cross at the age of seventeen—"

Jaufre's own age.

"—and traveled to the East as a Knight Templar. We were both on Ruad when it fell." Alaric hesitated. "It would be five years until Philip sent out the order to have us all arrested, but Robert—" He shrugged. "The Knights fell with Ruad, he said. He said it didn't matter if it was our fault or not, that we would be blamed." He spat over the walls. "And he was right, of course, but then Robert was an old head on young shoulders and he usually was."

"You were friends."

Alaric shrugged. "We were comrades, for a while. Enough to exchange personal histories." He looked at Jaufre. "His vocation was more expediency than piety, I think. He was the youngest son, his father had provided for him as well as he could. But he was bitter at our failures." He sighed. "We all were."

"What happened after Ruad fell?"

"Most of the Knights were killed," Alaric said in a voice devoid of emotion, as if he were reading from an ancient text of events hundreds of years before. "I was wounded. Robert stripped us both out of our armor and pulled me through the water to a coracle he saw floating a little way out. There was no paddle, so he used his hands to get us to the mainland." He looked down at his own hands, turning them back to front and back again. "I was in a high fever and delirious by then. I don't remember much beyond what he told me afterward. Somehow, he got us off the beach, where we were most in danger of discovery, and found a hayloft to hide in. He cared for me until I was well enough to care for myself."

"And then you parted company?"

Alaric raised his head. "Not at once," he said. "We made our way to Antioch and hired ourselves out as guards on a caravan to Damascus. We had to eat, and all we had to sell was our skill with a sword. In Damascus, Robert met Agalia." He fell silent.

"My mother."

"Yes." Alaric brooded for a moment, and then seemed to realize that more was needed, and to give it freely was a better option than to have it demanded of him. "She was the daughter of a merchant traveling with the Damascus caravan. Robert—as I said before, Robert's vocation was less than devout. He had always struggled with the vow of celibacy." He added, reluctantly, "And she was very beautiful."

"And so they were married."

"Yes."

"And then you parted ways."

"Yes. I didn't believe Robert when he said the blame for the loss of Jerusalem would fall on our shoulders." Alaric's shoulders straightened and his chin lifted. "We Knights Templar were heroes, soldiers of God, anointed by the Pope himself. It was inconceivable to me that we could fall so far so fast. I wanted to go home, to see my family, to take up the Cross again in some other way, for some other purpose."

"And you went home?"

"Yes."

"What happened?"

"Oh, they greeted me with loud rejoicing and went straight off to kill the fatted calf." Alaric stared across the valley. "And the next day came the men of Philip the Fair, who may have been fair to look at but was not at all fair in his dealings with the Templars."

"Your family betrayed you?"

"My father, probably. His nose was ever up some royal ass." Alaric shrugged. "And he had not wanted me to take the Cross in the first place."

"You were imprisoned?"

"I was, in my lord of Agenois' deepest dungeon." Alaric grinned, his face bleached of color in the light of the moon. "For one night. I had a sister, a sister who rivaled Agalia for beauty, no less, and she—convinced the guard to allow her in to see me. He didn't even search her. She brought me two blades strapped beneath her skirts, and I fought my way out and ran for it."

Jaufre wondered what had happened to the sister, but thought on the whole it was better not to ask. "And returned to the East?"

"Yes." Alaric made a show of dusting off his knees. "And took up my present occupation." He hesitated, and looked at Jaufre. "I did ask after your father, and heard word now and then. I sent it back, as I could. But I never saw him, or Agalia again. I had no idea they had had a son." He paused. "But the moment I saw you, I knew. You are his image."

A prickle on the back of Jaufre's neck told him that there was more to tell of this tale, or at least of Alaric's part of the story, but he sensed that now was not the time to press for it. "Robert of Beauville," he said instead. "Is Beauville a place, then?"

"No," Alaric said. "Your father's father is or was a landless knight. He married disadvantageously—"

Jaufre translated that as his grandmother having no dowry.

"—and he pledged his sword first to Henry and then to Edward, mostly in France, as I understood Robert to say. France, you will come to understand, has been passed back and forth between the kings of England and the kings of France for a hundred years, and it's like to be a hundred more before they finally settle who has title to it."

"Edward I?"

"Yes." Alaric gave Jaufre a curious look. "Why?"

"He was—he came to the East, didn't he? In, what was it, 1270?"

"He was only a prince then, but yes," Alaric said. "Why?"

Jaufre shrugged. "No matter," he said, but he was remembering the history of Marco Polo as it had filtered down to him and Johanna all through their childhood. Marco Polo claimed to have met a Prince Edward of England in Acre on his way to Cambaluc. It was dizzying to think that it might possibly have been true. And if that was true, how much more might be? He thought of the book in his saddlebag. Not the dog-face men.

Alaric yawned, jaw cracking. "Me for my bedroll, young Jaufre." He pulled himself to his feet, moving lightly and surely while balanced on the edge of a wall quite a thousand hands in height, which argued just how drunk was he. Had he wanted Jaufre to ask him about Robert? If so, why?

Jaufre sat looking out over the silver fields and the winding river for a while longer, and then followed Alaric's example.

Neither man noticed the figure that detached itself from a dark corner and followed Jaufre back to his yurt.

They were attacked twice more before Damascus, and both times Jaufre blooded his sword. He wasn't sick again either time. He was glad he acquitted himself well, and knew a growing confidence in his ability to do so in future, but he had also learned that a life by the sword was not the life he would choose. Trading, buying and selling, the exchange of goods to the profit of both sides of the bargain, that was work for a man. And he didn't feel like a piece of him had died when he sold a copper pan to a cook or a Homeric scroll to a scholar studying the classics.

He wondered how long the attacks would continue before one of the lords and masters of the East would see fit to put the bands of raiders down once and for all. He wondered how trade could continue if they did not.

Of course if Ogodei, or some other powerful lord bent on conquest appeared on the horizon, the matter of itinerant raiders would be moot.

Damascus was a once-great capital of an independent empire that had dwindled into a regional capital ruled from Egypt by the Mamluks. It didn't look particularly downtrodden and it had a thriving marketplace, with an entire section of the city devoted to the blacksmiths and their forges. Damascus steel was a legend over the known world. A blade forged from Damascus steel was said to be able to cut a single hair dropped across it, and to be able to cut straight through other blades of lesser make.

Jaufre didn't know that he quite believed any of the legends, but as he made the rounds of the forges he had to admit he had seldom seen more beautiful blades. Some looked as though the makers had somehow replicated ripples of water on the surface of the steel. Others bore leaf-like striations that gave the impression they were about to sprout. The grips were made from every material, steel covered in sharkskin like his own but also made from antlers from oryx and ibex and one the dealer said was from a unicorn and told Jaufre with a wink that it wielding it was guaranteed to enhance one's sexual prowess. There were handles made from every kind of hardwood that grew from Cambaluc to Eire, which Jaufre had never heard of, and even some from a kind of molded, hardened animal skin. There were blades with and without pommels and pommels with and without inlaid jewels. The hand guards of the swords were always of steel and as beautiful as they were useful. The daggers ranged from decorative to deadly and were always elegant, if you didn't count the cheap knockoffs made from pig iron one found in the less prosperous sections of the souk.

He decided not bring out the knives he had acquired in Kerman. He had the feeling that the farther away he got from Damascus, the better chance he had of making a profit on them, or any profit at all. He did produce his sword in hopes of having its maker identified, but after much pursing of lips and shaking of heads, and not a few grudging compliments, no one recognized the smith's handiwork.

None of the steel production was on view, of course, as the process was regarded as proprietary and each smith was very protective of his own techniques, but Jaufre did find one artisan in a tea shop who was willing to talk about it a little. Producing Damascus steel involved something called folding, unexplained, and even more necessary was a steady supply of raw material from the East, somewhere in the Indus, unidentified, and, more recently from Persia, unspecified. Jaufre's new friend lamented the steady decline of said supply and prophesied the end of steel-making in Damascus, probably in their lifetimes, to the incipient beggaring of everyone in the trade and associated with it.

But blades of Damascus steel—knife, dagger, and sword—were still plentiful in the city's marketplace, if prohibitively expensive, and Jaufre wondered if the rumor of short supply had more to do with keeping the price up than an actual lack of raw material.

He spent the next day making the rounds of the slave markets and the dealers in human flesh. Most of them had the courtesy not to laugh at him, but none of them remembered Agalia or the Lycian Lotus or anyone who sounded like his mother. Or would admit to it, because how could anyone trust anything a slaver said?

He lay wakeful in their yurt that night, listening to the others breathe. Seven, nearing eight years ago now, his mother might or might not have passed through these same streets. She could be living yet, caged in some harem, vying for the attention of her master. Bearing his children. He might have half-brothers and sisters. It was not a thought that had previously occurred to him.

After another five minutes Jaufre gave it up and slipped from the yurt. There were a few coals left in their fire pit. He coaxed them back to life with a few bits of kindling and stacked on the wood.

Overhead, a sliver of new moon rose steadily from the horizon, almost but not quite eclipsing the millions of glittering stars. It was a sight he had never taken for granted. He and Johanna both had always recognized the beauty of the world in which they lived, and acknowledged the good fortune that had made them children of that most tolerant and encouraging man, Wu Li of Cambaluc, and his most gracious and loving wife, Shu Ming. He missed them both, but he missed Johanna even more. Her absence from his side, laughing, fighting, trading. Surviving. It was an ache the proportions of which if he let it could subsume him completely. It was only at moments like these, when he was completely alone, that he allowed himself to conjure her face from the darkness between the stars, when he wallowed in the memory of every word she had spoken to him, from that first time in the vast aridity of the Taklamakan when she had brought him all upstanding and indignant out of his own self-dug grave by peeing on him.

He smiled at the memory, but the smile didn't last. Was she ahead of them on the Road, perhaps already in Gaza, or Jerusalem? Was she behind them, barely a day's ride ahead of Ogodei and Gokudo?

Was she even alive?

He was well now, fit, and able once again with his father's sword. And Johanna hadn't been missing as long as his mother. Perhaps it was time to backtrack. She might have left word with one of Wu Li's agents. And if North Wind were still with her, surely there would be tales to tell of a woman riding a white steed whose speed was only outpaced by the wind itself.

He had asked, of course. He and Shasha and Félicien and Hari, they had all asked, all along the Road, from Kabul to Kerman to Bastak to Damascus. There was still no word of woman or horse. But then, if they had escaped Talikan with North Wind, it was reasonable to suppose that the sheik would have been hot on their trail. Perhaps Firas was taking care to travel only along secondary routes, ones less traveled by those who would carry news of seeing them. That made sense to Jaufre and would explain the absence of news.

He felt comforted by the thought, at any rate. There was a rustle and he looked up to see Hari emerge from behind the yurt flap. The chughi shook his saffron robes in order, smoothed back his last wisp of hair, and assembled himself next to Jaufre in a complicated knot of knees and ankles. "Young sir," he said in a low voice. "It is a soft night." He looked up. "Such wonders we may see, if only we had the wit to look for them."

"You think people don't?" Jaufre said.

"'Make happy those who are near, and those who are far will come,'" Hari said.

"Buddha?" Jaufre said.

Hari smiled serenely. "That is a saying that comes out of your own adopted country, young Jaufre."

"I don't feel so young anymore, Hari," Jaufre said, and was horrified to feel tears pressing at the backs of his eyes. He restrained them by sheer force of will, and became aware that Hari had let his hand rest lightly on Jaufre's shoulder. As soon as Jaufre became aware of it, it was gone.

"Youth to adult is always a difficult transition," Hari said.

Jaufre gulped and tried to change the subject. "Was yours?"

Hari surprised him by laughing. "Oh, my very dear young sir! Difficult hardly describes it." He looked at Jaufre, still chuckling. "I was the only son. My duty was to marry and have many children and eventually take over the farm from my father, and see him and my mother safely into old age. When I was called, they were accepting, but they were never happy about it."

"Have you ever been back?"

Hari shook his head. "I am meant to go forward."

So far as Jaufre could see, Hari seemed at peace with his calling. Thinking of Johanna and where she might be and how he could find her, he said urgently, "How do you know, Hari? How do you know you are meant to go forward?"

"You desire to attain enlightenment, young Jaufre?"

Jaufre thought about it. "Insofar as I can come to understand myself," he said, "I believe so."

"Ah." Hari rearranged a fold of his robe. "Buddha said that you should steadily walk in your Way, with a resolute heart, with courage, and should be fearless in whatever environment you may happen to be, and destroy every evil influence that you may cross, for thus you shall reach the goal."

An answer, if not the definitive one he wanted, Jaufre thought. *Destroy every evil influence that you may come across.* He thought of Wu Li, who had taken Jaufre, an abandoned waif with no paternal or social claim, into his household without hesitation or reservation. Of Shu Ming, his wife, who had raised him like a son. He knew the face of goodness.

He thought of Gokudo, a mercenary, and of Dai Fang, a murderer. He knew the face of evil, too.

"You should be aware, young sir," Hari said, "that at this same time, the young miss walks her own Way as well."

Jaufre sat back, arrested. Hari watched him with a steady gaze, the flames of the fire flickering over his features, casting them now into shadow, now into light. "She won't be the same person I knew, you mean," he said.

"Nor will you be the same person she knew," Hari said.

Shasha, Hari and Félicien left Damascus for Jerusalem two days later. Jaufre was with them.

· Twelve ·

October, 1324 A.D.
The Holy Land

⊢——⊣

The convulsing woman screamed again. She had a painfully loud and piercing scream which the rock walls of the cave only enhanced. Everyone in earshot cringed. Some cursed. And there were those who looked as if they would as soon murder the woman out of hand than endure another episode of her fits.

"This," said their guide, in full voice which was still amazingly although barely audible over the screams, "is the Mount of Temptation, where our lord Jesus Christ fasted for forty days, and was tempted by the Devil to throw himself over the cliff."

It wasn't the oddest thing Jaufre had heard during the last two weeks.

They had gone to Gaza first, arriving there six weeks before, taking their leave of Rambahadur Raj. The havildar ignored Jaufre's attempts to express his gratitude, instead to congratulate him on Jaufre's rebirth as a full fighting man. "Not quite a Gurkha, no," he said jovially, clapping Jaufre on the back with a blow that would have knocked him to his knees were he still in his weakened state in Kabul. "But I believe you could hold your own with a Gurkha if it came to that, young sir!"

Alaric, too, took his leave of the havildar and seemed to consider himself a member of Jaufre's party thenceforward. He said airily that he'd had enough of the high desert and, besides, he had a hankering to see Venice again. Jaufre thought with inward amusement that Johanna's habit of picking up strays seemed to have lingered on even when she was not with them.

Because, to his severe disappointment, they did not find Johanna waiting for them in Gaza. However, one of the first stories they heard in the taproom of their inn was of a great race in Baghdad, won by a white horse with a woman rider who flaunted her hair uncovered like a bronze banner.

There were other interested auditors of that news in the taproom that evening, among them two of Rambahadur Raj's muleteers. They had also left the havildar's employ at Gaza, and one or the other of which had kept Jaufre in sight ever since, while taking care to remain unseen themselves.

Jaufre barely managed to contain himself until they were safely behind the door of their room. "It was her! It has to be!"

Shasha, too, looked lit from within, although she said, "I wish there was some mention of who else was with her."

"Firas will be with her, of course he will be," Félicien said, who seemed surprisingly glum at the news

Jaufre, unheeding, fought to control the sense of relief that nearly swept his legs out from under him. He found himself seated next to Shasha, with a cup of spiced fruit juice being pressed into his hands. Shasha put a finger beneath it and pushed it towards his mouth. He drank, and then drank again, deeply, and felt the better for it. He looked at Shasha and saw that she had tears in her eyes, and for a terrible moment felt a little shaky himself, big strong warrior that he was.

To have no news for so long, and then this. Johanna could so easily have been dead. What would have been even worse, they could so easily have never known what had happened to her.

Like his mother.

"Good news indeed, young Jaufre," Hari said, assembling himself into one of his complicated seated positions on the rug Shasha had spread out over the floor of their room. It had no beds, but she had decreed it to be the least vermin-ridden of the six inns they had investigated.

Jaufre looked at Shasha. "We wait, then. She will come here."

She nodded. "She will." She smiled. "It was always the plan."

He smiled, and then he laughed, and drank off the rest of the juice. All would not be entirely well in his world until Johanna was within arm's reach, but the sun was going down on a day infinitely preferably to the day before, and all the days preceding it since the attack on the trail down from the Terak.

"It's a fine port city," Shasha said, "with good markets. We should turn over what we can of our own stock and lay in new supplies. When she gets here, she will want to get on the first available ship for Venice."

This brought an abrupt silence.

"Venice," Jaufre said. In the trauma of attack and separation and injury and recovery, he had almost forgotten the impetus for their journey, of much more importance for Johanna than for him. He and Shasha's prime motivation was to get themselves and Johanna out of the reach of Dai Fang, Wu Li's murderously ambitious second wife, as soon as humanly possible. Johanna, after growing up in a place that had vilified her all her life for her height, her coloring, her hair, her odd eyes, her very foreignness, had only wanted to find her grandfather, and acceptance.

Jaufre thought of the book he had found in Kerman, and of Alaric's familiarity with it. Of Alaric's disdain for it, and for its author. How many Marco Polos were there, who had traveled to Cambaluc and seen twenty years' service to Kublai Khan? If he was the same man, how kindly would he look upon the unexpected appearance of an unknown grandchild? It was one thing to celebrate great adventures thousands of leagues away, and another thing entirely to have one of those adventure's land on one's doorstep.

He thought again of Dai Fang, of her inflexible determination to gather up the reins of Wu Li's trading empire into her own lacquered claws, no matter what it took, up to and including the premeditated, cold-blooded killing of her own husband. He could only hope that Marco Polo, also a merchant and as such someone who would value practicality and pragmatism above all other qualities, was not equally efficient in ridding himself of what could be a large personal embarrassment in the shape of his granddaughter.

None of these issues could be addressed until Johanna arrived, and not just in rumor but in flesh and blood reality. In the meantime, they had found lodgings in Gaza and settled down to wait with greater or lesser degrees of patience. Shasha disappeared into the bazaars for three days, and reappeared briefly to inform them that she had found an apothecary willing to mentor her into the mysteries of Middle Sea herbal lore. Félicien found a job entertaining at the largest local taverns.

After two weeks of this, Jaufre, edgy and snappish, and Alaric, thoroughly bored, greeted the arrival of two galleons from Venice full up to the gunnels with seasick pilgrims with positive relief. One of the galleons was captained by a cheerful rogue named Giovanni Gradenigo who wore a golden hoop in one ear and a black velvet jacket lavishly embroidered with gold thread. They met him by chance on the pier as he was overseeing the unloading and the housing and feeding of his miserable human cargo. He accepted their invitation for a drink and a meal at the quayside tavern and the three of them settled in around a corner table for the evening.

"I tell you, my new-found friends, for twenty years have I sailed the vast reaches of the Middle Sea, and yet never until now have I experienced a storm the force and fury of this one," he said, draining his tankard and refilling it immediately. "I thought we would break apart on the seas, which I swear by the Blessed Virgin's intact hymen were higher than the campanile of St. Mark's. My passengers…well. They are no sailors. Not," he added acidly, "that they took any comfort from my idiot crew, who behaved throughout as though we were headed straight for the bottom of the Middle Sea. Then a barrel of drinking water broke loose and rolled over the cook, who was trying to kill us anyway with the moldy biscuit he tried to pass off as ship's bread. I know he got a bribe from the vendor and I intend to prove it the minute we return. By the blood of Christ, this was a voyage bitched before it ever left the wharf in Venice." He drank more ale.

A plate of bread and cheese arrived, along with bowls of lamb stew. Conversation was temporarily in abeyance. Plate and bowls cleaned and tankards renewed, Gradenigo, much cheered—his was not a nature to brood for long—continued with his tale of woe. "We were meant to dock at Jaffa, but the weather proved as intransigent there as it had been in transit, so I brought us here. And now," he said, the omnipresent twinkle in his eye dying briefly, "here I sit in Gaza, a dozen leagues from my mules and my camels and my guards and my supplies. Which supplies I am sure the aforesaid guards began pillaging the day after I was due in port." He sighed, and cocked a weather eye at a passing barmaid with a pleasing waistline. He watched her out of sight and returned his attention to them, which included an appraising look at their weaponry. "But enough about me, my new friends. Yourselves, are you soldiers?"

Jaufre shook his head, but Alaric said, "Once, yes, but not now. We have been most recently employed as caravan guards."

"Say you so?" said Giovanni Gradenigo, sitting upright, and the rest was a foregone conclusion. Shasha, when they unearthed her at the apothecary's workshop, shrouded in a canvas apron with a large hole burned into the front of it, said only, "How long will you be gone?" He wasn't entirely sure she registered his answer.

Félicien made a spirited bid to accompany them, and won over the captain with an off-color version of his clerk's song. Hari gathered up his saffron robe in an authoritative manner and said he would accompany them as far as Jerusalem. Gradenigo threw up his hands and hired five other men in case the guards who were supposed to be waiting in Jaffa had wandered off, two of whom Jaufre vaguely recognized from their caravan. Alaric greeted one by name. "Hussein! I thought that was you. You left Raj's caravan, too? You're as mad as I am, to leave such a good billet. No one from here to Kabul feeds you so well on the Road."

Félicien's presence turnout to be a blessing, as his lute and his voice became the only things that made the entire trip endurable. The Gaza muleteers were surly and uncooperative and Muslim to a man, which meant they were hostile to the entire enterprise of Christian pilgrimage from the beginning. They only deigned to sign on by a doubling of the going rate, which came directly out of Gradenigo's pocket. He did not suffer in silence. By contract, he was obliged to get the pilgrims to Jerusalem and back again to Venice or suffer the loss of his pilgrim transport license. Long experience of overseeing the said trade had led those authorities to provide for every eventuality, as well as inspectors stationed in Palestine—"Spies," Giovanni Gradenigo said, as if the word tasted of excrement—to ensure and enforce the safe, secure and successful passage of all who had paid a fee for such passage before embarking from Venice. Punishment for abrogating any one of the clauses in his contracts lay in the hands of the Venetian authorities, whose city derived much in the way of revenues from the pilgrim trade. Their judgment was sure and fell, and to be avoided by whatever means necessary.

The captain might make a good living but he had to work for it, Jaufre thought now, especially when—after taking in the sights of Jerusalem under the stern aegis of its Saracen authorities—the captain's group of pilgrims had decided on a side trip to visit Bethlehem, the River Jordan, which had required a tortuous descent down the face of a canyon on a narrow trail twelve leagues long, and the caves of Quarantana, where they were now.

The woman's screams continued unabated. She convulsed again and fell to the ground, her limbs jerking and twitching, where she rolled temptingly close to the edge of the cliff that fell to the rocks a thousand rods below. Since Jaufre had been given to understand that every Christian pilgrim who completed the Jerusalem Journey was at death guaranteed a translation straight to their heaven, he didn't know but what he might be doing Mistress Joan Burgh a great favor if he helped her over the edge with the toe of his boot.

She was a woman in her fifties and not physically fit, and she wasn't supposed to be there at all, but when her companions had refused outright to help her climb that nearly vertical rock face, she had bribed a Saracen to carry her up. Upon achieving the top, she had been so overcome with ecstasy that she had fallen straightaway into the fit they were witnessing now.

Her companions, fellow pilgrims who had suffered Joan's presence all the way from England to this very spot, had explained at length to Jaufre and Alaric and anyone who would listen that they had been looking forward to visiting the caves without an accompanying one-woman chorus of screams, shouts, cries and exhortations. Jaufre, who had only had to endure Mistress Burgh since Jerusalem, felt a good deal of sympathy for them.

He met their guide's stern eyes, one Baldred, a Franciscan friar of middle age and miraculously even temperament, and went forward to pull Mistress Joan back from the edge. He took very little care for her comfort as he did so.

She rewarded him by grasping at his sleeve and shrieking, "I tell you the Blessed Virgin has baked bread for me in her own kitchen with her own hands!"

"Is there any left over?" he said. "I haven't had anything to eat since breakfast."

There were a few snickers and one outright guffaw.

"Sinner! You must repent, repent, before Jesus Christ our Lord!" Joan Burgh's eyes rolled back in her head and her body stiffened into a bow and she shrieked again. Jaufre dropped her unceremoniously to the rock floor of the cave and retired to the crumbling trail head in hopes that putting some distance between them would muffle the subsequent din. It didn't.

After that, Mistress Burgh was left to her visions and exhortations while her companions spent the afternoon exploring the caves where the saints had lived, seeing the remnants of a bed in a deteriorating piece of wood, a bookshelf in a niche carved into the rock wall above it. There was a faint painting here and there, only one or two with enough left to them to indicate some sense of the original whole. Some pilgrims surreptitiously chipped a shard from the altar of the chapel, others carved their names into the walls or wrote on them with chalk. Some got drunk on wine they had brought with them from Jerusalem. Some dickered with the few merchants who were hawking piles of dubious-looking relics they had hauled up the cliff on their backs in hopes of making a few coins from the pilgrims. "The little finger of the Blessed Virgin herself, I assure you, sir!"

Since the Blessed Virgin was alleged to have died thirteen hundred years before, Jaufre somehow doubted it. Besides, in the leagues from Jerusalem, if he had seen the bone from the little finger of the Blessed Virgin, he had seen a hundred.

A few of the pilgrims, the intelligent ones, he thought, had found an out of the way corner in which to curl up in their gray cloaks, although it was hard to see how they could sleep, given the amount and volume of sound. Between Joan Burgh's continuous shrieking and sobbing, the drunken laughter, the surreptitious chink of blade on stone, the ever louder prayers, and the steady increase in volume of conversation as the aura of holiness wore off the longer they stayed, there was no peace to be found on this barren hilltop. The Franciscan, Baldred, was holding a hurried Mass at the altar for those so inclined, and the rest of them lit tapers (available for sale) and tried not to stumble over scattered rocks and their own feet as they staggered around seeking out everything in the caves that looked even remotely as if it were once the site of someone doing something holy.

He became aware of Alaric's presence next to him, and looked around to see a disdainful expression on the Frank's face. "Peasants," Alaric said.

Jaufre didn't know what irritated him more, the emotional excesses of pilgrims like Joan Burgh or the supercilious superiority of the upper classes, with whom Alaric clearly associated himself. "Has this place no hold on your faith, then?" he said.

"I've been here before," Alaric said with the kind of weariness Jaufre could only describe as professional. "Many times. And I'd have had visions of the Devil, too, if I hadn't had anything to eat for forty days."

"Blasphemy!" shrieked Mistress Burgh. "Sinner! Repent, now, sirrah, before your soul is lost forever to perdition!"

"My good woman," Alaric said, looking down his nose, "look after your own soul, which will be in mortal peril if you continue to assault our Lord's ears in this cacophonous and most annoying fashion." His sword clanked as he stalked over to the altar, and bent his head in ostentatious obedience before Baldred's Mass.

From the cleft below Jaufre heard a feral roar, and he looked over the edge to see the distant undergrowth rustle. They had seen three lions in the leagues between here and the city, and a dozen wild boars who were the cause of their presence. He was hoping to descend in time to hunt for dinner, as the days in the blazing sun had spoiled all their food and all that remained to eat in his saddlebags was a boiled egg and a very worn pear, both of which were probably going rapidly bad. His mouth watered at the thought of some juicy roast pig, although he wasn't sure he would be allowed to eat one even if he caught one, since the Saracens were so set against the practice.

From the Holy Sepulcher in Jerusalem to the River Jordan, every second rock and tree was the site of an event in the history of the Christian faith. Here Jesus was arrested. There he wavered in his faith. That place was where he was crucified (whereupon much bewailing and cursing of the Jews, although after he learned the full story Jaufre thought the Romans didn't come in for near enough of their share of obloquy), and in there was where he rose from the dead. Here his mother lived with her sister Martha, both of whom lived not far from another Mary, this one a prostitute whose home had been replaced by a chapel, which in turn was now a goat byre. Next to this riverbank in those waters was Jesus baptized by John. This saint scourged himself here, another saint's eyes were pierced by arrows there, and that one was thrown to the wolves, professing his faith until his tongue was torn out.

It all sounded overwrought and highly exaggerated to Jaufre, who wished the heir to one of those wolves would appear now and make for Joan Burgh. "Your faith is very violent," he said to Félicien.

"I warned you," Félicien said. He looked glum, but then the pilgrims had forbidden him from playing his lute during the entire journey. It was sacrilegious, they told him, disrespectful of our Lord's suffering and resurrection.

A particularly loud and sustained screech made them both jump.

By now the pilgrims were exhausted from days of tramping through the dusty desert, weakened by a subsistence diet of eggs and fruit, when the hostile Saracen villagers would sell anything to them. There was little enough water to drink and none at all with which to wash and they could be smelled long before they were seen. When the last one of them had finally managed to scramble down the cliff—Mistress Joan employing the same Saracen farmer to carry her back down—they were all relieved to hear that the group would rest for the night next to a small spring nearby. Most of them were too tired to eat, which relieved Gradenigo, who said frankly that they would be lucky to find enough fodder for the animals to get them back to Jerusalem, never mind enough food for the pilgrims. Normally this would provoke outraged mutters and threats of retribution involving authorities in Venice, but tonight the pilgrims were too tired to bother.

Back to Jerusalem they went the next morning, clattering through Jericho on their way. They remained only one night in Jerusalem, long enough to collect Hari, who had spent the intervening two weeks there in the collection of unknown faiths. A representative of each appeared the following morning to see him off. Jaufre had never seen such a collection of old and wizened men.

They departed for Jaffa, where Gradenigo hoped the weather would by now have allowed his two galleons to meet them there. Alas, Jaffa was bare of ships, and with much cursing Gradenigo booted his increasingly sulky and recalcitrant charges back down the coast road to Gaza. They were all relieved, captain, guards and pilgrims alike, when they came over a rise to see the buildings of the bustling port outlined against the deep blue waters of the Middle Sea, and the small forest of masts bobbing there. The pilgrims, hungry, filthy, sunburned, exhausted, their gray robes in tatters and their sandals in need of resoling, altogether a sight fit to make their mothers weep, straightened up in a body and hustled down the road as if Gaza was their home village and there was a hot meal and a loving welcome waiting for every one of them. Which there wasn't.

Mistress Joan Burgh of course shrieked at the sight of the port town and their ships and nearly fell from her donkey in ecstasy. No one moved to catch her, since Father Baldred had been left behind in Jerusalem and could no longer shame them into it. Regrettably, she recovered her balance, resettled herself in her saddle, and moved back into the line of trotting beasts. "The blessed Lord Jesus is guiding me home! O, such riches he has in store for me! Surely to God I am anointed for sainthood in this world and destined for the Kingdom of Heaven in the next!"

"We'll all be sainted for having survived travel with you, mistress," someone said, and there was laughter, although it was much better humored now than the malicious laughter directed at her had been at the Cave of Quarantana.

Jaufre found himself kicking his horse into a faster gait, leaning forward in the saddle. Félicien and Alaric began to fall behind.

His eyes squinted against the brilliant sun, Jaufre tried to make out the figures gathering at the northern gate of the city. Word of their coming had gone before them, and Shasha met them inside. She met Jaufre's eyes and shook her head.

He scowled.

Alaric sidled up and said in a low voice, "Jaufre, for the sake of us all, will you please find yourself a woman and have done with this unseemly pining?"

Jaufre turned his back on the Templar and went to help shepherd their flock into an inn while Gradenigo rode ahead to the quay to check on his galleons. Mistress Joan slid from the back of her mule and dropped to her knees and raised her arms to the sky, eyes closed, singing a hymn which would have sounded better if she'd been able to carry a recognizable tune. The other pilgrims, long inured to this behavior, gathered their belongings and stepped around her to stream into the inn, where in a triumph of hope over experience they looked forward to hot water for washing, a hearty meal, and a vermin-free bed.

Mistress Joan continued as she was, where she was, and Jaufre, alas, lost his temper. "Will you, mistress, for the blood of this sweet Christ you adore so much, be STILL!"

There was a momentary, and somewhat respectful, silence from everyone but Mistress Joan.

An hour later, Gradenigo reappeared, full of wrath at the dismasting of one of his galleons by an early fall storm that had swooped in with great gusto on the very night they had left. His crew had botched the replacement so badly it would have to be done over again from the beginning. "By Christ's bones, gentlemen," he said indignantly, "I have to do everything myself!"

Jaufre, brooding over his ale, made no reply.

Alaric cleared his throat and said, "How long will your departure be delayed, captain?"

"A week at least," the captain said.

Alaric nudged Jaufre and said in a low voice, "Didn't you say you wanted passage to Venice? Perhaps by the time the captain is ready to sail, your Johanna will have arrived."

Félicien paused in the act of raising his tankard. "Or perhaps she will never arrive."

Jaufre glared at him. "You don't have to sound so pleased at the thought, sir."

Félicien was unabashed. "We haven't seen her for a year, Jaufre," he said. "Who knows who this woman is now?"

Hari had said much the same, he remembered. A year was a long time. They had not spent more than a day apart since they had met as children, outside Kashgar, seven years before.

It was a legitimate, if unwelcome, question. Clearly he was not the same man she had left behind on the trail down from Terak Pass. Who would Johanna be?

· Thirteen ·

October, 1324 A.D.
Gaza

⊢——⊣

I n Baghdad, an astute Firas arranged for them to leave with a caravan en route for the port of Gaza. He explained, not unreasonably, that he didn't want the Baghdadian euphoria over North Wind's month-long winning streak to erode into ennui and jealousy, which could lead to attempts at retaliation by those citizens who had bet against the stallion and lost. Everyone agreed that this made sense and started to pack.

The man who had been following them presented himself to the caravan master shortly after Firas' conversation with that same gentleman and asked for employment. He appeared trim and fit and wore weapons that looked well used and well tended. It was two hundred leagues to Gaza. Since the Seljuks paid more attention to law and order within their cities than without, the way grew more fraught each year, and the caravan master was pleased to have another blade to safeguard their journey. When asked, he named several well-known caravan masters as previous employers and said they would give a good account of him. This caravan master didn't bother to check. Few ever did.

Back on the Road, city and farmland gave way again to desert and the trip devolved to a forced march. The merchants in this caravan were headed single-mindedly for the coast and transport west, as it was growing late in the year and everyone wanted to get home before being caught at sea by the first winter storm. It was mid-October when they passed through the ruins of Jaffa and headed south down the coast on the last leg of their journey. The sky was clear and blue and the temperature unseasonably warm and the general mood improved with every league.

"Fresh droppings," Firas said, pointing. "We are not the first on this road this morning."

Indeed, they arrived less than an hour behind the travelers ahead of them, who were dismounting in the yard of the caravansary. Johanna was looking eagerly around them for any sign of Jaufre, of Shasha, of Hari, Félicien, anyone familiar to her.

"Johanna!"

Her head whipped around, a beaming smile spread across her face as she searched for the man who called her name so urgently. She found him. Her smile faded to a look of blank astonishment.

"Johanna!" A different voice, from a different direction. "Johanna!" She blinked, dazed, to see Jaufre thrusting through the crowd, his face bright with joy. "Johanna!"

"Johanna!" the first man called again.

Her hands went slack on the reins and North Wind moved restively beneath her. She slid bonelessly to the ground, grasping his saddle to remain upright.

Jaufre reached her first, his blue eyes blazing. "Johanna!" He half-raised his arms and realized her gaze was fixed on something over his shoulder. He turned to look, and went still.

The stocky young man, clothed in nubby dark blue raw silk and a round cloth cap, smiled all over his brown face. "Johanna," he said again.

"Edyk," she said, in a high, silly voice.

"I don't understand," Johanna said.

She had looked happy but bewildered at first sighting Edyk. Jaufre could understand the bewildered part, but the happy? Not his chief emotion, certainly. Now he saw that her happiness had faded a little, and was meanly pleased.

Shasha had arrived at the caravansary and taken in the situation at a glance. She scooped them up in a body and moved them bag and baggage to their lodgings, a small house in a side street with kitchen and necessary in the yard out back. They sorted themselves out in groups, Jaufre and Shasha, Firas nearby, Félicien and Hari, Alaric a little apart, Alma and Hayat close together but not so close that they would get in each other's way if they had to draw their weapons.

Johanna and Edyk stood in the center of the room, staring at each other. Edyk raised his arms as if to embrace her, and then looked round the room at the eight pairs of interested eyes trained on them. His arms dropped. "Johanna," he said, a break in his voice.

"What are you doing in Gaza, Edyk?" Johanna said.

Hari had been right, of course, and Félicien, too—damn him—this Johanna was not the girl Jaufre had last seen a year before on the trail down from Terak Pass. He couldn't quite lay his finger on the difference. She seemed not just older but taller. It wasn't her appearance so much as it was her attitude. This woman was confident, disciplined, in command of herself. He saw the short sword hanging at her side. Where by all the Mongol gods had she gotten that? And could she use it? *You carry a sword,* Firas had told him, a year ago and more now. Sooner or later, someone will force you to use it.

He glanced at the Assassin, who looked just the same. Or perhaps slightly more taciturn, if that was possible, and just as communicative, which was to say not communicative at all. He appeared to be waiting for an answer to Johanna's question. Shasha stood next to him, and she, too, waited for Edyk's answer. She looked troubled, which was not what Jaufre would have expected given the long-awaited reuniting of their party.

Hari and Félicien were eying Alma and Hayat. The two women wore sturdy men's clothing and also carried weapons, one a slim dagger, the other a short sword. Both women showed signs of recent outdoor life, but there was an indefinable air of refinement about them in spite of their travel-worn state.

Alaric stood near the door, pretending not to be there at all in hopes that no one would notice and throw him out before they got to the juicy bits. His eyes lingered on Jaufre for a moment, registering the younger man's unhappiness, traveled from him to Johanna, paused to consider, and then moved to the young man in the round hat. From his expression, he was not impressed.

Edyk the Portuguese, merchant and trader, veteran of many journeys along the Road, husband of two and father of three and Johanna's lover in a three-day goodbye before they had left Cambaluc, colored and shuffled his feet. "Perhaps we could speak privately."

Jaufre opened his mouth and felt rather than saw the look Shasha threw him. He shut it again.

"Just tell me what you're doing here, Edyk," Johanna said with a trace of impatience. Jaufre noticed nothing loverlike in her voice.

Edyk noticed that, too, and it was obvious that he was much less pleased about it. Undoubtedly he had also noticed the other changes in Johanna, which measured from Cambaluc to Gaza had to be even more remarkable than the changes incurred from Terak Pass to Gaza. "Well," he said falteringly. "Well. She sent me, of course."

Jaufre ceased to breathe. Shasha went very still. The others exchanged uneasy glances.

"She?" Johanna said, very quietly into the silence that had fallen on the room.

"Your honorable stepmother," Edyk said. "The widow Wu Li." He paused, and added hesitatingly, "Dai Fang?"

There was a long silence, as Edyk looked increasingly confused at the lack of response. Jaufre heard a distant drumming sound, which he took to be the thud of blood in his ears.

"Dai Fang sent you to Gaza?" Johanna said at last.

"She wanted me to find you and bring you home," he said. "She said she needs your help to continue your father's business. She understands that all young things are restless and seek adventure, but that it is time for you to come home now and take your place at her side." He looked around the room again, and took a step forward and dropped his voice. "You know it is the dearest wish of my heart that you will obey her in this, Johanna. We could marry. I promise I could make you very happy."

Edyk didn't know that Dai Fang and Gokudo had murdered Wu Li, Jaufre thought. Because they hadn't told him, before they left.

Perhaps they should have.

"Dai Fang sent you to Gaza," Johanna said.

"Yes," Edyk said.

"To find me," Johanna said.

"Yes," Edyk said. "Johanna, what is it?"

"To bring me home," Johanna said. She looked at Shasha and laughed. It wasn't a pleasant sound.

"Who came with you?" Jaufre said.

Edyk turned, a flash of anger in his eyes. "No one. Chiang only. Not that it's any business of yours."

"She would have had him followed," Johanna said to Jaufre. It was the first thing she'd said to him.

Jaufre found the hilt of his sword in his hand. "She would," he said. The drum of blood in his ears sounded louder.

"How would she have known about Gaza?" Shasha said. "That we would come here?"

Johanna, considering gaze fixed on Edyk's increasingly irritated expression, said, "It's the main port for Venice in this area. She would surely have heard enough stories of my grandfather from Wu Li. She couldn't know for sure, of course, but..." Her voice trailed off.

Shasha held up her hand, and such was the authority in the gesture that all conversation stopped. "Listen," she said.

At first Jaufre could hear nothing, and then he realized that what he had taken for blood thumping in his ears was actually the sound many feet approaching their front door at a run. Firas was first to draw, Johanna and Jaufre not far behind him and Hayat, Alma and Alaric following suit at almost exactly the moment the door was kicked in.

It bounced off the wall with a loud thud. Six men burst inside, weapons drawn. Three were obvious professionals with hard, unemotional faces, the other three paid bravos, who wore broad grins at the prospect of murder and plunder.

They paused when they saw that at least some of their so-called victims were ready to meet them with blades of their own, but only momentarily. The three professionals charged directly for Johanna. Alaric engaged the first bravo while Hayat tripped one of the others. He staggered and regained his feet and parried her blow hard enough that she staggered into the wall and dropped her knife. Another knife appeared immediately from her sleeve and a third from her belt. It was enough to give her attacker pause and in that brief second Alma tucked herself into a ball and somersaulted into the back of his legs. This time he fell. Hayat was on him before he could recover. Both of her blades flashed, silver first, then red.

"Wait!" Edyk said. "What?" He stood where he was, incredulous, staring as the battle raged around him.

Upon the unceremonious entrance of their six attackers, Félicien had stepped expeditiously to the rear of the room, holding his precious lute up and out of danger. Hari joined him, hands clasped before him and a stern, declamatory prayer issuing forth condemning all acts of violence against one's fellow beings and prophesying the certain return of all so engaged as cockroaches in their next lives. Shasha stepped neatly through the door into the back yard, where she remained, watching Johanna with an expression of increasing wonder.

For all three professionals had converged on her foster sister, whose sword was up and deflecting the blows aimed at her in positive blur of defensive parries. Shasha cast a quick glance at Firas, and was reassured when she saw him, scimitar drawn. He was watching Johanna, too, with what she would later realize was a critical gaze, like a teacher watching a promising student during her final examination.

But Jaufre leapt forward, to deflect a slashing cut that would have struck Johanna's arm off at the elbow. She parried her second opponent's thrust, at which he looked fleetingly surprised before he barreled in again. She was only a woman, after all.

"What?" Edyk said from behind her. "What!" He had not so much as drawn his dagger.

Alaric's bravo had had some training and he gave the ex-Templar some brief cause for alarm, especially in the crowded confines of a room where the walls had a tendency to get confoundedly in the way. Ah. He parried the incautious thrust and slid the point of his sword forward to slide between two ribs and straight on into the heart. The bravo's eyes widened in surprise and he fell, dead before he hit the ground.

Alaric stood back, wiped his sleeve across his forehead and looked around in time to see Jaufre take a cut on his left forearm. The ex-Templar watched approvingly as Jaufre ducked to avoid the return sweep of the blade, dropped to lean his weight on his free hand and kick the other man in the knee. The man shouted and staggered back against the wall next to Félicien, who nudged Hari. Both of them moved farther down.

The man managed to stay upright and to hold on to his sword and shoved himself away from the wall to slash at Johanna, catching her a glancing blow on her right thigh. The cloth of her trousers parted beneath it and so did her skin. Blood welled up and at the sight of it Jaufre went a little mad, hacking at the man with brute force and no finesse.

Unseen behind him, Firas clicked his tongue.

"What?" Edyk said. "What?"

The man fell back beneath the fury of his assault and Jaufre finished him off with a blow to his head. He didn't bother to watch him fall. A glance found Johanna still on her feet, and some of his rage abated, although it whipped up again when one of the others lunged at her.

Hayat pulled out her knife, wiped it on the tunic of the man she had felled and rose to her feet, holding out her hand to Alma. Alma gave the body a contemptuous kick in the face on her way up. He rolled over with a groan and lost consciousness. He was crippled if he lived. If he died, no matter.

"Well done," Firas said, who had yet to raise his weapon in earnest. "But please to remember that demonstrations of emotion are best left until the battle is won." The third bravo, smarter than the rest, was still hesitating in the doorway, his smile quite gone. Firas stepped over the body at Hayat's feet and said conversationally, "I think you should put down that sword, don't you?"

The bravos had been hired as a distraction, sacrificial lambs meant to draw attention while the professionals went after the real target. The third bravo realized this a beat after Firas had, and about two beats after the second of his friends had gone down. In the next moment he surrendered his sword and begged for mercy. Firas accepted the weapon, shook his head over its imperfect balance, and shepherded his captive out of the way.

There left the two professionals, the one currently hammering at Johanna and the one at his back, holding the others off while the first one finished off Johanna. That was the plan, at any rate. Later Jaufre would marvel at how little apprehension he felt. He watched the other man with slightly unfocussed eyes, the man's movements overlaid by the same ones made against him so many times by Firas and Ram and Alaric. He could see them coming, almost predict them as the other man moved. His opponent was older, had trained longer, had vastly more experience, but he had not had Jaufre's teachers. The end came suddenly and without any warning to anyone except Jaufre, who had been aiming for that particular target from the moment they had engaged. His opponent dropped his sword, looked down at the slashing cut that had opened him up from waist to shoulder, and could only watch as Jaufre's blade came on a backswing and sliced opened his throat. He fell with a look of vast astonishment on his face.

Behind him, Johanna's opponent hacked at her with increasingly desperate blows, as if he knew his only recourse now was to overpower her by sheer brute force. It wasn't a bad plan, but she foiled it by parrying the latest blow while pulling her dagger, stepping unexpectedly inside his guard and sending the dagger's blade into his belly. She twisted hard and yanked up.

"Uh," he said. He dropped his sword and looked down in disbelief, staring at the blood and bit of slippery intestine that pushed out of the jagged wound. His hands went to his wound in a vain effort to push the blood and guts back inside. The strength went out of his legs and he went to his knees and then down to the floor, Johanna's dagger pulling itself free with the movement.

From start to finish the fight had taken no more than ten minutes. And, Jaufre realized, it had all been very quiet. None of the yelling, screaming, cursing that had accompanied every fight he'd ever been in until today. There had been clangs of metal and thuds of feet, and of bodies, but nothing loud enough to alarm the neighbors.

Of course, he thought. Dai Fang's instructions would have been to kill Johanna and to bring back the bao and the book. Loud noises would have brought the authorities down on them, and subsequent explanations would have been most inconvenient to the conspirators. City fathers were not as a class generally complaisant to mayhem and murder committed on their streets. Explanations, and possibly detention while those explanations were made would have been time-consuming.

Dai Fang, unable to trade without the bao, had to be running very low on time, and assets, by now. Jaufre smiled to himself. How very unfortunate.

Johanna went down on one knee to speak to the man she had dropped. "How long have you been following me?"

"Johanna," Jaufre said. "We need to bind your leg."

She ignored him, her attention on the man laying at her feet. "How long?"

His breathing was labored and stertorous. "Not you." He coughed, and gave a faint nod in Jaufre's direction. "Him. I picked him up in

Kerman." He coughed again, and gasped. A full loop of intestine pushed out between his fingers. "But there were three of us, and we had a detailed description of all three of you. And the horse was easy enough to find, once you raced him in Baghdad. Sharif picked you up there. Bilal followed him, in case he found you first." Another faint nod, this time in Edyk's direction.

"Hussein," Alaric said. At Jaufre's look the knight said, "He was a muleteer in our caravan. I recognize him now. And," he added, in growing indignation, "he came with us to Jerusalem, in Gradenigo's employ."

"Yes," the man said. He mustered enough energy to smile up at Johanna, blood bubbling now from between his lips. "Who expects a woman to be armed? To fight? To win? I will be a laughingstock to the end of my days."

"Who hired you?"

"I never knew the name. The money was good, though." Another cough, followed by several rattling breaths, and a long, slow expiration. The man's chest ceased to rise. At least he had not had to suffer his humiliation for long.

Jaufre looked around. All three professionals were dead, and one of the bravos. A second bravo was badly wounded and the third was sitting with his legs crossed and his hands folded on top of his head. He looked terrified but unhurt. Shasha was binding a scratch on Alaric's forearm, and Alma had a spectacular black eye coming up. Other than that, plus the cut he had taken on his arm and the wound on Johanna's thigh, they seemed to have come off without injury.

It is always a mistake to underestimate your opposition, Jaufre heard Ram saying, and he smiled again, openly this time.

Johanna cleaned and sheathed her sword and smiled back at Jaufre with a fierceness he recognized, as it matched his own. "Whatever are we going to do with all these bodies?"

"She sent me after you," Edyk said slowly, making a visible effort to understand. "And she sent them to find you, too."

It was some time later. The room had been cleared and Firas and Alaric had disposed of the bodies under cover of darkness. No one asked where. The wounded bravo and his lone surviving companion had been dealt with, too, and again, no one cared enough to ask. The room had been scrubbed clean of spilled blood but the smell of it lingered in the air. They took rough seats placed around a splintery table beneath a cedar tree in the back yard, and Shasha had put together a scratch meal of fruit and bread and cheese. They were all downing copious amounts of hot, sweet tea, although Alaric was trading off with wine that he was drinking directly from a clay bottle.

"She sent me after you," Edyk said dully. "I didn't know she sent them, too." He looked up. "I believed her when she said she only wanted you back to help her run your father's business."

"The last strike of the dying serpent," Jaufre said, and laughed.

Edyk's voice rose. "But you knew when I told you that she wanted to kill you. Didn't you? Didn't you!"

"Yes," Johanna said in a level voice. "Yes, I knew. She killed Wu Li, Edyk. She and Gokudo." She looked at Jaufre, and at Shasha. "Gokudo is dead."

By her hand, it was understood, by them if not by Edyk. Jaufre watched her with an appreciative gaze. He wanted to the hear the story but it could wait, now that she was well and truly back. Or someone was. Johanna had been first his savior, then his sister, then an object of desire, but this was the first time that Jaufre had seen her as a companion in arms. He was a welter of emotions, beginning with incredulous delight, gratitude, lust, and, oddly, a kind of wariness. He had no idea what to expect next.

He found himself looking forward to it.

"Do you have my purse?" Johanna said, looking at Shasha.

Shasha unfastened it from her waist and handed it over. "I kept them safe for you."

Johanna smiled. "I knew you would."

She opened the little leather bag and brought out Wu Li's bao, the jade cylinder inscribed on one end in raised characters, and the tiny jade pot filled with the red paste the seal was dipped it before impression. "This is why she wants me back, Edyk," she said. She pulled out the small, leather-bound book. "And this. It's not because she wants me to run Wu

Li's business with her. It's because she can't run it without these, and I took them from her when I left."

Edyk looked from the bao to Johanna with a kind of horror. "You stole Wu Li's bao?"

She tucked everything back into the purse without replying.

"She can't run Wu Li's business without it, Johanna."

"I know," Johanna said, and smiled. Jaufre warmed to that smile.

Edyk appeared less enchanted. "What have you become, Johanna?"

"She has become a warrior," Alma said.

"Strong," Hayat said.

"Able to defend herself when attacked," Alma said.

"And capable of exacting revenge where it is merited," Hayat said. Edyk looked at her, his eyes wide, and her lip curled. "You have no reason to fear, little man. You are no threat to her, and therefore stand in no danger from us."

Alaric snorted, and drank more from his clay bottle.

"Hayat." Johanna's voice was warning. Hayat sniffed and subsided.

Johanna turned to Edyk. "Go home, Edyk," she said, her voice much gentler now. "There is nothing for you here."

His hands half rose in entreaty, and fell again. "What do I tell her?"

Johanna shrugged. "Whatever you wish. Tell you couldn't find me. Tell her I'm dead. Chiang has always been discreet, you can rely on him to say nothing. Dai Fang will never know, and she has no reason to fear you. You'll be safe from any further attention on her part." She rose to her feet, and perforce, so did Edyk.

"But—" It was obvious that Edyk the Portuguese had followed more than Dai Fang's instructions to Gaza. He had also followed his heart. That heart had loved a young girl once, high in the hills above Cambaluc, in a cabin next to a lake, in the springtime when the plum trees were in bloom. He looked for any trace of that girl in Johanna's face, and could not find her.

"Go home to Jade and Blossom, Edyk," she said, not unkindly. "They will be missing you."

Edyk stumbled twice on his way out of the lodging. Firas put a helping hand beneath his elbow and saw him safely back to the caravansary.

Exhausted, the company made up their beds for the night and rolled into them. Introductions and plans could be made on the morrow. When Firas returned, the lamps had been doused and all were deeply asleep.

All but one. A hand met his in the darkness and drew him into the yard. "You returned," Shasha said. "And you brought her back to me."

"She is your family," Firas said. "Which means she is now my family, too." He traced her features with his fingertips. "You were ever in my thoughts during my absence, Shu Shao of Cambaluc."

Her hands came up to his shoulders. "As you were in mine during yours, Firas the Assassin."

He heard the smile in her voice, and laughed soundlessly.

She had spread their blankets in the farthest corner of the garden.

The others might have had more comfortable beds, but Firas and Shasha enjoyed theirs much more.

· Fourteen ·

November, 1324 A.D.
Gaza

├───┤

That pilgrim herder and charming rogue, Giovanni Gradenigo, fell in love with Johanna at first sight. Of course North Wind succeeded her immediately in his affections, and he had nice things to say about the purebred Arabians, late of the Sheik of Talikan's stables, too. Like everyone else who first made North Wind's acquaintance, he offered Johanna a fortune for him. She let North Wind discourage him, too, which the stallion speedily did. Gradenigo took it well, partly because no bones had been broken.

The good captain had his mast re-stepped and re-rigged four days following the arrival of Johanna and company, after which they were forced to wait two interminable weeks for a favorable wind. His pilgrims, thoroughly bored with the delights of Gaza's bazaars and women, were impatient to depart. They said so, in steadily increasing volume, and with mounting threats to inform the authorities of his malfeasance once they were back in Venice. There were some truly colorful phrases that polyglots Johanna and Jaufre were quick to commit to memory. English was a great language for oaths.

Johanna and Jaufre and Shasha used this period of waiting to catch up on the past year, whose events seemed so distant and yet so immediate in retrospect. Jaufre and Shasha listened to the tale of Talikan with sober faces. Shasha's detailed account of the torturous journey from Terak to Kabul and Jaufre's slow recovery leached the color from Johanna's cheeks.

The tale of Gokudo's pursuit and his eventual death was met with a silence that was almost awed.

"Good," Shasha said at last.

Jaufre raised Johanna's hands to his lips and kissed them, one after the other. "For Wu Li, twice over," he said.

Johanna colored and pulled her hands free, ostensibly to drink more tea.

Jaufre produced the book written by Marco Polo he had found in Kerman, and watched Johanna leaf through it, her forehead puckering. "Have you told anyone why we're going to Venice?" she said.

He shook his head.

"Good," she said. "Let's keep it that way. At least for now."

"Why?"

She was slow to answer. "I'm not sure," she said finally. "We don't know what's waiting for us in Venice. If my grandfather lives there still. If he is even still alive. If he is in or out of favor with the authorities."

"Gradenigo might know all of those things."

"Let's not ask him." Her smile was fleeting. "Something tells me the good captain likes gossip too well. Word would fly ahead of us the moment we docked." She touched the leather purse at her waist and her smile faded. "Remember what it was like in Cambaluc. Remember what my father always said."

"That it was always better to be unknown at court than known," Jaufre said.

She nodded. "Let us go to Venice anonymous and unannounced."

She looked at Shasha, who nodded agreement.

"Very well," Jaufre said.

In the meantime Alaric became slowly accustomed to the idea of women warriors, especially after Hayat and Alma working together managed to dump him on his backside during a practice session. He looked on their joining morning practice with a less condemnatory eye after that, and he was certainly less smug when he faced them across a practice blade.

Not by so much as a quiver of a cheek muscle did Firas show how much he had enjoyed the scene. But then he was feeling very mellow these days.

Félicien took to the two women immediately, and they to him, Alma in particular because he was a student, Hayat because he was eager to learn all the songs she knew. Hari questioned them most stringently on the role of women in Islam. Alma struck up an instant friendship with Shasha, who, like Félicien she regarded as a fellow acolyte in scientific matters.

When the question was asked, it appeared that the entire company was traveling to Venice, each for their individual reasons. Johanna was going to Venice, and Shasha was going with Johanna, and that meant Firas was going, too. No further comment was made. None was needed. Everyone had seen the bed in the yard.

"I seem to have acquired a taste for travel," Alma said, and Hayat shrugged. "Where Alma goes, I go." She and Firas were very alike in that way.

Alaric had already declared his intention of returning to his homeland, ignoring Félicien when the goliard said beneath his breath, "To see if it has cooled down enough for him to go home, more like."

Félicien, too, had declared a state of homesickness. He looked at Jaufre when he said it, although no one noticed but Shasha and Hari. "It's been five years," he said. "I can't stay away forever."

Hari said simply that he had no option but to move forward as his calling bade him. He was on a lifetime voyage of exploration, and a little thing like a vast sea would not stop him. Besides, he had been told of an enormous temple in Rome, dedicated to the Christian god...

"Wait until you see Chartres," Félicien said.

"Eight then," Giovanni Gradenigo said when he was informed, adding up figures. He looked up with a broad smile. "Seven ducats each. That includes bed and board, of course."

This provoked the expected outrage, as forced intimacy with the pilgrims had taught them that seven and a half ducats was the going rate for the round trip from Venice to Jaffa and back again, weevily hardtack and sour water included. They beat him down to two ducats each, if they provided their own food. Shasha, who had volunteered to go among the pilgrims to treat their aches and pains, had had an earful of what kind of board Gradenigo provided and laid in stores accordingly. Further, she had prescribed a large dose of valerian tea every night for Mistress Joan, which seemed to promote a quieter attitude. Jaufre claimed, not without credence, that Gradenigo owed them all a reduction in fare for that alone.

Then there were the horses. Since four of Gradenigo's pilgrims had died en route, three on board ship and one in Jerusalem of the bloody flux, he bundled extra pilgrims into the second ship to make room for North Wind and the three Arabians on the first, although he charged them a fortune for it. Johanna would entrust food and water for the horses to no one but themselves, so it wasn't as expensive as it could have been.

Meanwhile, they waited for a favorable wind. "We could sacrifice a virgin," Félicien said. When the wind finally came—with all the Gaza virgins still accounted for—Gradenigo bundled everyone on board post haste and set sail before it could change its fickle mind.

Of course their group found themselves on the same ship as Mistress Joan. Of course they did. Johanna only hoped she wouldn't frighten the horses.

On the voyage she found herself most in company with Jaufre, who had a disturbing habit of watching her with a smile in his eyes. It had been a long year apart and they were both much changed, but now that she was back in his company, she remembered clearly the feelings for him that she had only just begun to discover before they were parted. The kind of feelings she had once had for Edyk.

And then he had been attacked, stabbed in the back and for all she knew killed, as she had been dragged off against her will. She knew an enormous relief that Jaufre had survived, and thrived, as well as an astonishment at the maturity—and the competent swordplay—of the man who had taken his place. But she felt as if she hardly knew him now. She felt, unbelievably, shy, a thing she had never felt before in her life, and something it had taken a while for her to identify.

And then there was Edyk. Seeing him had been a shock, if not for the reasons she might have expected. He was older than she was by several years, a more experienced merchant and traveler, and vastly more experienced as a lover. And yet in Gaza he seemed so young and comparatively innocent. It was as if their positions had been reversed, and she was now the elder and wiser and by far the more experienced of the two.

She had been happy to see him again, and she had gone to see him off when he left Gaza to return east because she could not bear to part with him on bad terms. But in the end, it was with a very faint fond remembrance that she watched him ride through Gaza's north gate. It had not been nearly as easy for her to leave Edyk at the summerhouse the previous spring.

"Do you want to take North Wind with you?" she had said, dreading the answer.

Edyk smiled. It was only a slight smile, but still, he did smile. "He would not come. And even if I compelled him, he would not stay with me." The smile grew wider. "I should never have let you help with his training."

They both laughed a little. He had said much the same before she left Cambaluc. His hand caressed her cheek briefly, toyed with a bronze curl. Then his smile faded and he kicked his mount viciously in the sides and galloped away from her for the last time, followed by the ever-faithful Chiang, who had pretended not to have seen Johanna at all.

She should feel sad, she told herself. But mostly what she felt was relief.

It was a violent crossing, the previous lack of wind compensated for by one violent fall storm after another. The two ships were brutally pushed along a course that more resembled the trail of a snake that the wake of a boat. The storms had the virtue of making it a quick passage, at least, and of drowning out the shrieking and exhortations of Mistress Joan en route. Johanna and Jaufre, wise to the ways of sea travel since childhood, remained on deck for the entire five weeks, one standing watch while the other slept, fending off the attention of crewmen interested in what might be in their pockets.

They saw few other ships. "I thought anyone who sailed the Middle Sea was at grave risk from pirates," Johanna said one day when the captain was passing.

A gust of wind tore at the sails and rattled the rigging so fiercely that for a moment she thought the whole mass would be torn loose and carried away, leaving the ship at the mercy of the storm with no means of propulsion or control. The ship listed sharply and a wave of water came over the gunnel to soak them both to the skin.

Gradenigo laughed and pushed his wet hair out of his eyes. He had to shout to be heard above the wind. "Signorina, no pirate in his right mind would be out in this weather!"

Except for the mandatory stops at Candia in Crete and Modon in Greece, when everyone staggered on shore for an hour of fresh air and a surface that didn't move beneath their feet, the rest of their party stayed below in their single cramped cabin with their heads over the communal commode. The resulting aroma only increased their nausea and multiplied the rats. Firas and Shasha were unaffected, and joined Johanna and Jaufre on deck, where they held hands longer and more tightly than strictly necessary to keep their balance against the heaving of the ship. Johanna reserved comment. She was, amazingly, learning discretion.

Several more of the pilgrims died mid voyage and their bodies were buried at sea in accordance with the rules as set out by the captain's contract. There were moments when Alaric, Alma and even Hari wished most heartily to have been one of them.

They disembarked with relief for the last time, on the Grand Canal in Venice one cold, gray morning in early November. Stabling for the horses provided for and bags left at an inn Gradenigo recommended, the first gondolier they hailed said, "The Polo palazzo? Of course."

They climbed gingerly into the long, narrow boat and penetrated the heart of the one of the stranger cities they had ever visited. Most of the streets were canals connected by bridges, and Johanna wondered if this was what Baghdad had looked like before its canals had been destroyed by Hulegu. There were few signposts and many people, all talking and gesticulating at a great rate. There were shops filled with every kind of merchandise and they caught quick glimpses into open doors of dazzling arrays of silk and gemstones and spices.

Their gondolier pushed them along with a long pole he went up and down hand over hand, more often than not ducking when they passed beneath the bridges, which did not seem to have been built with gondoliers in mind. After thirty minutes' worth of twists and turns down waterways that all looked—and smelled—the same to them once they got off the Grand Canal, he decanted them at the foot of a bridge on one of the smaller canals. He pointed at a massive double door made of wood set in the front of a grand stone house, accepted payment and a tip that Shasha thought was extortionate, and shoved off in search of his next fare.

"It doesn't look like a building occupied by a family out of favor," Jaufre said, inspected the elaborate carvings on door and columns.

Johanna wiped her sweaty palms on her tunic, that same tunic made of the raw silk dyed black that her father had brought back from his last trip to Kinsai. It showed its many leagues: Cambaluc to Terak, Terak to Talikan, Talikan to Baghdad, Baghdad to Gaza, Gaza to Venice, and the doorstep of her grandfather's house. She wore the tunic now like a badge of honor.

They gathered behind her, her fellow travelers, her compatriots, her friends. Her family. With them at her back she could do anything. Even knock on her grandfather's door.

She stepped forward, raised the large brass knocker and rapped the wood with it twice, three times. The sound echoed beyond the door. After a few moments footsteps were heard. The massive door swung back.

She and Jaufre had seized the few calm moments at sea to use Captain Gradenigo and those of his crew amenable to bribes to amass a rudimentary knowledge of Italian. What she said now had been carefully rehearsed, over and over and over again.

"Good afternoon," she said. "My name is Wu Johanna, late of Cambaluc in Everything Under the Heavens. I am looking for Ser Marco Polo. Is this his home?"

The man who had answered the door was obviously a servant, and an upperclass one if the quality of his clothing and the loftiness of his manner were any indication. "It is."

He offered no further encouragement. Nonplussed, she said, "Well, I'm glad we have found the right place." He did not return her smile and she lost interest in further politesse. In a manner even loftier than his own, she said, "Could you please inform your master that his granddaughter wishes to speak with him?"

"Ser Polo lies on his deathbed," he said. "And the occupants of this house have no time to spare for ragamuffins off the street purporting to be relatives."

And he shut the door in her face.

ACKNOWLEDGMENTS

As always, my thanks to reference librarian Michael Cataggio, freelance editor Laura Anne Gilman, cartographer Cherie Northon, and all those wonderful people down at Gere Donovan Press.

And a big shout-out to the readers who so recklessly spend their hard-earned after-tax dollars on my books. I couldn't do this without you, guys. Thanks.

Glossary

Note: **Bolded** *words included in entries have their own definitions elsewhere.*

Arabic and Persian I have used names from both languages interchangeably, but mostly Arabic because they are most available.

Balasaga An historical province of Persia, now Iran.

Bao A personal seal. Chinese.

Beda Bedouin.

Bible All verses quoted are from the Vulgate Bible, English translation via the website vulgate.org. The King James version was three hundred years down the road.

Blister Foot-and-mouth disease, which produces blisters on cows and camels and anything with a split hoof. It is highly contagious and was indeed used as a bioweapon.

The Silk and Song Bureau of Weights and Measures No two nations back in 1322 measured anything the same way, so here for the sake of narrative clarity and my sanity time is measured in minutes, hours, days, weeks, months and years, and no notice is taken of that error in Julius Caesar's 45 BC calendar that wouldn't be corrected until 1582 AD by Pope Gregory XIII.

Length is measured in fingers (about an inch), hands (about 4 inches), rods (16.5 feet) and leagues (3 miles).

Travel is measured in **leagues**, about three miles or the distance a man could walk in an hour.

Fabric is measured in **ells** from China to England. Smaller lengths are fingers (three-quarters of an inch) and hands (three to four inches).

Google "weights in the Middle Ages" and you get over 8 million hits. Here, I use drams (one ounce), gills (four ounces), cups (eight ounces), pints (16 ounces), quarts (32 ounces) and gallons (124 ounces) in ascending order of liquid measurement.

Dry weight pounds then ranged from 300 grams to 508 grams, so the hell with it, here it's 16 ounces or about 453 grams. Ten pounds is a tenweight, and yes, I just made that right up. A hundredweight is a hundred pounds.

Calicut Now Kozhikode, India.

Cambaluc Built by Kublai Khan. Became the basis for what is now the Forbidden City in Beijing, China.

Chang'an Now Xi'an, China.

Cheche Pronounced "shesh." A long scarf, usually indigo-dyed blue, worn by Tuaregs. It can be knotted many different ways to keep the sun out of the eyes and protect the neck and face from sunburn. The indigo leeched onto the face and hands of the wearer. Or, alternatively, depending on which story you believe, Tuaregs deliberately dyed their face and hands blue to protect themselves from the sun. I heard both in Morocco.

Cipangu Now Japan.

Currency Tael: China. Bezants: Byzantium. Drachma: Arabic. France: Livre, and I cannot tell you how much it delights me that today this word in French means "book." Now that's currency. Florence: Florins. Venice: Accommodate all currencies but rely on gemstones. In *A Distant Mirror: The Calamitous 14th Century*, Barbara Tuchman writes, "...the *non-specialist reader would be well advised not to worry about it, because the names of coins and currency mean nothing anyway except in terms of purchasing power.*" Surely a bargain in Baghdad that begins with a search for bezants to buy malachite beads which is then concluded with a horse race sufficiently illuminates her statement.

Edward I of England Yes, he was in Acre in 1271 at the same time as the Polos, and even as fellow strangers in a strange land are surely drawn together in faraway places even today, Edward and the Polos could even have met. Maffeo and Niccolo had already been to the court of the Khan and they could have dined out forever on tales of Cathay. Why not at table with kings? Marco certainly did after he got home.

Ell See **Bureau of Weights and Measures** above. The distance from a man's elbow to the tip of his middle finger, or about 18 inches. A standard unit of measurement for textiles in the Middle Ages, and never mind the differences between Scots, English, Flemish, Polish, German and French ells.

Shidibala Gegeen Khan The Khan in Cambulac when Johanna and company departed. I have waved my authorial wand and made his tenure in office even shorter than it actually was.

Gujarat Now a province in northwest India.

Ibn Battuta Berber slave trader, 1304-1369, known for writing *The Rihla* ("The Journey"), an account of his extensive travels throughout the medieval, mostly Muslim world. I have advanced his first visit to Kabul purely for the convenience of my plot.

Kabul Now the capital of Afghanistan. Holdout against attack from every invading force from Alexander the Great on, including Genghis Khan, the USSR and the USA. In spite of being a mile high, highs averages in the 60's (F) as soon as March.

Khuree The summer capital of the Mongols. Now Ulan Bator, Mongolia.

Kinsai Now Hangzhou, or Hangchow, China.

Koran, or Quran All quotations come from quran.com.

Lanchow Now Lanzhou, China.

League See **Bureau of Weights and Measures** above. The distance one person could walk in an hour. Also defined as about three miles. I have rounded up and down. The Khan's yambs were built every 25 miles, therefore in Silk and Song every eight leagues. The Khan's imperial mailmen rode 200 miles daily, hence sixty leagues. Close enough for government work and fiction.

The Levant From Wikipedia: "A geographic and cultural region consisting of the eastern Mediterranean between Anatolia and Egypt... The Levant consists today of Lebanon, Syria, Jordan, Israel, Palestine, Cyprus and parts of southern Turkey. Iraq and the Sinai Peninsula are also sometimes included."

Marco Polo Did Marco leave a grand-daughter behind when he finally went home? I'd be surprised if he didn't leave a dozen. In any edition of his memoir, it is clear that he loved the ladies, and the twenty years he was from home he must have gotten lucky at least a couple of times. If he didn't, yes, by Marco's own account Kublai Khan did in fact exact tributes of nubile young women from his various suzerainties, enjoy their company, and then award them as gifts to his vassals. Marco was a personable and capable young man, high in the Khan's favor. It is reasonable to suppose he might have been so rewarded, so I have the taken the liberty to suppose it here.

The Travels of Marco Polo Published as "Il Milione" in 1300, and Marco himself was nicknamed "Marco Milione" because of the exaggerated figures he used in description. His stories were at first disbelieved and derided, especially by comparison to Sir John Mandeville's book, which was of course the truth, the whole truth and nothing but the truth itself. Much later, when advanced scholarship discredited Mandeville as a fabulist and a plagiarist, Marco's far better informed star (and story) rose by comparison. That is not to say his story failed of effect in its own time, however. You can see Christopher Columbus' copy, with marginalia by Columbus himself, in the Biblioteca Columbina in Seville.

Middle Sea The Mediterranean. Also known as the Western Sea.

Mien Now Myanmar, or Burma.

Mintan A short-waisted, long-sleeved coat. Ottoman.

Mongol battle tactics and strategy Surrender or die. If you surrendered, you would continue to live, albeit under Mongol rule, which was, amazingly, pretty reasonable. If you fought, if you crossed them or betrayed them in any way, they would annihilate you with whatever means they had to hand. They mounted hundreds of thousands of soldiers with extensive training. Their engineers were superb. They didn't travel with siege engines, they built them from available materials when it came time to use them. They'd catapult anything into a city they thought would kill and spread terror, naphtha bombs, stoppered urns filled with poisonous snakes and spiders that burst upon impact, bodies dead from the plague (weapons that stretch back to antiquity, FYI, the Mongols didn't have to invent them). When the city fell, as it almost invariably did, the Mongols would send in execution squads to kill off any remaining survivors, including women and children. Sometimes they'd save the soldiers and the engineers and put them to work. Sometimes the conquered soldiers would be placed in front in the attack on the next besieged city, keeping the Mongols' own soldiers in reserve until the besieged ran out of ammunition. You really, really didn't want to get on their bad side.

Mongols and torture Yes, they did those things. Those exact things, and more.

Mysore Then as now, a city in northwest India.

Paiza The royal Mongol passport. The Mongols called it a gerrega. Also a yarlik.

Philosophy Science as a term would not be invented for another five hundred years. I have used "philosopher" here as a catch-all for anyone studying the hard sciences.

Sarik A headscarf. Ottoman.

Shang-tu The summer capital of the Mongols. Now Ulan Bator, Mongolia. Also called Khuree.

Shensi Now Shaanxi, China.

Silk Road A term that did not come into common usage until the twentieth century. Here I use the more generic Road.

Talikan I have appropriated the name of today's tiny (pop. 43) village in northeast Iran for Sheik Mohammed's great walled city of 1323, which exists somewhere south and west of the Terak Pass and south and east of the Caspian Sea.

Templars A lot of scholars have written an awful lot about the Templars, and a lot more writers have written even more novels about them. It is difficult to distill fact from mythology. They did indeed exist for nearly 200 years, from between the First and Second Crusades until their dissolution in 1307 (or 1312 or 1314, take your pick). They weren't all slaughtered, contrary to the wishes of Philip the Fair of France, and after the dissolution many were allowed to join the Knights of the Hospital and other orders. As late as 1338, former Templars were still drawing pensions in England (Burman). Surely others, perhaps those who felt themselves more at risk, must have seen the writing on the wall and decamped early enough to escape the coming purge. They were warriors, and it isn't much of a stretch to imagine them hiring their experienced swords out as caravan guards. It is no stretch at all to imagine some of them absconding with whatever treasure was near to hand on their way out the door. It was a rough and ready time.

Time See **Bureau of Weights and Measures** above. In Europe: divided into times for prayer. Matins: midnight. Lauds: 3am. Prime: Sunrise. Terce: Midmorning. Sext: Noon. None: Midafternoon. Vespers: Sunset. Compline: Bedtime.

Turgesh, or Turkic Turkey, or Turkish.

Umar al-Khayyam Omar Khayyám, author of the *Rubáiyát of Omar Khayyám*, a verse of which Johanna translates so ably under Alma's direction.

Bibliography

My intent as a storyteller is always to entertain, but this book also required a great deal of research over many years, and was influenced by the work of many scholars, without whose heavy lifting this by comparison light-hearted romp would not have been possible. Here's a list of just a few of the books that helped Johanna and Jaufre on their way.

Ackroyd, Peter. *The Canterbury Tales: A Retelling.*

---. *Foundation: The history of England from its earliest beginnings to the Tudors.*

Armstrong, Karen. *Jerusalem: One City, Three Faiths.*

Barber, Malcolm. *The New Knighthood.*

Bergreen, Laurence. *Marco Polo, From Venice to Xanadu.*

Bonavia, Judy. *The Silk Road.*

Boorstin, Daniel. J. *The Discoverers: A History of Man's Search to Know His World and Himself.*

Brotton, Jerry. *A History of the World in 12 Maps.*

Brown, Lloyd A. *The Story of Maps.*

Brown, Michelle. *The World of the Luttrell Psalter.*

Burman, Edward. *The Assassins.*

---. *The World before Columbus, 1100-1492.*

Cahill, Thomas. *Mysteries of the Middle Ages: The Rise of Feminism, Science and Art from the Cults of Catholic Europe.*

Cantor, Norman. *The Medieval Reader.*

Caro, Ina. *Paris to the Past: Traveling through French History by Train.*

Cawthorne, Nigel. *Sex Lives of the Popes.*

Chareyron, Nicole. *Pilgrims to Jerusalem in the Middle Ages.*

Chute, Marchette. *Geoffrey Chaucer of England.*

Collis, Louise. *Memoirs of a Medieval Woman: the Life and Times of Margery Kempe.*

Cosman, Madeleine Pelner. *Medieval Wordbook.*

Costain, Thomas. *The Three Edwards.*

Coss, Peter. *The Lady in Medieval England, 1000-1500.*

Croutier, Alev Lytle. *Harem, The World Behind the Veil.*

Crowley, Roger. *City of Fortune.*

Dalrymple, William. *In Xanadu.*

Dougherty, Martin. *Weapons & Fighting Techniques of the Medieval Warrior.*

Evangelisti, Silvia. *Nuns: A History of Convent Life.*

Foltz, Richard C. *Religions of the Silk Road.*

Fox, Sally, researched and edited by. *The Medieval Woman: An Illuminated Book of Days.*

Freeman, Margaret B. *Herbs For The Medieval Household For Cooking, Healing And Divers Uses*

Garfield, Simon. *On the Map, A Mind-Expanding Exploration of the Way the World Looks.*

Gies, Frances and Joseph. *Cathedral, Forge, and Waterwheel: Technology and Invention in the Middle Ages.*

---. *Life in a Medieval City.*

---. *Marriage and the Family in the Middle Ages.*

Gillman, Ian, and Hans-Joachim Klimkett. *Christians in Asia before 1500.*

Goldstone, Nancy. *Four Queens: The Provencal Sisters Who Ruled Europe.*

Grotenhuis, Elizabeth Ten, editor. *Along the Silk Road.*

Hansen, Valerie. *Silk Road, A New History.*

Herrin, Judith. *Byzantium: The Surprising Life of a Medieval Empire.*

Hollister, C. Warren. *Medieval Europe.*

Hopper, Vincent F. *Chaucer's Canterbury Tales: An Interlinear Translation.*

Hutton, Alfred. *The Sword and the Centuries.*

Johnson, Steven. *The Ghost Map.*

Jones, Terry. *Medieval Lives.*

Lacey, Robert & Danny Danzier. *The Year 1000, What Life was Like at the Turn of the First Millennium.*

Leon, Vicky. *Uppity Women of Medieval Times.*

Lewis, Raphael. *Everyday Life in Ottoman Turkey.*

Leyser, Henrietta. *Medieval Women: A Social History of Women in England 450-1500.*

Man, John. *Gutenberg: How One Man Remade the World with Words.*

Manchester, William. *A World Lit Only by Fire.*

Mayor, Adrienne. *Greek Fire, Poison Arrows & Scorpion Bombs: Biological and Chemical Warfare in the Ancient World.*

Miller, Malcolm. *Chartres Cathedral.*

Morier, James. *The Adventures of Hajji Baba of Isphahan.*

Mortimer, Ian. *Medieval Intrigue.*

---. *The Time Traveler's Guide to Medieval England.*

Newman, Sharan. *The Real History Behind the Templars.*

Norwich, John Julius. *A History of Venice.*

Ohler, Norbert. *The Medieval Traveller.*

Polo, Marco. *The Adventures of Marco Polo.* Many editions.

Robinson, James. *The Lewis Chessman.*

Rowling, Marjorie. *Everyday Life of Medieval Travelers.*

---. *Life in Medieval Times.*

Stark, Freya. *The Valleys of the Assassins.*

Starr, S. Frederick. *Lost Enlightenment: Central Asia's Golden Age from the Arab Conquest to Tamerlane.*

Tooley, Ronald Vere. *Maps and Map-Makers.*

Trask, Willard R. *Medieval Lyrics of Europe.*

Tuchman, Barbara. *A Distant Mirror, The Calamitous 14th Century.*

Turner, Jack. *Spice: The History of a Temptation.*

Weatherford, Jack. *Genghis Khan and the Making of the Modern World.*

Weis, Rene. *The Yellow Cross: The Story of the Last Cathars' Rebellion Against the Inquisition, 1290-1320.*

Whitfield, Susan. *Life Along the Silk Road.*

Wood, Frances. *The Silk Road, Two Thousand Years in the Heart of Asia.*

The first historical novels I read were bestsellers in the 50's and as such available in the 60's as tattered paperbacks in boat cubbies all over southcentral Alaska, which was how they swam into my ken. They include but are not limited to Anya Seton, Thomas B. Costain, Norah Lofts, Samuel Shellabarger, Georgette Heyer, Frank G. Slaughter, Grace Ingram, C. S. Forester, Rosemary Sutcliff and James Michener.

Nowadays I read Diana Gabaldon (*Outlander*), Sharon Kay Penman (the *Princes of Gwynedd* and the *Plantagenets* series), Sharan Newman (the *Catherine LeVendeur* series and one of two authors to be listed in both the fiction and non-fiction sections of this homage), Francine Matthews (aka

Stephanie Barron and the author of the Jane Austen history mysteries but also of many other fine historical novels, including one that might inspire you to take a pry bar to a certain tomb in England), C.J. Sansom (*Matthew Shardlake*), Imogen Robertson (*Westerman and Crowther*) and P. F. Chisholm (*Sir Robert Carey*), as well as the late Ariana Franklin (*Adelia Aguilar*), Ellis Peters (*Brother Cadfael*) and Elizabeth Peters (*Amelia Peabody*).

These are only a few among many. For a lifetime of enjoyment and for the inspiration to write my own, my heartfelt thanks to you all.

To Be Continued...

Silk and Song will conclude in

The Land Beyond

Available 2015